ALONE IN A CABIN

ALONE IN A CABIN

LEANN W. SMITH

Library of Congress Cataloging-in-Publication Data has been applied for.
First Printing, 2021

ISBNs: 978-0-578-92241-6 (paperback), 978-0-578-92242-3 (ebook)
This book also available in hardcopy: 978-0-578-92723-7

Cover design by Shelby M'lynn Mick

To Shelby & Lincoln.

To all artists living bravely,
telling stories even when it's hard.

Also by Leanne W. Smith

Leaving Independence

A Contradiction to His Pride

On a Dark and Snowy Night (short story)

"There is a spirit in every home that meets us at the door."

Laura Ingalls Wilder

Sometimes it's waiting on the porch.

I

A story begins with a disruption to the heroine's daily life—a major disturbance in the balance of things that throws her off her footing and sets her on her rump.

Maggie's gaze rested on Tom's throat, on the smooth-shaven ridge she used to press her lips against. *If I wrap my hands around his trachea—cut off his windpipe below his larynx—could I squeeze hard enough to shut him up? Forever?*

Tom had just butchered Maggie's heart with his words. He deserved to die...looked like he wanted to, even.

She pictured Tom's body lying in an open casket, the echo of his words gone silent. Was it normal for a wife to picture her husband dead when he was the one who flung a verbal dagger into her chest and severed their relationship?

I could be the one to put him there.

As Tom's pronouncement continued its mean slide down the back of her spine, the rising temperature of Maggie's blood came up through her own trachea, heating her so thoroughly she reached to loosen the top clasp of her blouse. She couldn't stand to look at him for more than a few seconds at a time.

"I realize this must come as a shock," he was saying. It was so trite she disregarded the rest. Maggie could no longer bear his voice now either. Whatever he was saying all she could think was *Really, Tom? That's the best you can do?*

The force of her anger was unsettling...strange. She knew if she gave in to the fury she could do it—she could leap across the sofa and pin him to the floor.

Maggie had once thought Tom so clever—certainly before she married him. He was going to make a doctor. That's how her father had put it. And he did; Tom made a doctor. At every family gathering Maggie heard her father say to someone, "Maggie has done well for herself. She married Tom, and Tom has made a doctor."

When her father died, Maggie searched to find a memory where he had ever stated her worth based solely on her own merits. But she couldn't find one. Her father was proud, though, of her status as a doctor's wife, proud she and Tom lived in a gated community in Franklin, south of Nashville, and proud Tom drove a BMW. *All the important things.*

Maggie forced herself to refocus on Tom at the opposite end of the sofa—same color as the seats of his BMW—and for a moment allowed herself a new mental fantasy: grabbing a knife from the kitchen and taking the sharp edge of it down the side of his Z4 Roadster. Killing Tom was too kind. But scratching his car? That would hurt him.

The word 'Bethany' cut into her daydream. *No. I'll save the knife for Bethany. Bethany is the one I'll kill.*

"How old is she again?" Maggie was surprised she could speak at all—surprised by the evenness of her voice, so out-of-sync with the swelling waves in her chest.

Tom squirmed. He couldn't meet her eye—he who told families the worst of news on a daily basis. "Twenty-six."

"Twenty-six," she repeated, watching his eyes flit to the picture over the mantle, to the smiling boy and girl. The twins had turned twenty-six in June. "And she's your nurse."

"Receptionist."

Maggie waited until his eyes came back to hers before nodding. "She's the one you'd rather be married to now."

Tom shifted on the sofa. "We're not really talking marriage."

She felt her head continue to nod. The nod seemed bitter. Bitter wasn't how Maggie wanted to be. *Caskets. Knives. Killing.* Those images were fleeting indulgences, unbidden as the bitter taste forming in her mouth and the sudden throb, as from a hard kick, in the pit of her stomach.

"But she's pregnant." Before Tom could respond to that she finished it for him. "And you want to live together to raise the child."

Tom took his elbows off his knees. "I'll get my things."

"No. I'll get mine."

He flinched. "I'm not throwing you out of our home, Maggie."

"Don't refer to it as 'our home' anymore, Tom. 'Our home' is a thing of the past, apparently."

'Our' anything.

Anger fueled Maggie's bloodstream. Adrenaline surged. The wave was rising now but threatened to crash and suck her soul out to sea. She had to get out of there.

Tom reached for her hand but she jerked it away. Maggie had already been forced to endure his eyes, his voice, his stomach-churning remorse. She stood and stepped away from the sofa, clutching her fury like a lifeline, willing it to stay at a crest for as long as possible.

Lord, don't let Tom see me cry.

She would pack a quick bag for now, and come back tomorrow while he was at the office to begin the parceling.

Parceling. The earth seemed to shift, the house to sway.

Rage, hurt, fear hit a peak and rolled into the crest while Maggie stuffed items into a bag. She wasn't sure what she was grabbing, she just knew she had to get out of the house. Waves crashing. Soul sucking. It was happening. She could feel it.

She raced through the kitchen, smacked the garage door opener, flung open the hatchback of the Subaru, and tossed the bag in. Tom's car was parked a little close. The sharp corner of her door left the tiniest nick in his Estoril Blue. Not as dramatic as the knife running along the side that she had fantasized, but satisfying nonetheless.

Maggie threw the car into reverse with a shaking hand and fled.

*   *   *

That same day Canon sat in his patrol car at the corner of Elm and Main when a hatchback rolled through the stop sign—plowed, more like it. Maybe the driver didn't see the sign. Or him. The rain had started an hour ago and now fell hard. He flicked on his lights, leaving the sound off, and pulled out to tail it—a Toyota Corolla.

The driver saw his lights about the time he—or she—passed the bank. A woman. He could tell by the ponytail. The car turned at the corner, pulled into the parking lot, and circled to get in under the overhang of one of the drive-through lanes.

After hours. The bank was closed. Out of town tags, which was unusual because Marston County was well off I-40.

He took the lane beside her, glad she had the sense to get them out of the rain, falling in drumming sheets now on either side of the roofline, and called it in to Shirley. Canon gave her the tag number, and waited. She was quick with the details, like always.

Keeping his eye on the driver's side window over the teller box, he slid the safety off his gun, only a precaution, watching the woman through the dripping glass as she shook her head and looked over at him, lifting her shoulders like she didn't know what she had done. She rolled down her window. A redhead.

Canon had his hand on the door handle by then, but paused. Redheads affected him.

She was young—a girl, really—carrying extra weight for her short height, the ponytail a mess like it had been slept on or done up in a hurry.

Taking a deep breath, he pushed opened his door and took long strides around the cruiser, noting that the Corolla, by contrast, was dented, dated, and rusting.

"What did I do?" the girl asked, eyes brimming for a cry.

"Ran a four-way back there."

"I'm sorry." The tears spilled out. "I didn't see it."

The tears were genuine, he could tell, and Canon had a feeling they were brimming long before she saw his lights.

"You're a long way from home." With Indiana tags that were soon to expire.

"I know." She looked away. The girl couldn't have been driving long.

"Why don't you come back to the station with me and we'll give your parents a call."

The girl looked up at him sharply, wiping one side of her face. "My parents don't know I'm here."

The phone sitting in her cupholder buzzed. Canon couldn't make out the entire text, but caught part of the choice language. He knew what was going on. Shirley had tipped him off.

"They will when you call 'em." He tried to keep the natural growl out of his voice and let the words fall softly.

She broke down then, washing the front of her blouse in tears. The girl might as well have stopped out in the weather after all.

Canon got her out of the car she had stolen from her mother, into the back seat of the patrol car, and down to the station.

* * *

Maggie wasn't sure when her tears started or when the rain began to pelt the roof. Soon both fell in torrents. It had already been a wet week in Middle Tennessee. The Harpeth lapped at the edges of its banks, eyed freedom, prepared to jump.

She had trouble seeing oncoming traffic through the blur on the windshield and didn't have a destination anyway so she got into the far corner of an empty school parking lot, cut the engine and crawled into the passenger floorboard. The storm muffled her sobs as she clamped down on the leather, her saliva collecting in a pool.

Thirty years.

Thirty years sucked down the drain like salt dregs after a comforting bath. And here she was standing in that moment—the shock of the cold wind rising from the vent after climbing naked from the water. Maggie had put her faith in a good book ending. But maybe happy endings were only a wisp, vapors destined to dissolve.

Sometime after dark, after the rain moved out, she wiped the seat with her sleeve, crawled back into the driver's seat and drove to a hotel on the other side of town, an out-of-the-way place that looked as bleak as her future. The night was moist—hot—Maggie's mouth dry.

The clerk took one look at her and planted his eyes on the counter. She was beyond caring, her head throbbing with a ticker-tape of questions. Would Tom tell the twins? Had he done so already? Or would Tom leave that task for Maggie? She checked her phone out of habit. No messages. She turned it off before any could come.

Sleep was elusive, a past luxury Maggie worried she might never know again...like love. Her head wouldn't stop swimming with visions of Tom, images of the Harpeth, sounds of the rain continuing to fall outside the hotel window.

Sometime after midnight she flicked on the lamp and picked up a hotel pen and pad wondering if the next chapter of her life was to be an epic tragedy...a horror story...or maybe a suspense. Maggie could legitimately claim it as a mystery, at least for now.

Nothing seemed real. But as she rolled the pen in her fingers and looked down at the writing pad with its smooth blank surface, waiting to capture whatever words she wanted—*needed*—to see on the page, Maggie realized the pen and pad were real. And holding the pair was an instant comfort. That's when Maggie knew: *writing* was the answer. Writing was her future. She would need to make a living. The time had come to take the road less traveled, the one she had been avoiding.

So she began, in a flurry of scribbled notes—her current reality sprinkled with flashes of past and future—as if the pen and pad were a lifeline that might save her. She marked off columns and rows, boxing in this set of words, leaving others free on the page, all offering her needed direction.

With a flourish of ink she decided to take the downstairs sofa. She and Tom had never made out on that one. The kitchen was hers, of course—that was a given. The bookcases built by a favorite uncle. Those were Maggie's, too, whether Tom liked it or not.

Overall, as she traveled from room to room in her mind, Maggie thought of few possessions she cared to keep. *Incredible.* Material things had never meant so little. Still, nothing sacred could be left in the house at the risk of Bethany carting it off to a thrift store. The thought of the petite blond inspecting her things caused fresh tears.

Flinging the pen and paper against the wall, Maggie buried her face in the pillows, wondering how long she would need to hold herself there to make it all go away. Housekeeping would find her. They would call the police who would go through her purse and call Tom. He'd call the twins.

No...Maggie couldn't hurt Robbie and Cal. She rolled over on her back and decided to breathe, filling her lungs in a yoga move. *One, two, three—hold for five—now release.*

She should have seen this coming. Maggie couldn't even remember the last time she and Tom had sex. He sent flowers every February, boxed roses with a card. Was last February his final overture? *Were he and Bethany already...*

Maggie had thought she and Tom were simply coasting. Normal mid-life stuff. Shame hung like a wet curtain, dripping down with her tears.

*   *   *

Canon sat with the redhead long into the night, hearing her version of it—an online romance gone bad—until her parents arrived from Indiana. The boy had looked better on the screen. Evidently she had, too.

After they left, he wrote up the report then stuck a Post-it on Shirley's monitor saying he would be in later than usual the next morning. Canon cut off the lights and walked out to his patrol car hoping the parents and daughter could resolve things. Life was too short—too uncertain—to spend it in a squabble with your family.

The house was dark when he got there, except for the light he left on over the kitchen sink. He stood and listened to the scanner while checking the mail, out of habit. Next he looked in the refrigerator...*empty*...then the freezer...*unappetizing*...before closing the doors and climbing the stairs for bed.

When he finally closed his eyes, he dreamed for the first time in years—of simpler days before social media allowed young people to get false impressions, back when dreams had been a more regular part of his life, a redhead usually making an appearance. But tonight the woman's hair was brown.

*   *   *

When sleep finally took her, Maggie dreamed of list-making, the taste of seat leather, and Tom making love to other women, all blond. But by nine o'clock the next morning she was showered, dressed, and on her second cup of in-room coffee.

Like Scarlett clutching a carrot, Maggie wrapped her hands around the Dixie cup knowing she would survive this. *So help me God.* The same way she survived the death of her father, the illness of her mother, the twins leaving home. Each had hurt like a knife twist, but Maggie had regained her footing following the initial bleeds. She would wrap a tourniquet around this thing and keep moving forward.

Tom would pay for anything she needed to rebuild a nest for herself. She knew that. And Maggie would let him...at first...as a form of restitution. But she didn't want Tom's money. She wanted to earn her own. If any work pursuit could offer peace as she sought to build a new life, it was surely the act and art of writing. *Fiction.* Maggie needed a diversion from the current cold truth of her life—one that promised hope.

She picked up the pen and pad that were still on the floor and looked down at her scribbled list-making. *Reality.* Time to go back to the house and divide the spoils.

*   *   *

By the time Canon woke the sun was well into the sky, the wall clock ticking its regular beat. He checked his phone. One message—Shirley—telling him to take the day off. *Lord knows you need the rest. How late were you here last night?*

Ignoring her instructions, he got up to shower. The numbers ran over him with the water. The Andersons from Indiana arrived at 3:38 and left at 3:57. He had finished the report at 4:26, cut off the lights at 4:32, and flicked them back on in the farmhouse at 5:00 sharp. Remembering numbers on the clock through a long night was nothing new. Shirley had texted at 6:49 when she opened the office. Canon usually beat her, unless he'd had a long work night. And when he did come in late, she told him to take the day off because "Lord knows you need the rest."

Shirley enjoyed her pet phrases.

In over thirty years Canon never had taken a work day off. Not one. Shirley knew that. But she said it anyway. Every time. He let her say what she needed to, for her own peace of mind, then he ignored her. It was their way.

Buffing a towel over his head, Canon pulled clothes from the chest of drawers and got dressed, taking a minute to glance up at the redhead with her frozen smile. Then he went back into the bathroom marveling at the intersections of the human heart and mind.

A runaway chasing false love. A brunette in a dream. What lonely souls wouldn't do to fill the aches inside them.

*   *   *

Going back inside the house wasn't as bad as Maggie had feared. Material items are only items, after all. Inanimate objects. None of them drove Tom's choices. Although...when she looked over to Tom's side of the closet she couldn't help but wonder what clothes he had been wearing the day he first cheated. Was it something Maggie had bought for him? Did Bethany enjoy the smell of Tom's *Versace*? If Maggie had known it would draw other women like fruit flies she wouldn't have let that clerk in downtown Franklin talk her into the larger 3.4 ounce bottle.

Outside the bedroom the parceling grew easier.

Maggie stared out the back window at the pool in the early August heat. Fourth of July decorations she never had brought in dotted the landscape. Leaves from the birch trees floated in the water from the hard rain the night before. She would miss those birch trees, her herb garden and the oak-leaf hydrangeas. But Maggie never had loved the house. Tom won that argument. The house was too large, too presumptuous, and didn't have nearly enough windows.

After making a trip to the local UPS store for sturdy boxes, Maggie packed most of the kitchen and marked the bookcases with a Post-it. She scooped clothes, shoes and purses from the closet, leaving the long dresses she had bought for Tom's medical conventions and that cruise five years ago, along with Christmas and birthday presents, the Coach bag with the tassel on the zipper.

Surreal.

Twenty-four hours ago Maggie hadn't known this was how she would spend her day. When she checked her phone that morning each of the kids had texted some version of *when should we be there?* She texted back *change of plans* then turned her phone off. Let Tom break the news.

Maggie's head throbbed. She found Tylenol in the medicine cabinet and dropped the bottle in her purse—the one of tan leather—the one she had bought herself.

On her way out, she grabbed the new gray blanket off the upstairs sofa. This August heat was a sauna now, but colder days were coming. Gray looked to be the new color of her life. Tom could have the rest—Tom and Bethany—and all the accidental children they wanted to conceive.

2

"Rustic cabin. Built in the 1850s. Original fireplace. New windows. Only 70 miles from Nashville. Perfect writer's retreat."
Airbnb description

Maggie held the steaming mug and studied her daughter across the table. They sat opposite one another in a hipster coffee house only a short walk from Maggie's new high-rise condo in the Gulch, one of Nashville's hottest real estate markets.

Robbie frowned back at her. "You're going to leave me and Cal?"

She had expected Robbie to be unhappy with her decision. But, as the therapist Maggie paid one hundred dollars a session to said, she was not responsible for her children's happiness. They had to claim it on their own the same way Maggie had to reclaim hers.

August to December had been a painful yet liberating blur. A lot of soul-searching. One day at a time. Maggie's world rotating on its axis.

"I've only rented the cabin for a few days. You've got Mark. Cal's engaged. I'm not abandoning you."

"But it's Christmas, Mom!"

"I'll be here Christmas Day and head to the cabin the day after."

"For how long?"

"Through the following Monday, day after New Year's."

Robbie's frown deepened. Maggie wondered if she was truly mad or just hurt. Either way, change had become their new normal, welcome or not.

"Since when are you so matter-of-fact?" asked Robbie.

"New me."

Robbie frowned at the table top, her finger picking at a bothersome nail in the wood. "Why go by yourself?"

Maggie gripped her mug a little tighter, its warmth a comfort. "Who else do I have, sweetheart?"

Robbie winced, and Maggie felt guilty for causing it. But she didn't turn away from her daughter's probing eyes. Robbie was a stunner. Long brown hair. Eyes the color of molasses. And it wasn't just Maggie who thought so. Heads turned toward their table and lingered.

Calvin was the masculine version, five minutes younger, proud to be three inches taller. Maggie had taken care not to overdo matching clothing when they were young, wanting each of them to stand strong as an individual. She and Tom had prided themselves that when giving them matching names—Robyn and Calvin—they had at least given Robyn the more feminine and unique "y." But then they fell into calling her Robbie.

"You've got to stop feeling sorry for me," Maggie said. "I'm fine. You and Cal are both in new jobs. Choose your own vacation days and let me choose mine."

"How long, exactly?"

"A week. Maybe longer if I get into a good writing groove."

"So you are planning to write?" For the first time Robbie stopped looking worried and showed interest.

"That's the whole point! And I've been given this great and unexpected window of opportunity." Maggie shot Robbie her best smile across the table.

But Robbie wasn't swayed by Maggie's forced enthusiasm. "I don't like you going out there alone, Mom. Cal won't either."

"It's not as remote as you're making it sound."

"Fifteen miles from the nearest town."

"Less than a marathon. I can run it if I have to. Did you look at the pictures?" Maggie pulled out her phone, but Robbie pushed it away.

"I believe you. It has wi-fi? Cell reception?"

"No Internet, but great cell reception according to the caretaker. There's a caretaker! Right down the road."

"Still...won't you be afraid at night?"

"Me? I'm a lioness."

Robbie rolled her eyes. "If you say so, Mom."

Maggie decided to let the eye roll go. She might not have demonstrated high levels of courage in the past, but hadn't she been fast-tracked into learning bravery over the last four months? "I'll turn on all the outside lights. And take a gun, if you want me to."

She was only joking about the gun, but Robbie latched on to it. "That's not a bad idea. Cal will want you to."

"I'll do it then. I'll do anything for you and Cal. You know that." Maggie reached for her daughter's hand, and this time Robbie didn't push her away. "Let me have this one thing."

Robbie couldn't say no to that. She knew how rarely Maggie had ever put her own desires before anyone else's.

Twenty-seven years ago, just before learning she was pregnant, Maggie had approached a local newspaper about writing a regular column. An editor there gave her a shot. Then twelve columns in the doctor said it was twins.

While Maggie knew she could still manage a bi-weekly column after the babies arrived, Tom—and her parents, his parents—felt the commitment was too much. So she gave it up. She couldn't explain to them then, like she couldn't explain now, how the opportunity had briefly—*exquisitely*—fed her soul.

But then the twins arrived and her heart had a new focus. Only...as Maggie sat in school pick-up lines and drove the kids to piano practice she would catch herself daydreaming, ordering phrases in her head, hearing bits of dialog. She never really stopped writing that column.

As Robbie and Cal grew older and began to need her less, Maggie turned to reading and cooking. Deep in her bones she knew she should be doing something with the words that were forever sorting themselves out in her head, but the newspaper she had worked so briefly for went out of business. The world changed. Technology moved fast. Maggie worried about keeping pace. She didn't have a resume and wasn't sure how to write one.

She hid behind the twins' homework, ballgames, and the cupcakes needed for bake sales so long that if Tom hadn't forced her into stoking the old fires of her writing dream Maggie might never have returned to it. But here she was. Journaling, which had actually proven better than therapy, became the first floating ring she had clung to. Reading books on writing was the second. Now Maggie was eager to actually dive in on a fictional story.

The idea to rent the cabin had come to her at Thanksgiving. Maggie was still getting used to the smaller kitchen of the condo, and parking wasn't easy downtown, so she didn't invite the larger circle of family and friends to join them. Just a quiet meal with Cal and Yvette, Robbie and Mark, followed by a visit to her mother in the nursing home who, with the dementia, didn't know not to ask about Tom.

Now Maggie was an official *divorcee*, as of one week and three days ago. Tom knew a lawyer who knew the judge who pushed it through quickly. As Christmas loomed, she was wrung out and shamed out. Writing had become the last crumb of her shattered self-dignity. If Maggie couldn't get this right, she didn't have a second option.

This was it. This was huge. This was everything. But she didn't know

16

how to say all of that to her daughter. So instead she said, "Neither of us chose this, Robbie, but it doesn't all have to end in tragedy."

Maggie watched as Robbie picked up her Mayan Mocha, a sign of resignation. Then she pondered how long and deep were the ripple effects one person's life could have on another's.

3

After the inciting incident kicks the heroine to the ground, she has to decide whether to lie there or stand up and put one foot in front of the other. If she can rally the reader has cause to cheer.

The cabin was perfect. Maggie had begun to think she would never reach the old log structure on the winding dirt road through the countryside, but there it was suddenly in a burst around a corner through a clearing.

The Outback bounced through the final puddles left by recent rains and came to a halt in a dirt patch in the yard. As she stepped out, Maggie heard a truck ambling up the road behind her. That sole cottage she passed two miles back must have been the caretaker's.

The truck pulled in. The rusty hinges of his door protested as a man swung it open and got out with the help of a cane. He was as weathered and nicked as the green Ford pick-up he drove.

"You must be Mrs. Raines." The man grinned, his voice little more than a whisper. Larynx cartilages hardened and the vocal cords shrank with age. Maggie knew this because Tom was a throat specialist.

She reached to take his gnarled hand. "Pleasure to meet you, Mr. Thompson."

"Been caretaker of this place fifty years," he wheezed. "Still cut the grass in summer. Takes me longer'n it used to. Keep the pipes from freezing in winter. She's cozy. Fella in Florida owns her now, but he don't come up here much."

He pointed toward the door with his cane. "Let's have a look-see."

Maggie popped the trunk for her suitcase, deciding to wait on the crate of kitchen supplies.

Mr. Thompson glanced over. "Need help?"

"Thank you, I've got it." She closed the trunk, embarrassed for him to see the gun case. Cal insisted she bring it along, as Robbie had predicted. "I'll bring the rest in after I make a trip to the store." She pulled the rolling bag behind her over the hard-packed ground.

The porch sat wide—a swing on the right, two rocking chairs to the left—with a "welcome" sign dangling from a nail on the door.

"These are from original trees on the property." Mr. Thompson knocked his cane against the porch rails as he thumped up the steps. "Hickory. That's a strong wood. They's hickory trees all over these parts."

Maggie let her eyes fan over the surroundings and felt her city leanings, unable to name most of the trees she saw, though she did recognize an oak, some maples and dogwoods. "Are they the ones with rough bark?"

The old man's eyes twinkled. "You know a thing or two, don't you?"

She didn't tell him about helping the twins gather leaves for a fourth grade project. Mr. Thompson's comment was generic, but it made Maggie wonder what the older man saw when he looked at her. She had once resembled the Jaclyn Smith of *Charlie's Angels* acclaim—it was her high cheekbones—but in more recent years all she saw in the mirror was a middle-aged woman whose more attractive days had fled. Maggie didn't want to be preoccupied with her looks, but was sensitive to her status as a woman replaced.

Mr. Thompson put the key in the lock, swung the door open, and stepped back so Maggie could go inside. A wood fire crackled in the fireplace. At her raised brow the old man's eyes lit up again. "You said you'd be here about noon, and it's noon. So I snuck down here and built you a fire."

On impulse she hugged him, pleased Mr. Thompson was the caretaker. No other neighbors were in sight, but having a kind old man down the road was enough.

The hug seemed to catch him off guard. Recovering, he swept a hand over the room. "She's old, but as you can see, a beauty. Solid. And she's been modernized, all but the fireplace." He grinned back at her. "Do you know how to build a wood fire, Miss?"

"Been a while, but I'm sure it will come back to me." The twins had been in Scouts. Building fires, filleting fish, roasting S'mores, and spending a few nights on the ground in a pup tent had been part of it. Mostly fathers went on those trips...and Maggie.

Not that she was ever a natural. Maggie had been happy enough to let those fathers build the fires. But now that she was on her own, she was determined that she would...*she could*...learn whatever was necessary...whatever was required.

"Well, you call me if you have any trouble. My number's by the phone in the kitchen. Look over the place and let me know if you have any questions 'fore I take my leave. I know you didn't come out here to gab with me."

Mr. Thompson leaned on his cane as Maggie walked through the cabin.

So perfect. Like the pages of a magazine. Cushy red couch and ottoman in front of a big stone fireplace on the right. Braided rug beneath them. Quilt rack in the corner by the front windows. TV cabinet to the left. A narrow dining table and four chairs flanked the far wall with a cutout over it that held a view of the kitchen. Another cutout, long and narrow, sat above eye level between the living room and bedroom. Maggie could see the cutouts allowed the heat to circulate.

The path from the front door to the back split the log structure neatly in half. Running a hand along the ancient logs, she stepped through the main room toward the kitchen. Small, but ample counter space. Red barstool near an old-fashioned phone on the wall. A washer/dryer combo sat to the left of the back door, an upper shelf running over it with supplies. A hallway on the left led to the single bedroom and bath. Maggie peered into the bathroom first, with its all-white, footed tub, then the bedroom, with its dried vase of lavender on the bedside table, king bed, white matelassé coverlet and red pillows. Exposed beams ran overhead. Nothing on the walls, no clocks, no pictures, just windows—lots and lots of windows—with simple lace toppers.

"That bath used to be a second bedroom. It's newly redone," she heard Mr. Thompson call from the living room as she turned from admiring the bedroom back to the bath. Gray slate floors. And a glass shower large enough for two. Maggie wondered how many couples came here for romantic getaways.

Mr. Thompson didn't ask her why she was alone and Maggie was grateful. She knew she might as well have 'divorce' inked on her forehead. Her left hand still felt strange without the golden band she wore there thirty years. She often caught herself reaching to straighten the marquise diamond that no longer twisted on her finger.

"The windows," Maggie cooed as she returned to the living room, unable to pull her eyes from them. Even skylights overhead. Among all the Tennessee cabins listed, she had chosen this one for its light. Though the wooden logs were rustic, care was taken to install modern windows. The noonday sun lit each room with golden brilliance.

"Everybody loves the windows," he said.

The pictures on the Internet hadn't misrepresented things. The longer blurb had described the cabin as one of the oldest standing structures in Marston County, built by a man named Micah Patterson for the bride he brought here from Sacramento.

"Don't let those windows make you afraid at night." Mr. Thompson stepped toward the front door. "See this switch? At night, you just flip that switch up and folks can't see in. You can see out, but they can't see in. Also helps tint the windows if it gets too bright. Works on every window in the cabin, even the ones in the ceiling. I don't understand how, but it does."

He opened the door. "You'll want to test it, more'n likely. Folks always do. Nobody's up this way to see inside anyway, but that'll give you privacy if you want it."

"Will the fire be okay while I go to the store in town?"

"Oh, sure. You won't be gone more'n two hours, I reckon. That stone hearth is wide. Sometimes a wood piece will pop a spark out, but it don't get past that hearth. It's a solid-built cabin."

Mr. Thompson looked to the sky as he went out. "Looks like snow clouds. I hope it don't snow," he muttered.

Maggie heard the door of his pick-up creak again as he climbed back in. As the sounds of his Ford jostling back down the road died out, she went to inventory the kitchen, to see what kind of pots and pans it had before making her grocery list.

*   *   *

Shirley stepped into the frame of Canon's doorway, causing him to look up. "Let's go on, before it gets dark." She held out his jacket.

He stood and stuffed his arms into the sleeves, then poured himself another cup of coffee, one for the road.

"That's not decaf," she said.

"That's alright."

Her face twisted into that look she had been giving him more of lately—her disgusted look. "Tell me you're not plannin' to come back here and work all night."

"I'm not plannin' to come back here and work all night."

Shirley's face twisted again as Canon moved to the outer door. "I can tell when you're lyin', you know."

He nodded at Amos, the deputy on duty, which Amos knew meant to call him if he needed anything. Shirley was still muttering when she got into the passenger seat of the patrol car. Canon turned the radio up to drown her out. He wasn't lying—Canon *never* lied. He simply had a different definition than Shirley of what "all night" meant.

They drove out of Marston on the main highway, down the familiar curves of Highway 47. The farther they drove, the quieter Shirley became. Canon was quiet by nature. Seven miles out, he pulled off the main road onto gravel that changed to dirt as it wove through the countryside.

Shirley swore suddenly, which really wasn't like her.

"What?" Canon asked.

"I had new flowers at the house I meant to bring."

"They won't care."

"I know they won't care, but I still meant to bring 'em."

"You can bring 'em next time." They did this four times a year, on the birth days not the death days—never on the death days.

The cemetery came into view on the right side of the road, behind an old country church, white, with the windows boarded up. Canon pulled the cruiser into the overgrown lot.

"The paint's peelin'," noted Shirley.

"I'll get down here and put a fresh coat on it when the weather turns."

Shirley shot him a look, her did-you-leave-your-brain-back-at-the-office look. Winter had only begun in Tennessee. The weather wasn't likely to break anytime soon. "Be a good summer project for Kyle."

The part Shirley didn't say...*this time*...was that she thought he worked too hard. But work was Canon's solace. "We can do it together."

Shirley got out first. Canon sat with his memories a minute before following. They walked together over the hard-packed earth until they reached the markers. He stooped down and pulled a wad of weeds that covered one of the names, then smelled of his hand—the smell of plants and soil...a comforting smell...*a pain-filled smell.*

They stayed some minutes, looking out over the cemetery and the fields beyond, neither of them talking.

"Herb still cuttin' the grass?" Shirley finally asked.

Canon nodded. The grass hadn't needed cutting since October, but Herb came a few times through the winter to mulch the leaves and keep things looking neat.

"Lord, I sure do miss 'em." It was another of Shirley's pet phrases.

*   *   *

Maggie hauled the bags of food in, along with her kitchen crate and the gun case, and slid the case beneath the bed beside her emptied rolling bag. Not many clothes had been needed...jeans and sweatpants mostly...cozy slippers...fuzzy socks...some workout clothes for running and yoga...a journal for writing longhand, a computer for typing, a stack of books to read and study.

She placed her clothes in a cedar chest at the end of the bed, hung her robe on a hook in the bath, set out her toiletries, and stacked the books on a table in the living room. By the time she was settled the sun hung low. Maggie flipped the switch for the windows and stepped outside to check around the cabin like Mr. Thompson had predicted. Sure enough the windows were opaque now.

Back in the kitchen, she put two eggs on to boil, chopped multi-colored vegetables on a cutting board, and washed greens for a salad. The water felt colder than at home—more pure. Maggie mixed oil, vinegar, and spices for a dressing and poured it on top of the eggs. She wasn't much of a drinker but did like to cook with wine and thought a few glasses this week were justified. So opening a Chardonnay, she filled half a goblet before sitting down to eat and plan her week's cooking schedule. Raising the glass she offered a toast, "To time alone in a cabin. New year. New life. New me."

Then she reached for her journal.

Tomorrow I'll bake a loaf of bread, and the day after that make pasta.

*   *   *

It was well after dark by the time Canon dropped Shirley at her place, went back to the office to finish reports, and finally drove home. Shirley had invited him in for supper. "There's still leftovers from yesterday."

But he declined. "No, thanks."

This time, as he pulled off the main road onto gravel that turned to dirt, instead of driving past his place to the cemetery, he turned into the winding drive.

When he got out of the patrol car Canon flipped his collar up against the December wind and walked around to the front of the house, stopping at the end of the walk to stare down into what was left of the flower garden. *The smell of dirt.*

After a while, he sat on the front steps and stared into the night, wondering how much longer he could keep this up. Life was short, but too long to come home every night to a stack of mail addressed only to one person.

*   *   *

When the sun peeped over the hill the next morning, Maggie lay awake watching it.

She was an early riser by nature and often slept fitfully the first night in a strange place, even after staying up late to read in front of the fire—a true-crime thriller that didn't make it easy to creep back into the bedroom. But now Maggie was glad to be awake. The windows captured the dawn like a fairy tale, the naked branches of a large oak tree dancing over the skylights.

Suddenly the cabin shone brilliant with daylight. The sun had tipped over the horizon. She threw back the coverlet and set her feet on the floor, savoring the brush of the rug fibers along the bottoms of her feet.

In two days Maggie had a pattern. Watch the sun come up. Curl toes in the rug beside the bed. Go for a walk/run down the dirt road and breathe in the frosty air.

It was thirty minutes to Mr. Thompson's brick cottage to wave to the older gentleman if he happened to be about, then thirty minutes back. Maggie liked to run part of the way, just to feel the chest stabs of being alive.

The colder it got the better. She liked to see her breath roll out and hang in the air in front of her. After breakfast she showered, twisted her brown hair in a towel, and built the fire back up. Then Maggie picked up her pen or opened her laptop and played with words for the next few hours.

Her journal was for rambling. Longhand. Personal thoughts. *So...I'm alone in a cabin in the woods.* Her computer was for the first book idea she had decided to tackle, a story about the man who built the cabin for his bride: *Micah Patterson. 1850s.* Maggie didn't have much to go on, but those two details were a start. If only the rough old logs could talk. She imagined a dark-haired man cutting them, hauling them, stacking them.

Why? For the woman he loved...to make provision for her. *Oh, to be loved like that.* Surely his devotion had seeped into the walls. Maggie could feel an aura of hope hanging over the rafters. Would that hope bless her? And would it bless her writing?

Yes, she decided. *Yes to both.*

Maggie had devoured several books on the writing craft over the past few months and was eager to carve out a process. Her goal for the next week was to get the shell of the idea down. Micah Patterson would be fatherless...misunderstood...befriended in childhood by the woman who would later become his wife. Character sketches...basic plot line...act one...act two...act three...interspersed with personal journaling.

A woman, following Thoreau's much-tested call, went to the woods to see if she could remember how to live. She longed to drink deeply again, to savor and be deliberate--to look for proof she still had a working pulse.

After conversations with writer friends Maggie knew everyone's process was different. She was anxious to find her own rhythm, see if she had the chops to pursue the calling. Could Maggie make enough money to support herself? It didn't promise to be easy, but what had ever proven easy in life?

Her stomach would eventually make her stop and eat—something light, something quick—then supper would be her slower indulgence, her eyes feasting on the deep reds, yellows and greens of the vegetables, her hands savoring the silky texture of oil. After the numbness of the preceding months, Maggie's senses were awakening again. Or maybe her heightened sensitivity to colors, textures, smells, and taste was some-how connected to the hypnotic state of writing. She had never allowed herself this much freedom with the written word.

After supper she read back over her notes, unless she was hot on the story thread. When the words were coming she went back to the computer, her fingers skimming the keys as the fire popped in front of the ottoman where her feet sat propped. When her eyelids grew heavy she crawled under the coverlet in the bedroom and waited to relive the peace and stillness again.

Peace and stillness proved to be the exact liniments Maggie's body had needed. Robbie worried she would be lonely, but Maggie loved the stillness. She could feel it healing her, holding out a window that framed a hopeful future.

Or maybe it was only the calm before the storm.

4

Nothing can remain as it first appears. If it does, the reader won't turn the page. If the reader doesn't turn the page...well...what's the point?

On Wednesday Maggie's cell phone rang. Robbie's voice came through in a rush. "You okay, Mom?"

She had been skimming the first pages of a historical novel, studying the author's opening. "Why wouldn't I be?"

"The weather."

Maggie had noticed a temperature drop that morning. A thermostat with large numbers clung to a porch post. She passed by it each morning, after flipping the switch down and locking the front door. Then she passed by it again when she stepped back onto the porch, resting a moment on the swing or in one of the rockers as she stared at the wooded landscape, letting her breath return to normal before going back in. Maggie liked the swing best. It allowed her to see into the living room and study the cabin, letting the thoughts stirred from her walk float down.

She went to the window and looked out past the swing at the sky. "I'm not worried about the weather." Although it did look snowy.

"What if you lose electricity?"

"This cabin has a big fireplace that puts out a lot of heat. It's wood-burning."

"Do you have a flashlight? Candles?"

"Plenty. Why all the fuss?"

Maggie glanced at the cabinet that held the television she had never turned on, wondering if she should check out the forecast. Might be nice to hear other human voices. It was good to hear Robbie's voice. She had spent so much time in her own head the past three days it was strange to hear herself talking. Maybe it was time to watch one of the movies she had brought.

"They're predicting ice, then snow," said Robbie. "Temperature's dipping down to the single digits. I hate you're out in that cabin alone."

Maggie cradled the phone in the bend of her neck as she rummaged for the flashlight and candles she had seen in a kitchen drawer. Then she went back to the front window and peered out again. "This place looks like it's been through its share of ice storms. And the Subaru handles well in the snow. It's all-wheel drive. You know that."

Robbie sighed.

"Really, Robbie, you sound like me. This is the kind of stuff I'm supposed to say." Maggie went back to the couch in front of the fire. "What about you? You ready for an ice storm? You going to leave your cabinet doors open and drip your water?"

"If I get snowed in I won't be all alone."

"Trust me, I'm well supplied, plenty of food—too much, really. If I get snowed in, good for me. Maybe I'll stay longer."

Robbie's voice dropped. "You're getting impossible, Mom."

"Would you rather I was needy? Wouldn't that be harder on you and Cal?"

Robbie didn't say anything for a minute. Maggie could picture exactly how her daughter would shake her head, casting around for just the right response. "What about the writing?"

"I have ten thousand words."

"Ten thousand! Is that good? How much do you need for a novel?"

"Eighty or ninety."

"Still...at that pace you could have a third of it by the end of the week."

"I feel myself slowing down...second guessing. I wish I had someone to tell me if it's any good."

"You know you're a good writer, Mom. What if you're the next Kristin Hannah?" Robbie knew *The Nightingale* was one of Maggie's favorites.

"How about I be the next Margaret Raines?" She felt Robbie smile on the other end of the line. Robbie was the one, after all, who preached the importance of non-comparisons.

"Fair enough. You sound okay."

"I *am*! Better than okay."

"I just wish the weather wasn't turning bad with you out there by yourself."

"I'm not in Iceland, Robbie. I'm still in Tennessee."

"No one knows how to drive on slick roads in Tennessee."

"That's not true. Who taught you how to drive on them? Stop worrying!"

Robbie grew quiet again. Then she said, "I'm not used to you this way."

"New me." *I'm choosing my life and my attitude. I'm living deliberately.*

"If you say so, Mom."

After they said their goodbyes Maggie decided to mix up a batch of molasses cookies. At the country grocery there had been a whole section of Amish goods. She hadn't been able to resist the pure cane sorghum like the kind her grandmother had kept in a jar on her table for biscuits.

Maggie used to make cookies and cocoa for the twins when it snowed, no reason for her not to have some now.

When the dough was ready, she rolled it and wrapped it in foil so all she had to do was slice and bake tomorrow. Ice began hitting the roof.

A tin roof in an ice storm. The steady ping was better than rain.

After bundling up, Maggie went outside to gather in wood. A large cord sat stacked between two trees in the yard. Scooping several armfuls, she piled them on the porch under the cover of the overhang. She brought more inside, to stack near the fireplace, enough for a couple of days. On her final trip outside, she stopped to stare at the graying skies, suddenly giddy with the anticipation of snow.

*   *   *

Canon was still sitting at his desk catching up on paperwork when Shirley leaned her head in. "Ice is hittin' the windows. You want me to stay?"

"Get on home before it gets bad." Last thing he needed was for Shirley to end up in a ditch. There would be plenty of that without her adding to the mix.

Canon got up and walked from his desk to the door while Shirley got her coat so he could see the ice for himself, get a gauge of how long his night was about to be. The ice was falling thick. Fast.

Shirley, ever thoughtful...*maternalistic*...left the scanner turned low. He could hear the reports droning in from the county to the west. Reporters on the television in the corner were gearing up for a long night, too, with more excitement in their young voices than Canon was feeling. Only eight more years and he was eligible for retirement. That was one number he didn't used to know. Amos and Becky were the spry ones in the office.

"Any more news on that escape from Turney Center?" Canon asked Shirley as she reached for the door. Turney Center was a minimum security prison. Escapes weren't entirely uncommon there. Dickson deputies typically handled them, but the Dickson sheriff had called midday to let Canon know about it, on the chance the guy went south-west toward Marston. Uneasy memories had plagued him ever since.

An ice storm and a prison escape.

"Everybody's gone quiet on that story with all this," said Shirley, wrapping her gray hair under a scarf. "They say it's goin' to be bad, Canon. You sure you don't want me to stay?"

Amos was off and Becky was out working a wreck. He ought to put Amos on alert, but Amos was likely keeping an eye on the weather. Amos and Becky were both good deputies.

"Get on home," he told her.

"I'm cookin' beef stew if you want to come get some while you're out."

"I might do that." Canon knew she knew he wouldn't, but it was nice of her to offer. Shirley fed him plenty as it was.

He watched her get in her Camry and leave. Cars were slowing down on the turns around the square. The falling ice made downtown look magical in the courthouse lights, the white building stark against the deepening sky. Who was that painter? Kinkade. Marston County looked like a Thomas Kinkade painting. Like a dreamland. But Canon knew ice, in reality, was deadly.

The switchboard lit up and the phone started to ring. Canon reached for his jacket.

*   *   *

By the time Maggie finished with the wood she had worked up a sweat. Ice came hard now with snow mixing in. She couldn't resist sticking out her tongue so she could taste the falling flakes.

Maggie was filled with sudden desire to take a bath in the claw foot tub. Once she and Tom had gone to Maine in the winter. The resort where his medical conference was held had private cabins with hot tubs on the porches. There was nothing like being in a hot tub with snow falling all around you. Maggie wished she could drag the tub outside to sit in it naked while snow fell on her eyelashes.

She went inside, turned on the faucets and took some of the candles she found to the bathroom. After lighting them, she slipped out of her clothes and into the steaming water.

* * *

Amos beat him to the fifth accident. Canon pulled the cruiser off the road, put a tired boot on the snow-covered ice, and walked up to get a read on things.

"The driver's calling his wife." Amos pointed toward his patrol car where the man sat. "And a wrecker. If he can get one."

Amos drove the new Explorer, Becky the old. That left Canon the Taurus—an old man's vehicle, they teased him. But they knew it was because of his father so they didn't tease him much.

"Good of you to come." Amos was single and there wasn't a lot to do in Marston County. Working for the sheriff's office was the most exciting thing that had ever happened to the younger man. He often showed up for calls when off the clock.

Amos leaned his head toward the driver talking on his phone. "He's not from around here. Cuttin' through from a job in Memphis. Lives in Franklin. Thought he could beat the weather. Didn't know this is a nasty spot."

Amos had already set out the orange markers to let drivers know this bend was trouble.

He pointed. "Herb Taylor's Bronc in the ditch over there. He walked on home."

Canon had assumed as much, recognizing the Bronco. Herb only lived a half mile down the road. Even the locals had a hard time here when the pavement was slick. He studied the banged up nose of the Franklin man's Jetta. "He okay?"

"Cussin' plenty for the inconvenience, but he's fine."

"You mind stayin' 'til the wrecker comes?"

"Don't mind a bit."

Canon checked his watch. "Things ought to quieten down, but I just got a call Tim Drexler hit a tree near his waterin' hole."

"From drinkin' or the roads?"

"Combination. I'll get him home then write this one up when I get back to the station. Let me know when you leave."

Peering into the window of the Explorer on the way back to his car Canon made sure the man on his phone didn't match the description of the prison escapee from Turney Center.

He didn't.

*　　*　　*

As she sat in the bath and watched smoke rise from the candles Maggie tried to remember if she had flipped the window switch back up when she came in after her run that morning. Darkness had fallen now.

Worried she might have forgotten, she stepped out, wrapped in a towel, and padded to the living room. Sure enough it was down. She flipped the switch and rechecked the locked door, then headed back to the warmth and comfort of the water.

Thonk!

Maggie froze. In three days she had learned most of the cabin's noises. This was different. This was a hard knock that sounded like it came from the woods behind.

The fireplace provided the only light in the room. Straining to listen, Maggie eased to the kitchen window and peered out into the woods. It was hard to trust that no one could really see inside with the switch up, even after testing it.

As Maggie tiptoed from window to window she saw a thickening blanket had covered the ground, the Subaru, the front and back steps of the porches, and the trees all around. But nothing seemed out of place. She replayed the noise in her mind, like the whack of an axe or a piece of wood hitting against a tree trunk, the thud amplified in the frigid air.

It didn't make sense, though. This place was so isolated. No one should be in these woods at night, especially not a night like this. Maybe it had been a buck knocking its antlers against a tree. But...no animal should be out of its shelter either.

The wind didn't appear to be blowing to have knocked tree limbs together. Or could the ice have caused a dead tree limb to fall? That seemed plausible...that a heavy tree limb could have fallen nearby. Although there had been the faintest something. An *oomph*? Or was it only the wind's howl?

But the wind wasn't blowing. When a mind tried to replay the unexpected it was tempted to fill in the cracks with imagination. Maggie wished now she had not started reading that true-crime novel.

Her body trembling from the cold, Maggie made her way back to the bath and eased into the warmth again, adding a few drops of lavender oil. A woman alone in a cabin needed every relaxation trick she could find, especially with an unexplained *thonk* in the air, and her eyes playing tricks on her as she peered into the snowy night over the side of her porcelain tub.

The snow picked up. Maggie watched it fall until the water went tepid. By the time she pulled the drain plug the land was a postcard. *Robbie didn't exaggerate the weather.* Pellets of ice mixed in the snow continued to plink against the roof and windows.

Maggie told herself it would be beautiful in the morning. It was beautiful now. But she still felt uneasy about the noise she couldn't place. She wondered if she should have headed on home to Nashville when Robbie called. Had she been foolish to think she could ride out the storm alone?

She was tempted to call Mr. Thompson, but hated to ask him to get out on such a night with no more cause than a single *thonk*. If it had been a tree limb falling, it didn't cause any damage that Maggie could see. She would call Mr. Thompson tomorrow...unless she heard the noise again.

Maggie wondered how old Mr. Thompson was and if he could really be a help to her. Then she remembered she had Cal's gun under the bed. That was some small comfort.

Most likely a tree branch falling.

After dressing in her flannel pajamas, robe and slippers, Maggie opened the cabinet doors and dripped water in the faucets. Best to be on the safe side. Finally, she settled on the couch beneath a blanket, a flickering candle on the table near her head, and opened the true-crime novel.

The pinging of ice pellets on the roof after the soothing lavender in her bath soon lulled her to sleep.

5

An artist must prepare for the unexpected. Entering a new realm is frightening, a risky proposition with a real chance of failure, including the chance of harm and damage to your soul.

Canon saw a man talking to a tree as he pulled up. Tim Drexler was likely scolding the maple for his own bad choices. Or did he think the tree was a person?

Tim was a regular. Canon had resisted the urge to tally up just how much Tim cost his department on an annual basis, but knew it was a sizable figure. The man had plenty of ghosts in his closet, like most folks from Marston.

Canon got out of the cruiser, slid down the bank and reached for him. "Come on, Tim."

Tim slurred his words, trying to hug Canon, happy to see him, pointing to the tree and his pick-up. Canon didn't see how Tim's old truck would keep driving after this one. It didn't take an ice storm for Tim to end up in a ditch.

Hauling him up the bank, Canon got him into the back of the cruiser, where Tim lay over and cuddled the seat like a lover. He reeked of alcohol and unwashed armpit. The snow had doused him pretty good, but not enough to dilute Tim's natural odors. Tim was raised on Lick Creek. His family didn't have running water for a long time. When Tim finally got it, he conserved it in bathing to save more for the stills.

Twenty minutes later, with the low hum of the scanner and Tim's snores making background music, Canon pulled in front of an old farmhouse missing a front shutter. Still, it looked pretty in the falling snow. After several knocks, Tim's wife, Tina, came to the door, looking like she'd gone to sleep in her waitress outfit.

Tina took Tim's arm without saying anything, long ago having given up on scolding him. Canon stood at the door until she got Tim settled inside and returned, looking older than she really was. "I'm sorry you had to get out on such a night, Canon. I don't know what I'd do without you."

"Tell him the truck's on Lick Creek. And it's probably not going to drive home this time."

Tina shook her head, her eyes cast down, and closed the door. Canon felt bad for her, and made a mental note to call Seth Jenkins tomorrow to see if Seth could pick it up in his tow truck. No telling when Tim would get to it. Maybe Canon would tell Seth to go on and fix it if it was fixable, and send him the bill without saying anything to Tina.

*   *   *

Maggie woke with a start to banging on the door. Fear shot through her. The candle flickered on the side table. She never should have gone to sleep with a candle burning.

Straining, but not hearing anything but the hard knock of her own heart, she decided she must have only dreamed the banging on the door. Then it came again—*a hard pound!*

She lay still on the couch, not sure what to do, reaching for her cell phone but it wasn't on the table. She must have left it in the bedroom. *No one should be at the door.*

More banging. Maggie jumped.

She thought of Cal's gun, but groped toward the closer phone in the kitchen, squinting to see Mr. Thompson's number on the wall. *More banging!* She dropped the phone receiver then set it back in its cradle, deciding it had to be Mr. Thompson at the door, come to check on her.

What time is it? Where was her cell phone?

A moan stole through the walls followed by a hard thump at the base of the door as if someone kicked or threw their weight against it.

Maggie willed her feet toward the front window. A heap lay at the door. She had to open it. *She couldn't.* But she had to. The thermometer outside read eight degrees. She looked for Mr. Thompson's truck, but the only vehicle outside was her own.

With trembling hands she turned the lock.

A man lay curled on the porch shivering, wearing only a light jean jacket. No hat. No gloves. His hands stuffed under his armpits. His thumbs red. His head and clothes dusted in snow and ice. When Maggie cracked the door open the man slowly twisted and looked up at her.

"Help me," his blue lips mouthed.

*   *   *

Canon finished the last report and looked at the scanner. Quiet. Finally. Then he hit the blinking light on the voice machine.

"I knew you wouldn't come get that stew, but I saved you some and I'll bring it tomorrow. I would have had Jack run it over to your place, but I's worried about him gettin' stuck and keepin' you out longer. I hope you're not workin' past midnight. Go home."

Even as a kid Shirley had leaned toward bossy.

Canon checked his cell phone. No messages. 12:58. Close enough. He would tell Shirley it was midnight. She worried enough about him.

He reached for his jacket, turned off the lights and was out the door by 12:59. So he didn't see the single line of text that rolled across the bottom of the scanner at 1:00: *Man spotted on foot near Patterson Road.*

*　*　*

Maggie flung the door wide and pulled the man inside, dragging him by the back of his jacket toward the fire. He was heavy and yelped at the harsh treatment, as if his limbs had begun to set in a curled position and she was torturing him by trying to straighten him out.

"I'm sorry! I'm trying to get you closer to the fire." She reached for a quilt from the rack and threw it over him, using it to rub his frozen limbs.

"Easy!" he hissed, jerking his body away. "It's too much."

"I'm sorry." Maggie felt of his hands, stiff and bent as frozen boards. "Tell me how to help you."

His face clenched like his body. "Just let me lie here."

She stepped back to study him, wondering if this was really happening or if she was in the middle of a vivid dream. The man began to shake. Maggie pulled another quilt from the rack and tucked it around him. Feeling the cold herself, she closed the cabin door, locked it and stood to the side marveling at the sudden change to her evening, still wondering if it was real.

*　*　*

Canon's patrol car left tracks in the winding drive. He stamped his snowy boots on the back porch of the farmhouse and flipped on the lights in the kitchen.

He could smell the Pine-Sol clean of the counters before he saw them. That meant Thelma, a neighbor down the road, had come even though it was a holiday week. Canon was a little surprised, but knew she needed the money. Thelma came every second and fourth Wednesday. He was thankful she brought in the mail and thumbed through it as he opened the fridge, making a mental note to drop a check in Thelma's mailbox on his way into the office tomorrow. In case her family was low. Thelma's husband, Frank, worked at the plant and this was their slow season.

The shelves of the refrigerator were bare, Shirley's leftovers from Christmas long gone. Canon opened the freezer next and stared at the plastic selections, his stomach rumbling at the thought of Shirley's stew. Oh well, she'd bring him some tomorrow.

None of the bags looked appetizing, so he closed the door and went up the stairs.

*   *   *

Maggie's heart thumped wildly as the man continued to shake on the floor, more violently now. Had she waited too long? *Tom never once talked about hypothermia!* How should that be treated?

"I'll call an ambulance," she offered, stepping toward the kitchen.

"No!" He tried to rise. "No ambulance."

"Okay. Okay." Maggie came back and knelt beside him, her brain flailing for solutions. "Hot coffee?"

He groaned. "Soup?"

Maggie had brought some tomato soup from home. "I'll go warm it." She hurried to the kitchen. *Where did he come from? And what was he doing out in this weather?* She was anxious to put the questions to him, but felt she should help him get thawed out first.

Think, Maggie!

When the soup was on the stove, she pulled cheese and butter from the refrigerator and sliced the homemade bread. She would make him a grilled cheese sandwich, too. That was good with tomato soup. Maybe two sandwiches. How long had it been since he'd eaten?

Maggie watched the man through the cutout then stuck her head back through the door to the living room. He was still shaking, his limbs rattling against the floorboards.

"How about a hot bath? That would be the quickest way, wouldn't it? To get you warm?" She knew from recent experience.

The man moaned like an animal. What had he been through?

"Yes," came the whisper from where he lay curled on his side.

Maggie ran to fill the tub. With the water running and the soup simmering, she came back to help him up. A tear slid off the end of his nose. His pain-filled gaze pierced her. She could see his eyes were blue and his grizzled cheeks gaunt. His hair, matted with ice and snow, light-colored underneath.

"Thank you," he whispered. His face broke into a sudden smile. "I must have scared the bejeebies out of you."

Maggie laughed, from relief not joy. "I was asleep. Not expecting anyone."

"I guess not."

Putting her hands under his arms, she helped the man stand. He yelled again, tensing. The quilts fell off. That's when she noticed the blood on his leg.

He must have felt her stiffen. "I fell on the ice. Into a broken post. I don't think it's bad."

Fear trickled up Maggie's spine. A stranger...in her cabin...in the middle of the night...injured...nearly frozen. And now she was helping him to the bath. But...she couldn't leave a man writhing in pain...freezing...on her porch.

She walked him slowly toward the bathroom thinking about the gun beneath her bed.

Lowering the lid on the toilet, Maggie helped the man sit while she checked the water. "I hope it's not too warm." The faucets squeaked as she twisted them off. "You can add more hot as you can stand it."

From where he sat curled tight the man nodded. Maggie wondered if they would ever get him straightened out again. His hands looked use-less. He tried to move them, but they didn't appear to be working. She told herself there was nothing to be alarmed about. This man was docile as a kitten, and seemed genuinely grateful for her help.

"I hate to ask you this," he said.

"It's okay." Maggie knew what he was going to say and almost added *I'm a mom*, but thought better of it. This wasn't a child she was about to undress. It was hard to tell the man's age. It was hard to even get a good look at him, the way he sat hunched and shaking.

First Maggie peeled the jean jacket off his shoulders, taking care in pulling the sleeves over his frozen hands. He groaned as she moved his stiffened limbs.

"Like knives!" he said, with a grimace. She knew he was talking about the blood flowing back.

When she had the jacket off of him, Maggie unlaced his shoes, old canvas Converse, and peeled off his icy socks. His clothes were ill fitting and no match for the weather.

Where was his car? Why was he on foot? Why was he not dressed to be out in this weather? Where had he come from? And where was he going?

The man's feet were well shaped and masculine, as ice-chilled as his hands. Maggie stood and pulled his shirt from the waistband then leaned in to unbutton it. The only man she had ever undressed was Tom, and Tom was not this tall, not this muscled...nor had he ever shaken like a leaf while she unfastened his clothing.

She worked the man's arms out of his shirt, then his undershirt, and peeled the latter up over his head. A thin tattoo ran under his collar-bone, from his right to left shoulder, the word "everlasting" in rolling scroll. Maggie tried not to stare at the letters or hairline that reached up to encircle them.

Violent spasms shook his body. They needed to get him in the water. She helped him stand. The only thing left was his pants.

"The shower might have worked better," Maggie said. "I just thought—"

"No, you were right." His breathing jerked, as erratic as his movements. "That would have been like icepicks." His hands groped the clasp of his jeans, but his fingers were wooden. "If you'll just get me started," he whispered, "I think I can manage from there."

"Okay, but shouldn't we get you closer?" Based on his mobility, she didn't see how he could get himself to the tub.

He glanced at it several feet away in front of the large windows along the wall. "You're right."

Nudging her shoulder under his arm, Maggie inched him over.

"Get me started," he whispered again, his mouth near her ear. She felt his face break into a grin. "Just don't take advantage of me."

"Of course not." Maggie avoided his eyes and unfastened his pants, sliding her hands along his quivering sides, inching the trousers down until the bones of his hips showed. She tried not to notice, but from all indication, the lower part of his body was as well defined as the top.

His breath stirred the top of her hair. "That should do."

Without looking up again, Maggie made sure his arms would hold him to the side of the tub, then she left the bathroom and closed the door. She stood in the hallway some minutes with her back to the wood trying to calm the rapid drum of her heart.

Did I just undress a stranger?

She could hear him grunting and working to get his pants off on the other side of the door, so it must have been happening. Maggie looked down at her hands, remembering the cold of his skin, the ice in his shoes and socks. He was talking to himself on the other side of the door, but she couldn't make out the words.

In a moment of panic, Maggie feared he would pull the tub over. But surely it was weighted enough by the water to support his heavy lean against it. Finally, she heard a splash and knew he'd rolled over the side. She pressed her ear to the door to make sure he wasn't drowning. Presently, the sloshing of the water stilled and Maggie heard a clear "ah-hhh."

That's when she tiptoed across the hall to the bedroom and slid Cal's gun case out from under the bed. With trembling hands she unsnapped the case cringing at the loud pops it made. She took the gun out then looked for a place to hide it. Under the pillow didn't seem especially clever, but Maggie couldn't think of any better place so she tucked it there and went to check on the soup.

Soon she heard more water running.

*   *   *

Canon wasn't a dreamer. Sometimes work crept into his nighttime thoughts, but dreams? Hardly ever. That one from back in August had lingered in his mind because it was so rare.

This one started with him in the woods helping Tim Drexler up the snow-covered bank. Then he was in an unfamiliar woods. Instead of helping Tim, he watched another man—a thinner man—dragging a body up a bank. The body was a man on the ground who wasn't dead yet, but soon would be if he didn't get in from the cold. He'd been knocked in the head with a fallen branch, knocked in the head by the thin man dragging him.

How did Canon know all this? He just knew. Dreams ran that way. He was a silent observer, watching. He may not have seen the thin man strike the other one down, but in his dream he knew this had happened—knew it with conviction.

Canon watched a killer disposing of a body.

*   *   *

Maggie watched the snow still falling outside the kitchen window and tried to get her heightened nerves to calm down. Then she went from the kitchen to the front windows to study the man's tracks wondering if he had made the noise she heard before falling asleep. If so, why stay out there? She couldn't make sense of it.

There wasn't a single track around the house that she could see. The man must have come up the dirt road, but the white blanket outside was undisturbed...pristine. The snow was falling hard, but it didn't seem possible it would have fallen hard enough to cover the route he had taken in so short a time.

She went back to the kitchen, pulled out a frying pan and assembled his sandwiches. Once they were searing she picked up the phone to call Mr. Thompson. As it rang, she heard the water drain, surprised the frozen man didn't stay in the bath longer. Or was Maggie not keeping good track of time? The clock on the microwave said 2:36.

*　　*　　*

Canon watched as the killer strained, pulling the body up the wooded hill, leaving a deep swath in the snow. Canon was a mist that floated behind, leaving no tracks of his own.

When the thin man finally reached the top of the embankment—the top of a ridge—he stopped to catch his breath and look back down the hill. Canon followed his gaze. A cabin lay nestled in a clearing below, soft light flickering in a window. He couldn't see inside.

The man on the hill began pulling again, hauling the body over the edge, shoving it hard, sending it rolling down a ravine. Canon watched until the spiraling body came to rest below, then watched the man reach down to pick up a handful of snow, using it to wash his hands. His breath came in hot vapors. The killer started back down the hill. Canon followed.

As they got closer to the cabin, Canon could see that the window was steamed—clouded—but light flickered on the other side as if made by the dance of a candle. A woman was in there bathing—a dark-haired woman—the same dark-haired woman Canon had seen the last time he dreamed. He could not explain how he knew this.

Then Canon was inside Ollie Thompson's cottage. The old man was drunk. *Of course he was, it was snowing.* Empty beer cans littered the place.

Ollie's phone rang, but the old man couldn't hear it. Canon tossed fitfully, his hand reaching for the phone. The dark-haired woman was in trouble. Ollie was closest, but Ollie couldn't help her.

Canon's breath grew short. He reached for the phone again but his hands wouldn't work. He couldn't pick up the beer cans either. He couldn't wake Ollie. He couldn't see the scanner. He couldn't help the woman. His hip radio wouldn't come off the set.

Canon wanted to yell—to shake the old man with his fists. Hadn't they had enough of this? Would Ollie not *ever* be over his grief? But even as Canon cursed the old man, he understood. *Grief is a ghost that never leaves your mind.*

Then Canon woke, the sheets of his bed soaked in sweat.

*   *   *

Maggie counted six rings, but Mr. Thompson never picked up. When she heard the knob on the bathroom door twist, she hung up the phone and reached for the spatula. As she turned off the burner she heard steps in the hall.

There he stood, the mysterious man, a towel wrapped around his waist, *everlasting* scrolled across his chest. "My hands work." He flexed them to show her. Blood dripped below the towel down his injured leg. He followed her eyes and saw it. "Sorry. I didn't have a bandage."

As he looked around for something besides the cloth at his waist to blot the blood, Maggie pulled off a wad of paper towels and handed them to him.

"My clothes were wet with snow," he explained.

"Come eat and I'll find something to wrap that wound." Maggie had a first aid kit in the trunk of her car, but maybe there was one in this cabin.

Instead of sitting at the table while she checked, the man picked up one of the sandwiches, devoured it in four quick bites, then picked up his soup bowl and sipped from the rim as he followed her to the bathroom.

Maggie checked every cabinet—no bandages.

"I have a first aid kit in my car." She scooped up his clothes and stepped past him to the dryer to pitch them in and start it running.

Then she stepped past him again to get the keys from her purse in the bedroom.

A man wrapped in a towel is in my cabin. 'Everlasting' on his chest. I'm not sure this is really happening.

As Maggie reached for her coat the man's hand was suddenly on her wrist. Her skin was already pricking from the way he had followed her. Now he had her by the arm. When Maggie had brought him inside, the man had seemed so helpless. He wasn't helpless now.

She went still.

6

"Where can I go from your Spirit? Where can I flee from your presence?... Search me, God, and know my heart...lead me in the way everlasting." Excerpts from Psalm 139, NIV

"You'll come back, won't you?" he asked.

"Of course." Maggie's heart rapped hard against the cavity of her chest. "I'm just getting the first aid kit." She looked down at her purse, wondering if she should take it with her, make a run for it. But the weather didn't lend itself to a hasty exit, plus...Maggie felt strange, like a fog had moved into her mind, like she was still half asleep despite the events of the night.

The man smiled and let Maggie's wrist go. She could still feel the urgency in his fingers, though, as she walked through the living room. He stopped at the dining table and finally picked up the spoon for his soup.

Perhaps she was over-reacting. The man might simply feel needy or frightened to think she would leave him. Still, it was an odd feeling to open the door and walk out of the cabin. What if the man closed and locked the door? Maggie had her car key. If he did, she *would* make that exit, hasty or not.

I'll be okay.

An icy blast met her on the porch. Thick snow swirled. There must have been four inches on the ground by now. Twice going down the steps Maggie caught herself on the rail.

Slowly—gingerly—she made her way out to the car, popped the trunk and grabbed the first aid kit. Tom had insisted she keep the kit in her car, but she had never once used it. Maggie wasn't even sure what was in there.

The biting snow stung her cheeks. It was colder now than when she had gathered the wood. No wonder the man had nearly been frozen. How long had he been out here? Where was his car? And why were there no tracks? It was as if he had materialized on the porch.

If Mr. Thompson's house wasn't so far down the road Maggie would have made a slog for it. Or was Mr. Thompson even home? Could he have gotten caught by the weather on a trip to town? Maggie hoped not. That would mean she was truly alone with the man in her cabin.

For how long?

Maggie made her way back to the porch steps clutching the kit to her chest. The man watched her from the door and held it open as she came inside, helping to brush snow from her shoulders and hair.

For the first time Maggie thought about how she must look. She hadn't expected to see anyone. No makeup. Hair piled loosely on her head. When she pulled off her coat and boots she pulled out the tie that held her hair, shaking snow and ice to the floor in front of the fire.

She felt the man watching her as she tied it back up.

"Longer than I imagined," he said.

Maggie wasn't sure if he meant her hair, or the time it took her to get the first aid kit.

The man shivered and pulled a fleece blanket off the quilt rack to wrap around his shoulders, pointing to the dancing flames. "I put another log on. And added the wet blankets to the dryer."

Maggie heard the hum of the appliance. "You need some clothes. I have a pair of sweat pants and an oversized t-shirt. I'm sorry I didn't think about it before." She set the kit on the table. "I'll patch that hole in the leg of your jeans if I can find some thread."

"I'd be grateful." The man smiled again. It was nice, his smile, though his front teeth were crooked.

Maggie went to get her largest shirt and sweats, both black. He didn't follow her this time. Coming back, she laid the clothes on the table in front of him and opened the first aid kit. He pulled a chair around for her then reached for another to prop his wounded leg. The soup and sandwiches were gone.

The wound, just above his right knee, was a deep gash that looked like it was made by a sharper object than a piece of wood. But Maggie didn't question him about it.

"What is your name?" The man's eyes bore into her. "I always like to know the name of a woman who undresses me." He grinned when Maggie looked up.

How many women had undressed him?

"Maggie. Raines."

"Short for Margaret, or Margarite?"

"Margaret."

He stuck out his hand. "I'm Zeke, Maggie. Short for Ezekiel."

Maggie put her hand firmly in his and smiled. "Good to see your hands working, Zeke." She wasn't sure she really meant it, but it seemed polite to say.

He hesitated in letting her hand go.

She reached for a bottle of Peroxide. "On the chance you still have debris in the wound."

"Do it," he said.

Maggie doused several cotton balls and cleaned the wound, dabbing it lightly at first, until he pressed on her hand. "You don't have to be gentle with me, Maggie. Not now that I'm thawed out."

"It could use stitches," she said.

"It'll be fine."

Maggie poured Peroxide in the bottle's cap and dripped it into each cut until the bubbling stopped. Then she opened three large gauze pads, smeared them with Neosporin, and pressed them over the wounds. Next she took a roll of gauze and wrapped it around his leg to hold the cut skin together, and so the bandages wouldn't come loose. She cut the end of the gauze and tucked it into a fold. "I'm not a nurse by profession."

"Could have fooled me. Looked like you know what you're doing. You have kids, Maggie?"

She nodded. "Twins."

"How old?"

"Twenty-six."

"*Twenty-six!* Did you have them when you were ten?"

Maggie blushed and repacked the kit. "I'm not even wearing makeup."

"You should never wear makeup. Shouldn't tie that hair up either."

Her cheeks flushed again. *What am I, a blushing girl? Was I fishing for that compliment?* Maggie held up the kit. "I'm going to put this in the bathroom."

She stepped down the hall, set the container on a shelf, then went to the bedroom to put her key back in her purse and get him the Tylenol. As Maggie's hand closed over the bottle she glanced at the side table where she remembered she left her cell phone. She ought to text Robbie and Cal about what happened.

But her phone wasn't there. Maggie's heart skipped a beat. She lifted the pillow where she had hidden the gun. It was gone, too.

Maggie's mind and body went numb. She stood still, trying to think what she should do. A floorboard creaked behind her. She turned. Zeke knew she knew the gun was gone, she could read it in his eyes.

He had donned the t-shirt and sweat pants and the fleece blanket was wrapped around his shoulders again. "We should probably talk, Maggie."

7

"It is not death that a man should fear, but he should fear never beginning to live." Marcus Aurelius

Maggie wasn't a screamer...wasn't quick to excitement. She killed her own bugs, set her own mousetraps (that first year of college, renting an old house with three other girls—mice were never a problem living with *Tom*, of course), and once when grease in a pan on the stove caught fire, she calmly grabbed the handle, set the pan in the sink and used a box of baking soda to douse the flames. Just like they tell you to.

On the inside Maggie's blood could boil or freeze, and on the outside she would look the same—unfazed, collected.

She neither flinched nor blinked as Zeke leaned in and put his mouth close to her ear. "While we're in the bedroom..." but a chill did trickle down her spinal cord, "...do you have an extra pair of socks?"

Maggie, conscious the chill had landed and settled in her hip joints, stepped around him to the end of the bed. She lifted the lid of the cedar chest, pulled out the first pair of socks she saw—fuzzy, with stripes of pink and blue—and laid them in his outstretched hand.

"Thank you." He put them on and followed her down the hall. The pants were short on him, gathered several inches above his ankles, so he needed the socks. Cool air skimmed the wooden floors of a cabin, especially on a bone-chilling night like this one. "How about that coffee now?" he asked as they passed the kitchen.

Maggie's hands remained steady as she opened the cabinet. "Decaf or regular?"

"Decaf. I don't know about you, but I could use a good night's rest."

He was planning to stay then? *Where will he sleep?*

Maggie's mind remained numb as she measured beans into the grinder and pushed the button. "How many cups?"

"Only one for me, thanks."

She put two rounded spoonfuls into the basket and poured water in the carafe, then stood by the coffee maker waiting to see if he had more instructions. He watched her. She couldn't read his eyes, but thought she detected a note of disappointment. Or was it sadness?

Will he kill me? Rape me? Where did he come from? What is he doing here? Talk about bad timing for a week alone in a cabin. Maggie had chosen this one for its light. And now the darkest cloud since the day Tom told her about Bethany had formed just over the roof.

Tom and Bethany are the reason I'm here.

Ripple effects.

Maggie rubbed her forehead. Where was Mr. Thompson? Would she get another opportunity to call him? And if she did, would he answer? Should she run out of the house and take her chances in the snow and ice?

She opened the refrigerator door for the Half and Half. "Cream? Sugar?"

Maggie had saved a few drops of white wine to add to a salad dressing. Her eyes landed on the bottle. *If I grab that Chardonnay, could I smash it against the counter and use the jagged edges to fend him off?* Tactics like that seemed to work in the movies.

"Neither," he said.

He used words like 'neither.' Said 'thank you.' Had teased her not to take advantage of him by the tub. He was docile at first, helpless, seemingly frightened when she went out to the car. Maggie kept trying to wrap her head around the changes, the strangeness of this night.

When she closed the door to the refrigerator and turned back to the counter, she noticed the knife block. Empty. All the knives were gone.

A slight tremor started in her hands as she filled two mugs with coffee—hers with added cream—and handed him one. Zeke's eyes lingered on the tremor, but he didn't comment on it, just nodded his head toward the living room.

*   *   *

Canon was asleep again...dreaming again. Same dream. Same players.

The man who pulled the body up the hill was now standing in an all-white bathroom. Canon still couldn't get a good look at his face. All he could see was the dark-haired woman undressing the man. Then she was undressing Canon, unfastening the buttons on his shirt.

Her slender hands—beautiful hands—were now tending to Canon's wounds, pouring Peroxide on a bandage, laying it over his chest.

How did she know?

Canon reached for her. She was in his arms. But it was no longer the dark-haired woman. It was Rita, red curls pinned up.

When Canon looked past Rita, who'd grown limp in his arms, he could see the white bathroom in the distance...the man walking out, then into a bedroom, slipping a gun from beneath a pillow the color of newly spilled blood...picking up a cell phone...removing knives from a block.

*   *   *

Maggie and Zeke walked in and sat at opposite ends of the red sofa. She remembered that last visit with Tom. Anger had fueled her, helped her get out of the house. Could she summon enough fury to escape this man's clutches? Fear and fury, it was suddenly clear to Maggie, didn't mix well. Fear presently ruled. Fear had the upper hand.

Zeke stretched his legs to the fire. Maggie curled hers beneath her, making herself as small as she knew how. It would have been comical to see him wearing her clothes and fuzzy socks had he not taken her phone...Cal's gun...the knives.

Silence hung like a mist, filling every crevice of the room. The only sound, besides the hissing and popping of the fire, was the sound of Zeke sipping his coffee until Maggie finally swallowed and said, "I'm listening." Her coffee sat untouched on the table beside her.

Zeke turned to her, grinning, holding the mug close to his chin. "I like that about you, Margaret Raines. You're a calming presence, a capable woman." He took another sip. "And you make a fine cup of coffee. I looked for a wedding ring in the bedroom and didn't find one. But you have children." His eyes searched hers. "Are you divorced or widowed?"

Maggie didn't know what to say. How could he do that? Talk like they met at a coffee shop. On an arranged date. *What is this?* Her eyes watered against her will.

Zeke saw it and winced. "Oh, Maggie, don't cry. That'll kill me! I like you."

She shook her head, questions looming large. "Who are you? What are you doing here?"

He looked behind him, grabbed a box of tissues off the table and handed them to her. "I'm trying to figure out the same thing, Maggie Dearest. What are *you* doing here?"

It didn't feel safe to be transparent. Maggie stared at him, mute, as a long tentacle of silence curled in the air between them.

"I understand," said Zeke finally. "I haven't gained your trust."

"Where's my cell phone?" Maggie's voice wasn't much more than a croak. Fear, like age, tightened the vocal cords.

Zeke reached behind the sofa cushion to his back and pulled out her phone. "You mean this? Someone named Cal sent you a message while you were outside. Is there a code?" He looked down at the cell phone as if he'd never seen one before, as if it were a marvel.

Without thinking Maggie lunged. Whether she was going for the phone or his throat she couldn't have said. But her hands never made it. Zeke grabbed her arms and pushed her back on the sofa. He was on top of her now, pinning her hands down with his elbows.

*   *   *

Canon tossed in his sleep. Straining. His brow knotted, slick with sweat. He was younger...a deputy...knocking on Ollie's door, snow falling around him.

Now he was pounding. "Ollie!" Canon tried the door. It was open. He found Ollie in the bedroom, beer cans scattered over a nightstand and rug.

Canon lifted the old man's head in his arms. Then the dream turned to Rita—it was Rita that Canon held now, her head flailing like Ollie's to the side, her straw hat fallen to the ground. But she wasn't drunk.

Pulled weeds littered the grass around her. Canon could still smell the upturned soil.

*   *   *

Fear spread through Maggie's body like a grease fire. She didn't know this man, Zeke, and suddenly couldn't see her future. Was this to be her final night? *Lord, don't make Robbie and Cal suffer this, too. Don't make them bear my death.*

Tom would be sorry. Served him right.

Zeke's low laugh in her ear sent another unwelcome shiver down her spine. This time it settled above her tailbone. "You're a quick one." He put his head mere inches from her own. "I don't want to hurt you, Maggie. Not after you've been so good to me."

Confusion bubbled hot inside her, and sudden rage at being pinned down. Maggie strained to free her hands, but Zeke held them in a vice-grip.

Could she kill this man? Could she do it to save her own life?

Probably not.

Tears of frustration scratched the sides of her cheeks.

But can he kill me?

Maggie didn't want to force the answer. She squeezed her eyes shut to stop the tears—to keep from having to meet Zeke's eyes. She'd already noted how blue they were and was furious with herself for noticing. And his teeth were brilliant white, although those on the bottom overlapped. And he could use a shave.

She felt him shift his weight, then he was wiping her tears with one of his hands. Did a man bother to wipe a woman's tears if he was planning to kill her?

Maggie's eyes flew open. "Who are you?" she whispered. The vocal cords were really folds. Enough air had to push up and out between the folds to cause a vibration for a voice to work.

Zeke looked hurt. "I told you my name, Maggie."

"I still don't know who you are, or how you came to be on the porch."

All at once he released her. She sat up and hugged the box of Kleenex on her end of the sofa. Zeke settled back on his side, still holding Maggie's cell phone. "I notice you didn't say 'my' porch. Is it still a rental?"

He knows this place? Maggie nodded.

"How long do you have it rented?"

She pressed her lips together, refusing to answer.

Zeke studied her several moments. Maggie glared back. She wouldn't die or be cowed into answering his questions without a fight.

He was the first to crack. "Are you expecting someone?" Zeke held up the phone. "This 'Cal' person?"

"No!" The thought of Cal driving up to check on her sent an icy shiver through Maggie's heart. "What did the text say?"

"It's called a what? A text?"

How does he not know this?

Zeke studied the phone. "Is there a code to unlock it?"

Maggie stared at him.

"The code, Maggie. And I'll read it to you."

She took her time answering. "Zero eight, zero nine."

An eyebrow lifted as he punched it in. "That's not terribly original. Twins' birthday?" She didn't answer. "Your birthday?" She nodded. "How old are you, Maggie?"

"Fifty."

Both of his eyebrows lifted this time. "I never would have guessed that. Was it special? Big party?"

Tears welled up again. "No. No party." *Just a bittersweet walk through the house I once lived in, to parcel out my things.*

Zeke frowned. "Why not?"

Maggie studied him. He didn't look like a killer, he looked like the guy next door—the good-hearted hippie who would help you get a snake out of your garage, or fix a leaking faucet.

Zeke crossed his arms and stared back at her with all the calm of a therapist. "Tell me about it."

"You said you'd read me the text."

"Patience, Maggie. I want to know what's making you cry. It's not me this time."

Maggie pulled out a tissue and blew her nose. "This *cannot* be happening." She finally took a gulp of her coffee. The warmth felt good sliding down her throat.

"Why are you sad, Maggie? What made you rent this cabin?"

So she told him. What else was she supposed to do? "I spent my birthday walking through my house to see what I was going to keep. Anything that didn't have Tom's mark on it."

"And Tom is..."

"Tom was my husband."

"How long?"

"Thirty years."

"Why did it end?"

"He got his receptionist pregnant."

Zeke winced. "So Cal is one of the twins? Boys?"

Maggie shook her head.

"Girl and a boy." Zeke was quick. This did nothing to make her feel better. "How old is the receptionist?"

Maggie felt her forehead furrow. The answer sent a shame wash through her every time. "Twenty-six."

Zeke's breath caught. "Same age as the twins?" Then his face grew dark. "That bastard!"

Maggie looked up at him.

Zeke leaned forward. "I'd kill him if I thought it'd make you feel better, Maggie. But it wouldn't. Trust me." His face went darker still, his blue eyes icy.

I'd kill him if I thought it'd make you feel better, Maggie.

The words cracked back and forth in Maggie's mind like an ice tray. She remembered the day she sat on the sofa across from Tom and pictured him in a casket. Yes, in that single moment Maggie had wanted Tom to die. She had even wondered if she could do it.

But...Maggie didn't wish Tom dead. Not anymore. She'd gone through the worst of it already...people knowing...the twins knowing. In the beginning, when she first learned about it, the thought of Tom's death was simply kinder than the realization of his betrayal.

She felt Zeke watching her but didn't say anything, the memory of that awful day replaying in her mind and heart, re-cracking open the wounds.

Finally Zeke said, as if he sensed what was going through her mind, "Tom is an A-one idiot, Maggie. But that's no reflection on you."

"You haven't seen Bethany. She's beautiful."

"I'm looking at Maggie. She's beautiful."

Maggie rubbed her forehead, as if subliminally checking to see if she could still feel her own skin. *This cannot be happening.*

Zeke's next words came to Maggie's ears as through a tunnel. "And it's more than her brown eyes and long hair and how good it felt to have her try to get this phone out of my hands. There's a strong light in you, Margaret Raines. I could see it from a long way off."

A dozen emotions fought for control of Maggie's mind. She studied

Zeke more closely than she'd allowed herself to previously. He was tall, fair-headed, his hair still drying from the bath. It was a little long and the cut reminded her of someone...*Rick Springfield*. He looked like a fair-haired Rick Springfield with a shag from the eighties, his eyes rimmed in thick brows and lashes.

Zeke's age? Hard to tell. Younger than her, but older than the twins. Mid-to-late thirties?

Maggie went to a Rick Springfield concert once, when she was sixteen, in Nashville. Her friend got them seats near the stage. Maggie remembered being appalled at the screaming girls around her, right up until the moment she stood in her own seat and screamed alongside them.

"I'm sure it had more to do with brokenness than beauty anyway," Zeke said. "*His*, not yours. That always seems to be the case." He tapped his coffee mug with his finger, looking once again like a therapist.

*   *   *

Now Canon was in his patrol car. No Rita. No brown-haired woman. No killer dragging a body up a hill. No Ollie. No beer cans. Just the race of the pavement under his wheels as he sped down Highway 47, the words coming through the radio piercing him. *Stand-off at the Handy-Mart at 159. Hostage situation. Sheriff on the scene.*

Canon was only a deputy then.

As he took the final curve, going so fast the car came up off its wheels on the right side, the radio crackled with urgency: *Shots fired! Shots fired!*

For the third time that night, just as the Handy-Mart came into view, Canon woke in a shiver-inducing sweat.

*   *   *

As Maggie stared at the strange man on the other end of the sofa and fought to make sense of his words, something loosened inside her.

She could feel it, like a worrisome thorn being slowly worked out from deep within her flesh.

Maggie had always been uptight. While she took pride in her ability to hold it all together, there were a few times, like that Rick Springfield concert, when she let herself give in fully to the moment. When she flung pride and reservation aside and stared down the fears of her most private demons. When she said, in essence, *caution be damned.*

From the moment Tom had gotten the words out, *I need to talk to you, Maggie, I have some unwelcome news,* as though she were one of his throat patients—the test results were back and she was the one with cancer, not him—Maggie screwed a tight lid on her heart.

Lord, don't let Tom see me cry.

After that initial tidal wave in the car, Maggie thought she'd done an admirable job of tamping down her emotions. Keeping a brave front for the children. Avoiding going anywhere or being around anyone who might ask unwanted questions. *What happened, Maggie?*

She didn't need looks of pity from her nearest friends...extended family...those glances people meant to be sympathetic but that she knew would only cause her to lose her composure when she got back to her car or newly leased, modern, sharply outfitted, cold and empty condo.

Maggie had tried to convince herself the clean lines of contemporary housing would do her good. But uncluttered and unfettered simply meant unattached. She wasn't really a clean-line person. Maggie was old-fashioned at heart. She loved what a home represented, the shelter...the safety...its history. People lived their lives inside the walls of a home. That romanticism was what had drawn her to the cabin.

How awful for Zeke to say, *I'd kill him if I thought it'd make you feel better, Maggie.* And yet that's exactly what she had wanted when Tom first told her. *Yes! Kill him and kill Bethany, even it means the child dies, too.* That child, after all, was the evidence of Tom's betrayal.

But—*oh, what a relief!*—Maggie didn't feel that way anymore.

"I don't hate Tom," she said, staring into the pool of Zeke's well-lashed eyes, as if she was realizing it for the first time, or...rediscovering it. As the words left her throat, she felt actual relief, a tangible burden lifted.

She felt her lips curling into a smile, Zeke's outburst lying delicious in her ears. *That bastard!* Maggie giggled. Then she was doubled over on the sofa, laughing.

Tom is an A-one idiot, Maggie.

Then she was crying again. How long had it been since anyone had validated her? Or told her she was pretty? *Too long. Not even the therapist, at one hundred dollars an hour.* All the self-blaming...the embarrassment around friends...the pain in her children's eyes that she knew she somehow caused without meaning to. Mothers were responsible for *everything.* Weren't they?

In nearly five months, Maggie hadn't allowed herself to *feel.* After that first awful night, she had hardly shed a tear. Why now? Why were the tears—*mixed with laughter, no less*—flowing out of her now?

"What did I do to make Tom stop loving me?" she whispered. So much so that he would seek solace in another woman's arms—a woman hardly more than a girl—a girl no more than their daughter's age.

Hurt pierced Maggie like a stab wound. She felt Zeke's hand on her back.

But...what if it wasn't Maggie's fault? What if it had more to do with brokenness, like Zeke had suggested? Tom's, not hers. What if she wasn't the true source of the cancer? What if Tom was simply an ass?

"Poor Bethany," mumbled Maggie, not realizing she'd spoken aloud. Poor child in that twenty-six-year-old's womb.

Then she was back to fresh tears. *I am the fool who first married Tom, the ass, and lived with him for thirty years. How long will it last for Bethany?*

She shook her head at the thought. No...Tom wasn't an ass. Not really. "He took no pleasure in hurting me," she felt the need to explain to Zeke. "And he will pay for his indiscretion for the rest of his life. He has to carry that burden like a ball and chain." *I feel sorry for Tom.* Part of her would always love him...and miss him.

Divorce was exhausting. Maggie hadn't been prepared for that. While she might have looked on the surface like she was taking it all in stride, she had mentally run around this issue from every angle casting for some way not to be a victim or a failure in this story—her story! "Isn't it my story?" she raised up and asked Zeke forcefully. "Don't I get to say?"

He watched her with a bemused expression. She knew her comments weren't making sense to him, but they made sense to her. Zeke held out the tissue box again. Maggie took one, then another.

Part of what had driven her back to writing was her need to resume control. Writing put her in the seat of command. Let her fly the plane. Didn't it? First the twins grew up and left her. Then Tom pushed her out. Wouldn't that lead anyone to fight for control?

"Death seemed kinder than divorce. That's why I fantasized about how Tom would look in a coffin." Maggie blew her nose. If death had separated them, like they claimed would be the case when they took their vows, Maggie could have been mad at death instead of Tom. If death had been the perpetrator, Tom could not have *chosen* Bethany, and Maggie's pride could have remained intact.

Tom is an idiot.

"Exactly!" Maggie slapped the sofa cushion—the kindest words she had heard in months. Zeke, a stranger who had pinned her arms to the sofa and wiped her tears, wasn't looking at her like she was a thing to be pitied, but like she was a woman who had the right to feel her rage. A stranger seemed to realize this. A stranger, who had hidden the knives but who also said, "I don't want to hurt you."

Maggie rocked herself on the sofa until her emotions played out—fear, relief, pain, forgiveness, acceptance, then something like peace. Finally, she lay still knowing she was really alone in the cabin. But just as she started to doze off, she felt movement at the other end of the couch. She wasn't alone. So she sat up, blew her nose again, and looked down the sofa at the man jerking her heart around with his remarks and unexplained presence.

"I'm having trouble wrapping my head around this...around you," she said.

Zeke grinned, looking like innocence personified. "What's to wrap your head around, sweetheart? A man showed up on your doorstep. He was in need. You helped him. He's grateful. He'd like to do you more good than harm."

Maggie studied him again, then said through swollen nasal passages, "Then why did you move the gun?"

"Because you moved it. I heard you click it open when I was in the tub. Didn't want you to make any decisions you'd regret."

"Where is it?"

He smiled. "Somewhere safe."

"How do I know you won't use it on me?"

"Maggie!" That look of hurt again.

She covered her face with her hands. "You're confusing me, Zeke, and you know it!"

He didn't say anything. The way he looked at her infuriated her suddenly. "What did the text say!" she yelled.

Zeke reached behind him for the phone and punched in the code. Then he turned it so she could see the message: *Keep your doors locked. There was a prison break not far from your cabin.*

8

There is something sexy about a man in uniform. Prison garb does not count. Nor does clothing from the eighties.

Maggie stared at the words on the screen, then at the man holding her phone.

"You need to respond," Zeke said, matter-of-factly. "Let Cal know you're safe."

"Oh? Am I safe, Zeke? Am I really safe?"

He smiled. "I like to hear you say my name, Maggie."

She stood. "I'll get my keys and head out, then. You keep the gun and knives. Keep the phone, too. But I'm going to head out now."

Zeke stayed on the couch while Maggie went to the bedroom to get her purse and keys. She was shaking all over, as if she were the one thawing out this time. All her emotions were on the surface. They'd been set free on the couch and she couldn't screw the lid back down. For one blessed moment she had felt peace, had almost fallen asleep. Now fear was charging the hill again.

When Maggie turned, Zeke filled the doorframe.

"I responded for you." He held the phone out. "See what you think of this: *I'll keep them locked, Cal. Thanks for loving me enough to let me know!* I used an exclamation point. Took me a little bit to figure out how to—"

Rage flared and surged past Maggie's fear. She slapped at the phone, trying to knock it from his hand, then she slapped at him, trying to move him away from the door. *Don't trap me!*

But when he grabbed her arms, she realized her mistake. Zeke obviously wasn't sane, Maggie shouldn't have made him mad.

He wrestled her to the bed. *He's going to rape and kill me now. My children will pay for my stupidity.*

Zeke pinned her arms with his hands and her ankles with his shins. "You know I can't let you leave, Maggie. It's dangerous."

"More dangerous than being here?" Her face crumbled. Maggie hated being trapped. She could feel the mattress below her and the closeness of his taut body above. Her world was closing in. *Are these my final moments? Am I about to die?*

Zeke laid the top of his head on her chest and rolled it side to side. Was he weighing his options? The smell of her shampoo on his hair wafted up her nose.

"Dammit, Maggie! Could we just get a good night's rest and talk about this in the morning? I am so *tired.*"

The vice grip in his hands and knees didn't make it seem like he was tired, but Maggie had to admit his blue eyes looked it when he raised his head back up.

"Don't be foolish," Zeke said.

"You mind clarifying 'foolish'?"

"I think you know."

"I don't."

"You do."

Maggie breathed in and out, studying Zeke's face. His sideburns were a little long. Maybe she wasn't about to die. "And if I promise not to do anything foolish?"

He rolled off her and stood, putting a hand to his leg where she knew his wound was beneath the sweats. "Then we'll be fine."

Zeke turned to go.

"Were you the only one?" she asked.

He looked back at her.

"The prison break." Maggie's breath was still coming fast. "Were you the only one?"

The line of his lips grew thin. "You don't have to worry about that other guy. Now get some sleep, Maggie." Zeke shut the bedroom door behind him. There were no locks on the inside doors. She knew this already.

Maggie lay in the dark, watching the snow outside the window continue to swirl and fall. Hours must have passed as she went back through the events of the last five months, the events of that evening, each word Zeke had uttered, the oddness of his being here. Maggie wove dozens of escape plans in her mind, but lacked confidence in her ability to execute a single one.

Sometime in the night, feeling sorry for herself and more alone than she'd ever been in her life, Maggie's eyelids grew heavy and she gave in to sleep.

***

Maggie woke with a start. Had she heard a noise? Where was she? Outside the windows snow was still falling.

Zeke! The cabin was as silent as the snow outside. Maggie lay still, her body paralyzed with fear.

She looked at the bedroom door. It was closed. Had the earlier events of the night really happened? It wasn't Maggie's habit to close the bedroom door. Her bladder screamed for relief. She wanted to go back to sleep and wake to sunshine, warmth, and the realization that it had only been a nightmare, the Chardonnay gone bad. But her bladder wouldn't cooperate. If Maggie didn't go to the bathroom her body would explode.

Easing the covers back, she put her sock feet to the floor. Maggie never slept in socks. She tiptoed to the door and eased it open. As the door swung into the hallway it bumped against something. Maggie's breath caught.

Zeke sat up and looked at her from a pallet of blankets and a pillow he'd borrowed from the couch. It was true then. *Zeke had really happened.*

"I'm sorry," she whispered. "I need to go the bathroom."

He rolled to the side and let her pass.

She went in and closed the door, knowing he would hear her. Hadn't there been a moment when her fear of him had completely dissolved? When she felt relief and joy from his words? Maggie wanted that moment back. Having a man in her cabin was as tiring as divorce.

She flushed and washed her hands, wondering if there was anything in the bathroom she could use to win her freedom. Maggie's shoulders sagged. She decided to wait and figure it out in the morning. Zeke hadn't killed her yet. Perhaps he wouldn't tomorrow.

She eased back by him in the hallway, feeling a little sorry for him on his blanket on the floor. "Did I ever give you the Tylenol?" she asked.

"I'm okay. Thanks."

Maggie didn't know what happened to it anyway. She couldn't tell what time it was. Zeke still had her cell phone. The only other clock in the cabin was on the microwave and she couldn't see it from the hallway. For all the snow and ice outside, the air was surprisingly warm.

"You must have put another log on."

He grunted in affirmation. She'd been afraid to let the fire keep going through the night. Now, on the coldest evening since she'd been in the cabin, it felt the warmest.

"Would you not be more comfortable on the sofa?" she asked.

"I'll sleep here until I've won your trust, Maggie."

Was Zeke worried she would escape out the back door if he was on the couch? Or that she'd open one of the bedroom windows? If she did, he would feel the cold air of it pull from under the door here in the hallway.

Maggie wondered if she could raise herself through the cut-out over the head of the bed without him hearing her and get to the front door. But if he'd heard her open the gun case while he was in the bath, Zeke was sure to hear her shimmy up through that cut-out in the wall.

Not knowing what else to say, Maggie went back into the bedroom and closed the door. She didn't bother with any more escape plans. She simply closed her eyes and prayed for protection. Then Maggie went to sleep.

9

Stephen King said in Secret Windows that writing allows you to step into another world, to "be someplace else for a while."

When Maggie woke again, the bedroom was flooded in light. A deep snow covered everything outside the window, and though the skies were still overcast, sun streamed through cracks in the clouds. The world was awash in brilliant white.

The bedroom door stood open, letting in the smell of coffee, the sizzle of bacon, and the hum of the washing machine running. Maggie's first days in the cabin had been so silent it was strange to hear noises originating from someone else...yet oddly comforting. She realized how much she had missed that—noises originating from someone else—a clear indicator you are not alone in the world.

Maggie went to the bathroom, washed her face, and smoothed her hair. When she came out, Zeke said, "You're up! Hungry?" He didn't look at all like a man who had slept on the floor. He didn't look like a murderer or prison escapee, either. But things always looked less threatening under a canopy of sunshine.

Why were you in prison, Zeke? Did you hold another woman hostage?

Until now Maggie had only seen him in dim lighting. He was freshly shaved, his hair damp again, like he'd showered. How did the sound of running water not wake her? He was back in his old clothes rather than her things, but still wearing the socks. He had patched the hole in his jeans himself.

She realized now his clothes were reminiscent of the eighties, like his hair. Was that why they seemed ill-fitting? Men wore fashions trimmer now.

A large fire crackled from the living room. Maggie leaned her head in to look. Zeke had brought in more wood.

"How long have you been up?" she asked.

"Long enough to work up an appetite." He lifted what was left of her baked bread off the counter. "Did you make this? It's not in a store wrapping." Had Zeke's eyes grown bluer in the night?

"I'm not a half-bad cook."

"I'll say! You're going to have to make us some more. I'm in love with it." He talked like they'd come to the cabin together, a getaway for Zeke and Maggie.

"How do you like your eggs?" he asked, setting a cup of coffee on the counter in front of her. The cream was already added. It was exactly the right color tan.

Maggie stared at the coffee with a crease in her brow. How did he know how much cream she liked? Was he really that observant? What if he had poisoned it?

"Did I not get it right?" he asked softly.

Maggie picked up the mug and drank. "It's perfect. I'd like to take a shower before I eat." She'd had a bath last evening, but all that crying left her grimy.

"Alright. I'll wait and eat with you." He put the egg carton back in the fridge.

"Omelettes." She turned toward the bedroom for her clothes. "I like omelettes: mushrooms, spinach, sun-dried tomatoes, and feta."

Maggie twisted the shower faucet and peeled off her clothes, remembering how she undressed him in this same bathroom the night before. She stepped under the spray feeling every slide of the droplets. Showering suddenly felt more sensual than it had in a long time. There was no lock on the bathroom door. If Zeke opened it and came in, what would Maggie do?

Invite him to join me?

* * *

Canon was the first one into the office. Memories of Rita rode in with him.

Shirley was next in, hauling a crock pot of stew. "Made extra. Knew you'd all be comin' in half-froze. It'll be in the kitchen when you're hungry."

The office kitchen wasn't much bigger than a closet, but it had a plug and held a card table. When Shirley came back in the main office she stood in Canon's doorway with her hands on her hips.

"Lord, look at those bags under your eyes." Many of Shirley's pet phrases began with 'Lord.' "What time did you get home last night?"

Canon looked down at his notes. "You hear any more on that prison escapee, you let me know."

"I knew it'd be past midnight."

Luckily, Becky came in and distracted her.

* * *

What was wrong with Maggie? There was a strange man in her cabin! Shouldn't she be quaking with fear? Figuring out how she was going to get away from him? Certainly not imagining him in this shower built for two. But somehow, having survived the night and now feeling the sun through the windows, Maggie's pulse beat stronger.

She turned off the water and stepped out. Dressing in jeans and a sweater, she combed out her hair then blew it dry. Remembering Zeke's comment about her make-up, she kept it minimal.

When she returned to the kitchen he was reading one of her cookbooks. He looked up from the pages and stared. A slow smile spread over his face as his eyes fell down to her feet and back up to the hair left loose on her shoulders.

"You are a vision, Maggie."

It was exactly what she had wanted him to say. The whole day, in fact, played out like a dream. Maggie floated through it start to finish in something like a daze. But a daze wasn't to be confused with a fog. Her mind and body weren't functioning *poorly*, quite the opposite. They'd flowered open. But the day still held a dream-like quality.

They stood in the kitchen, Zeke washing the remnants off their breakfast plates and handing them to Maggie to dry, when Robbie texted. He pulled the phone from his pocket and held it up for her to see: *You making it okay?*

"How do you feel about the word 'swimmingly'?" he asked.

Maggie nodded her agreement and he punched it in. Robbie texted back: *Great! Happy writing.*

"So you came here to write." Zeke washed the coffee mugs next. "What are you writing?"

She shook her head. "I'd rather not say."

"Maybe I can help."

Maggie concentrated on drying the mugs as he handed them to her. If Tom had ever helped her wash the dishes, it was so long ago she couldn't remember it.

"How old are you, Zeke?"

"I forget exactly."

"What is your profession?"

"You mean other than escaped con?"

Maggie set the mugs in the cabinet then twisted the cotton towel.

Zeke pulled it from her hands and snapped it at her playfully. "Let's go sit by the fire."

She followed him to the living room where they settled in their chosen spots on the couch. He leaned his head on one hand to study her. "You don't strike me as a romance writer. Fiction or non-fiction?"

"Fiction."

"What genre?"

She cocked her head. "You know about genres?"

"Even prisons have libraries, Maggie. I've done quite a lot of reading the past few years."

"Who's your favorite author?"

Zeke grinned. "Margaret Raines."

"You don't know if I'm any good. You don't even know what I write."

His eyes fanned over her face and hair. "All fiction is a hero's journey isn't it?"

"You know Joseph Campbell?"

"Heard of him. For you, I'm guessing, the hero's journey is in the form of chick lit. Strong female heroine...beautiful, of course...who wants to be known and loved for who she really is. Everyone's story when you think about it."

Maggie squirmed beneath his gaze. "So were you a psycho-therapist before you were a..."

"Psychopath?" Zeke grinned at Maggie's flush. "That's what you were thinking, wasn't it?"

"Are we going to play mind games, Zeke?"

"Let's not. But since we're on the topic of psychoanalysis, I want to raise one question that's been on my mind."

"Okay."

"Do you really not hate Tom for what he did to you?"

The question surprised Maggie. Then again, everything about this man surprised her.

"I was plenty mad when he told me. Do you have any idea what an administrative nightmare it is to get all your accounts separated?"

The question was meant to be hypothetical, so Maggie was surprised again when he said, "I have an appreciation for it, yes."

"Are you divorced, Zeke?"

"No."

"But you had to get your accounts separated from someone's?"

"Divorce is not the only reason for that."

Zeke was perhaps the most matter-of-fact person Maggie had ever met, and still maddeningly mysterious.

"Why were you in prison?"

"We're not talking about me, we're talking about you."

"You said you wanted to raise a question that's been on your mind, well I've got questions, too."

"I asked mine first."

"Divorce has involved a lot of things I never thought about before."

"Such as..."

"The legal nightmare. All the paperwork. And..." Maggie stopped.

"What? Say it."

Maggie didn't want to be *that* honest. But she plunged ahead. "Wondering if I can make it on my own financially. That's the biggest question."

"And..." he waved his hand for her to go on. "The *other* questions."

Maggie looked away from his probing eyes. "Wondering if I'll ever love anyone again, and if they'll love me."

Zeke waited for her to continue.

She took a sip of coffee though it was now lukewarm. Maggie once read you couldn't cry and drink at the same time. "Wondering if I'll die alone. My mother has dementia. Is that to be my fate? Will I end up being a burden to my children?"

Maggie felt him studying her. She chanced a look. A grin simmered in the corners of his eyes.

"Yes," he said. "Prosperity is in your future. So is love—sex, even—good sex. And no, you won't die alone. You won't get dementia, either."

Maggie stared at him. He wasn't smug, just knowing.

"And you know this how?"

A twinkle jumped in his eye. Maggie looked away again. Why did Zeke remind her so much of Rick Springfield? *It's that silly haircut.*

"I know things, Maggie. My vision has become amazingly clear."

That was no kind of answer. Maggie started to press the point, but sensed it wouldn't do any good. She decided to go back to the 'not hating Tom' part of the conversation.

"I feel sorry for Bethany," admitted Maggie. "She's so young. She doesn't know yet how mad Tom's going to be when that child wakes him in the middle of the night. Or how bad he is about vacations. He doesn't even know how to pack. And Tom has to face his grown children with the shame of his betrayal for the rest of his life."

"Tom's an idiot, remember?" Zeke pointed his finger at her. "He deserves any inconveniences that come his way."

"Does he?" A thread of guilt Maggie was well-familiar with crept into her voice. "Did Tom come to his choices all on his own, Zeke? Or did I push him there?"

"Don't act like it's your fault, Maggie. Don't act like you did something to deserve it."

"How do you know I didn't?"

"You're not the type."

Maggie shook her head. "You don't even know me."

"Anyone who is around you five seconds can see what a jewel you are."

Maggie looked to the ceiling and shook her head.

"What?" he asked.

"This is the strangest enigma of my life, Zeke. *You* are the strangest enigma of my life!"

He smiled. "Thank you."

Maggie shook her head again. "That wasn't necessarily a compliment."

"But I chose to take it as one."

"Why?"

"Why not, Maggie? So much of life is simply what we *want* to believe, isn't it?"

His words hung in the air.

"We look out of a prism," he continued, "but what if it's not the right view? One quarter turn to the right changes everything."

Maggie didn't answer.

"You know I'm right about this."

Maggie stared at the fire, not disagreeing with him so much as feeling confused. "I don't know how to have a conversation with you."

"But we *are* having a conversation. Quite a fine one, too."

"Fine for who?'

"Whom."

Maggie glared at him. "You're correcting my grammar?"

"Well if you're going to be a writer, Maggie, you need to get that straight."

"How is it that *you* have it straight, Zeke?"

"I've had some years to observe things."

"But you don't know how old you are. Or you just won't tell me?"

His expression was impossible to read. "I haven't been keeping track. My perspective changed, Maggie. The things that are important to me changed. Yours would, too, if you were in my position."

"Help me understand your position, Zeke. What is it, exactly? And what changed it?"

He stared at her, amusement dancing in his eyes. After several seconds passed he sighed. "I feel badly that I've interrupted your work time, Maggie. I simply wanted to compliment you on not being mad at Tom. It lets me know you're going to be okay." He pointed behind her. "If I read one of those books on your stack could you get some writing done?"

"Why do you do that?"

"Do what?"

"Switch gears like that? Where did that come from?"

"I got to thinking about what you came here for, not to gab with me, but to get started on your book."

Not to gab with me. That was a phrase Mr. Thompson had used. Was that simply the way folks talked here in Marston County? Was Zeke from Marston County? *He knew this place was a rental.*

"I don't remember mentioning that I was working on a book, per se," said Maggie.

"Isn't it obvious? You came here to write so you must be writing a book. And you weren't expecting a man to show up in the middle of the night. You'd likely be working on that book right now if I wasn't here to distract you."

Maybe this was an *out* for her. Maybe he was going to leave now. "Can I drive you somewhere, Zeke? Home, perhaps?"

He looked around at the window. "In this snow? I don't think that would be a good idea."

"My car handles well in the snow."

He shook his head. "No, I don't think so."

"Weren't you on your way somewhere?"

There was that impossible to read expression again, like he knew a secret and wasn't telling. "I was on my way *here*, Maggie. I saw your light."

Maggie took a deep breath. "Okay. So you're here. Now what?"

Zeke lifted his hands innocently. "I need to let you work. Get back to writing!"

"I don't think I can concentrate."

"I'll sit in the kitchen. Pretend I'm not here."

When Maggie didn't answer, he leaned over her and picked up her laptop. His upper body grazed her shoulder. "This is your computer, isn't it?"

For a moment, as he looked into her eyes, she thought he was going to kiss her. She held her breath, but he looked down at the MacBook Pro instead, turning it in his hands. "These used to be so large." After inspecting it, he set the computer in her lap and opened the lid. "Work," he whispered.

Then he jumped off the couch, selected one of the books she'd brought—a copy of Patrick O'Brien's *Master and Commander*—and went into the kitchen. She heard the barstool by the phone scrape across the wooden floor, then creak under his weight.

Maggie stared at her computer screen.

After a moment he called, "I don't hear any writing, Maggie."

"It doesn't make a lot of noise."

"It does on a computer. Use your computer." She started plucking the keys to quiet him.

I don't hear any writing, Maggie, Zeke called from the kitchen. And who is Zeke, you ask? Well...that was the question with which Maggie was currently grabbling. Zeke's true identity remained shrouded in mystery.

Twenty pages and two hours later, he was standing in front of her. "You hungry, Maggie?"

She jumped, having forgotten that he was anything more than a fabrication.

Zeke checked the fire and folded the laundry, then came to look over her shoulder in the kitchen. "Is that dough going to be another loaf of your wonderful bread? Any chance we could add raisins and cinnamon?"

Maggie's hand stilled. She had just been reaching for both items in the cabinet. "Okay," she said, having a déjà vu feeling, as if she were writing all this instead of it really happening.

He opened the refrigerator door and pulled out the roll of foil. "What's this?"

"Molasses cookies."

When he turned to her his eyes were big. This time he did kiss her, on the forehead, so fast Maggie didn't have time to react. "How did I get so lucky?" He grinned like a boy, his face filled with wonder.

For lunch they made chili, topped with shredded cheese and corn chips, followed by hot molasses cookies. Zeke ate so many Maggie was surprised when he appeared in front of her computer again four hours later, ready to help make supper. This time it was penne pasta with chicken and vegetables.

"My word!" Zeke exclaimed, drizzling a balsamic dressing Maggie mixed up over a green salad. She added in those last few drops of white wine—that was a Margaret Raines secret. "Where did you learn to cook like this?"

Maggie didn't answer, just handed him a bottle of Pinot Noir. He uncorked it and filled two glasses. She lit candles. They sat with knees touching on the sofa afterward and watched the film version of *Master and Commander*, each tearing up when Captain Aubrey was forced to make the hard decision to cut the rope resulting in the loss of a young seaman.

Zeke handed her a tissue from the box.

As the movie ended she blew her nose. "Now you know how it ends. You won't want to finish reading the book."

"No, I'll finish. Tomorrow. I figure I have one more day."

Maggie had nestled into the crook of the arm Zeke threw across the back of the sofa, but raised up now to look at him. What did he mean by that? Zeke had been in the cabin one day and part of a night and he felt like...well...like he *belonged* there...like they'd been friends a long time and now would be forever.

He reached in his back pocket. "Do you have a charger for the phone? Battery's nearly dead. That's what this little bar means, right?"

Maggie turned off the television and went to get the charger. When she returned Zeke was standing at the window looking out. The sky was black, the land a white carpet. The pasta, the wine, more warm cookies, and a blanket over their feet during the movie had wrapped Maggie like a glove all evening.

She came to him and held out the charger. He took it and kissed her on the forehead again, slower this time, with lips that pressed like silk against her skin. No one had kissed Maggie in months. *When did Tom and I stop kissing?* She missed it.

"Thank you, Maggie. This was all so lovely."

She held her breath as Zeke held her head in his hands. *One twist and he could kill me. This man could break my neck.* One of Tom's friends was a chiropractor who insisted one person couldn't really break another's neck with a sharp twist. That was a trick solely for Hollywood. But Maggie wasn't sure she believed him.

Even as these thoughts ran through her mind, others...unbidden...crowded in. *I want him to kiss me. I want to be touched. I want this man to undress me this time.*

But he didn't. His hands dropped down to hers and gave them a squeeze. "Good night, Maggie."

"Good night, Zeke."

She walked past the fire, past the dirty dishes on the dining table she would worry about tomorrow and went to the bathroom. After getting ready for bed Maggie eased under the coverlet and went to sleep.

10

The Shirelles first asked the question in 1960 and women have been wondering ever since: "Will you still love me...tomorrow?"

Canon stood in his kitchen cooking eggs. It was still dark out. He threw three sausage patties in the pan. Shirley tried to get him to switch over to turkey bacon, but Canon liked pork sausage. He bought it local, fresh ground.

He ate standing, looking out the back door at the porch where he liked to take his coffee in warmer weather. Snow still covered the farm, and would for a bit longer. Temperatures weren't predicted to rise for another couple of days.

Rita was on his mind again...Ollie...a killer dragging a body up a hill...a dark-haired woman...a clawfoot tub. Two nights in a row he'd had snippets of the same dream sequence. He couldn't figure out why.

Not that Canon put much stock in a dream. He was nothing if not practical. Life had taught him that. Rita taught him. His father. Canon's livelihood was built on facts, not fiction. So he didn't put any stock in dreams. But he'd never had one two nights in a row like that.

Every now and then someone brought information to the office built on a cloud. They had a dream. They had a feeling. They might have seen something. They thought they heard a noise, a voice. Like the folks who claimed they could hear laughter near that old Indian mound on Treetop Ridge.

Whatever.

Canon couldn't arrest on a cloud. He couldn't build cases on dreams or sounds near an Indian mound just because it made the hairs on the back of someone's neck rise up. So Canon didn't know what to do with this dream.

He knew he needed to go check on Ollie, but there would be more accidents today. That prison escape wouldn't leave his mind, either. He'd like for that to be resolved before riding out to Patterson Road in case Ollie saw it on the news.

When the eggs and sausage were gone, he set the pan in the sink. Canon rarely bothered with a plate. Why dirty another dish?

On his way back up the stairs, through the bathroom door from the bedroom, he glanced at the picture of Rita on the wall. The calendar would flip over in a matter of days. Another year without her. Canon didn't know why he had started keeping track of the years until his retirement. More time to knock around the farm might not be a welcome thing.

*   *   *

The next morning Maggie woke to the smell of coffee and bacon frying. The room was flooded with light again. She stretched luxuriantly.

A strange man is still in my cabin. And she was strangely at peace with that.

Mid-day found her sitting at the dining table. She had abandoned her initial project and began writing about her strange visitor instead, trying to capture his spirit, his mannerisms, his dialog.

Zeke walked slowly through the cabin, the cut on his right leg causing a slight lilt in his gait. He seemed to be taking stock of things.

"What's this switch for?" Zeke stood at the front windows. He looked outside, then back over his shoulder at Maggie. He had already tested the porch light. That switch plate was on the right side of the door.

Maggie hesitated, wondering if she should tell him.

"What's it for, Maggie?" he asked again, his eyes boring into hers. "I know you know."

She'd grown pretty comfortable with him by now and didn't think he intended to hurt her, but still...Zeke hadn't answered a lot of *her* questions.

"It makes the windows opaque from the outside."

"Ah," he said, as though a mystery were solved.

The switch was up, but now he raked it down. He glanced at her before opening the door. She didn't move as he stepped out onto the porch and peered back in through the front window. *I could run lock the door and call the police.*

But she didn't.

Zeke came back inside. "Does it work on all the windows?"

"I think so."

"What about the skylights?" He stepped under the living room skylights and inspected them. They were still covered with snow.

"Mr. Thompson said they did."

Zeke whipped his head toward her. "Who?'

"Mr. Thompson. The caretaker who lives down the road."

"The caretaker." Zeke stared at her, unblinking. "When was the last time he was here?"

"The day I arrived. The day after Christmas."

"Christmas." Zeke's brow furrowed. "When was Christmas?"

How could he not know this?

"Sunday," she said.

"What day is this?"

"Friday."

"Tomorrow is New Year's Eve?" Zeke had worn a lot of looks since he'd been in the cabin—tired, amused, knowing—but not confused. This was the first time Maggie had seen him confused.

She nodded. Maggie expected him to ask what year it was next—2016 until midnight tomorrow—but he didn't.

Strange.

Zeke walked back through the cabin to the kitchen. Maggie heard him open the back door and step out, apparently checking the windows on the back of the house. He presently came inside again and locked the door. Then she heard him open cabinets in the kitchen, the bathroom, as if he were cataloguing items in the cabin.

He poked his head through the door to the living room. "You have some paper and a pen I can borrow?"

Maggie pulled a sheet from her journal and handed it to him, along with a pen. He went back to the kitchen. She heard a creak. The red stool had become a favorite perch for him.

Sometime later—Maggie kept losing track of time—he looked in again. "What do you want for lunch?"

Her computer said it was after one o'clock. Maggie's stomach confirmed it by rumbling.

"We still have some chili," she said.

"Don't get up. I'll fix it."

In less than two days they had developed an odd rhythm, the words on Maggie's screen coming so effortlessly—the hours on her laptop clock flying by so quickly—she could hardly believe it.

Maggie listened to the comforting sounds of Zeke pulling out a pan and opening the refrigerator door. Soon the smell of the warmed-over chili and fresh grilled cheese sandwiches filled the air.

Maggie cooked dinner later that day: Brown Sugar Salmon with asparagus and baked potatoes. They finished off the Pinot—a whole cluster from Oregon's Willamette Valley Maggie had brought from home. Tom used to order it by the case. It was Maggie's favorite.

As they lingered at the dining table, swirling the red liquid in their glasses, listening to the fire, Zeke said quietly, "Leave that switch down on the windows, Maggie. Promise me." His gaze bore into her. "Don't ever be afraid to let folks in."

Maggie was still mulling over this instruction when he added. "And remember, there are stories all around you."

Before she could think of a good response, he spoke again. "If you could go back and make different choices, right from the beginning to avoid the pain, would you?"

"No."

"Why?"

"Because I wouldn't have Robbie and Cal. And..."

"Yes?"

"Look, I think I know where you're going with this. Even if we'd never had Robbie and Cal, I wouldn't go back and choose not to love Tom. Loving Tom was never a mistake."

"Exactly!" Zeke was back to his knowing look...training her...instructing her. "Loving *anyone* is never a mistake, Maggie. Remember that."

"But it hurts that Tom didn't love me back."

Zeke cocked his head. "Who says Tom didn't love you back?"

"He betrayed me, Zeke. He slept with his receptionist."

Zeke nodded slowly, as if sifting and weighing her words. "If a person doesn't honor their commitment to you, you could call it betrayal. But I think of it as a forfeit instead—a forfeit of the sanctity of what could have been. *'Those who cling to worthless idols forfeit the grace that could be theirs.'"

Where had Maggie heard that quote?

"What's happening with that other person is often the greater tragedy," Zeke continued. "We're all flawed, Maggie. Every one of us forfeits gifts that are right under our noses. Prison was one of the greatest gifts I ever received. Remember to include that. It offered the maturing of my soul just like Aleksandr Solzhenitsyn claimed."

"Who? What do you mean by that?" Maggie hadn't told Zeke she was writing about him.

"Just file that away. You'll know what to do with it."

Maggie was typically a one-glass-of-wine woman, but tonight she'd had two. How was that even possible? A glass for her and Zeke the night before, and a glass for each of them tonight. Weren't there only four glasses in a bottle? But somehow she had two. And while Zeke's comment seemed strange on the one hand, on the other it was smooth...natural...and settled on her ears like the warmth of the fire on her skin. She didn't question it, only lounged in its comfort.

At some point they moved to the couch for another movie—*The Lake House*, one of Maggie's favorites—about a man and woman separated by two years in time, but who connected through letters delivered through the mailbox of a rental house.

Then Maggie was asleep. Zeke was kissing her, real kisses this time. Warm. Faintly familiar. Pleasant. She was thinking how intimate it felt, lying so close beside him on the couch, like she was lying in the very palm of his hand, her body molding perfectly into each rise and bend of his. Maggie had wondered every night since Tom's pronouncement if she would ever be held again...*held...cared for...known.*

Then strange visions. Tom was on the phone talking to Cal, and Cal was upset. Maggie knew it was because of the prison break.

"No, it's fine," she wanted to tell them. "Zeke is not a danger to me." They didn't know him the way she did.

Cars were in the yard suddenly, pulling in fast, surrounding the cabin. *No!* Cal called the police! Maggie had to hide Zeke. They wouldn't understand.

Gun shots!

Zeke running. Blood dripping in the snow. It wasn't his leg this time, but his chest, a gaping hole, blood staining the white. Zeke falling, rolling down a ravine. Police officers standing over him.

Suddenly Zeke lay curled on the porch again. Frozen. His lips purple, no longer moving. No longer kissing her.

11

There can be no
resurrection if there is no
death. Conclusion drawn
from the study of Ezekiel
in the Bible

Canon woke in a sweat. Third night in a row. The dream again. More
vivid this time. The dark-haired woman dressing a leg wound then slap-
ping at a man's hands. The man pinning the woman down. Ollie's phone
still ringing.

The clock beside Canon's bed said it was 3:38. Regardless, he threw
the covers back.

Enough.

He hardly remembered yesterday, had hardly had a chance to eat.
Everything from helping Mrs. Jamison change a flat to driving out to
Turney Center to hear the latest briefing. He had a long talk with the
Dickson sheriff after. Good chance to compare notes.

When he got back to the office Shirley had handed him a Post-it. A second caller said she saw a man walking near Patterson Road about the time the snow started. High time Canon got out there. He called Ollie twice yesterday, but each time the line was busy. Canon needed to lay this thing to rest.

He showered then went downstairs. It was too early to eat but he wanted coffee for his thermos. The thermometer under the light on the porch said it was fourteen degrees. So he grabbed a knit hat.

Before going out to the cruiser he checked his Glock and made sure there was an extra magazine in his belt.

*   *   *

Maggie woke with a start. Blue lights swirled over the walls.

Her heart pounded. It was only a dream. *Where is Zeke?* He no longer lay beside her on the couch.

There was sudden banging at the door! Maggie's heart caught. *Not again.*

"Zeke?" she called in a low voice. "What's happening?" Had he gone to the bathroom?

No reply.

Maggie eased from beneath the quilt and put her feet on the floor. She was wearing her pajamas and robe. *But didn't I fall asleep in my clothes?*

Zeke wasn't in the kitchen, hall, bathroom or bedroom.

More banging!

That must be him at the door. But...how did he get locked outside?

As Maggie passed the dining table she noticed only one dirty plate from supper, only a single wine glass. Blue lights continued to throw patterns over the walls. Hadn't the blue lights been part of her dream?

Yes...no...the blue lights are real.

Maggie suddenly felt cold. The fire had died down in the fireplace. How long was she asleep? She was at the window now.

It wasn't Zeke at the door, but a police officer instead. Sensing movement, he stepped to the window and peered in at her, motioning for her to open it. Maggie looked at the switch on the wall...down where Zeke had left it. She shivered, pulled the robe tighter, and opened the door.

The man's eyes went wide. He took a step back and searched her face. He didn't flash a badge, but the blue lights of his squad car felt official enough. As his eyes pored over her face and hair, he said, "Sorry to bother you, ma'am, but I need to ask you some questions."

I'm saved...the police are here...I'm not alone anymore. Or was it a bad thing that the police had come?

"What's wrong?" she asked.

The officer hesitated. "Mind if I come in?"

The thermometer behind the officer read fourteen. He wore a thick brown uniform jacket and knit hat, but looked cold, and for good reason.

"Of course." Maggie stepped toward the hearth to stir the fire.

He threw out an arm. "Wait." The officer's eyes held both her and the room under scrutiny. "I'd like to look over the place first."

Was he asking permission, or telling her?

Maggie stood mute, feet rooted to the floor, while the officer looked up and studied the cut-out to the bedroom. He unhooked a tie on the gun at his side before running his eyes over the dining table, then stepping into the kitchen. Maggie's pulse picked up again as the officer checked the lock on the back door and peered out the window. He checked cabinets. Maggie even heard him open the refrigerator door. Then he stepped back in the open doorway and looked over his shoulder at her.

She shivered, whether from cold or fear she couldn't have said. When Maggie looked up at him the officer moved on, going down the hall to the bathroom and bedroom, the floorboards creaking under his weight. He was tall and broad-shouldered.

He'll find Zeke. Any minute now.

Maggie braced for it. How would she explain she'd harbored a fugitive? Should Maggie have tried harder to escape? But there were no sounds to indicate Zeke's discovery. Had he fled before the officer arrived then? But how had Zeke known this man would come? He obviously sought to erase evidence he had ever been in the cabin.

The police officer came back to the living room holding Maggie's cell phone.

Zeke left my phone.

"The code." The officer had a deep voice—a voice of assurance—but there was a faint note of something. Hesitation? He seemed like a man who did more thinking than talking. His roving eyes didn't miss a thing.

Maggie told him. He punched it in and checked her messages. Then he handed the phone to her, looking sheepish. "I apologize for disturbing you. Just trying to make sure you're safe. I'm looking for a felon from Turney Center—that's a prison not too far from here. We've been huntin' him three days. I needed to know he didn't come here."

Zeke.

Maggie stood dumbly.

"But he might have come to this area," continued the officer. "I need to scout around once it's light outside."

The cold seeped up through Maggie's feet from the floorboards. She rubbed her arms. "Can I build a fire now?"

"Oh." The officer swept off his knit hat and reached for the kindling. She could see he was graying at the temples. "Let me."

As he knelt to make the fire she studied his broad back. The officer knew what he was doing. The kindling caught quickly. He stacked larger pieces on top. When the flames were strong and popping, he finally stood, his gaze swinging between satisfied and apologetic.

The blue lights continued to fan over the walls. Maggie didn't know what to say. They stood awkwardly, each staring at the fire as it continued to lick and build.

"What time is it?" she finally asked.

"'Bout four-thirty." He checked his watch. "Nearly five." The officer sounded tired. Had he worked all night? Why come here at such an hour?

"Would you like a cup of coffee, Officer..."

"Dale. Canon Dale."

Maggie smiled in spite of the strangeness of his being here at this hour and the erratic beating of her heart. Would it ever find its normal rhythm again?

What happened to Zeke? Should Maggie tell this man—Officer Dale—about him? "Your first name is Canon?"

"Buchanan, officially. Canon for short. One 'n' like a law, not a weapon. Canon is actually my second name. My first name is Tom...Thomas. But..." there it was again, a look of satisfaction, pleasure almost, then apology, "nobody ever calls me that."

The string of words appeared to be more talking than the officer was used to, but if it was nervous chatter, it didn't seem to fit his character. And really, what would he have to be nervous about?

Leave that switch down on the windows, Maggie. Don't ever be afraid to let folks in. Had Zeke not told her that, she might have invited this man to leave, just for having the first name of 'Tom.'

"Would you like a cup of coffee, Officer Dale?"

His shoulders relaxed then. Definitely a look of satisfaction now. "More than I know how to say."

As Maggie went to the kitchen to make coffee, the officer went out to his car to turn off the swirling lights. If Zeke was out there hiding, those blue lights gave him plenty of warning to leave.

The officer came back in stamping snow off his boots, picking up where he'd left off as he stepped into the kitchen. "Nobody calls me 'Officer' either."

Maggie opened the refrigerator door for the cream. "What do they call you?"

"Sheriff."

She held the carton in the air. "You're the sheriff of Marston County?"

He nodded.

Maggie sensed he didn't tell her because of ego, but because he was a man who liked to get the facts straight.

"For the past twenty years anyway...a deputy twelve years 'fore that. Hoping to retire in another eight." He grinned. "If I live that long."

Canon Dale was a nice looking man, his jawline more hardened, no doubt, from the hardness of his line of work. His presence filled the cabin in a way Zeke's hadn't. Maggie didn't mean to start a mental comparison of the two, but the differences were so striking—so palpable—she couldn't help it. Zeke's presence caused her both peace and fear. This man was stirring peace and fear, too, but in a different way...for different reasons.

What was it about a man in uniform? Maggie had grown used to sterile white jackets and stethoscopes long ago, but had to admit the deep brown of his sheriff's shirt beneath the bulky jacket was nice, too. She couldn't really tell how large Canon Dale was...*taller than Tom Raines, certainly, and taller than Zeke*...so tall the sheriff's head nearly came to the top of the inside doorway.

"My name is Maggie," she said. "Maggie Raines."

She set the cream on the counter. Would the sheriff notice she was getting things out of order? She should have made the coffee first. On the inside Maggie was rattled...confused. On the outside she was trying to appear normal.

As she reached to open the cabinet door for a filter, Maggie noticed there was only a single mug in the drainer. This was how Sheriff Dale had seen things—nothing in his search to indicate the presence of another.

Maggie looked to the end of the counter. The cookbook Zeke last flipped through was back in the stack, as if never opened. The page she tore from her journal for him was gone, the pen lying loose on the counter. If Maggie suggested Sheriff Dale get his dusting powder and sprinkle it over the countertops, would he find evidence that Zeke's fingerprints had ever been there? Was *this* moment happening? Was the sheriff really standing in her kitchen now?

"How do you like it?" she asked, opening the bag of coffee. Gourmet. Italian roast.

"Strong. Hot. Black."

Maggie poured beans into the grinder and water in the carafe. He removed his jacket, stepping to the dining room to hang it on the back of a chair, then sat on the red stool at the end of the counter to watch her. The badges, the gold stars, the words and stripes sewn into his uniform were all evident now...intimidating...there was even a gold star pinning his tie down.

"I thought police officers wore navy."

"Municipal officers do, but we're a county sheriff's office. Tan and brown. Colors of the soil. Deputies wear tan, I wear brown."

Maggie tried not to stare. *Zeke was the last one to sit on that stool. Or was he?*

"How many in the prison break?" she asked.

"Just the one."

That didn't fit. Zeke seemed to indicate there were two.

Maggie put her back to the sheriff under the guise of getting a second mug from the cabinet. She didn't want him to see her eyes. "What did he look like?"

"Tall, lean."

Maggie's heart skipped a beat.

"Hispanic fella in his mid-twenties, name of Rodriquez."

She let out the breath she didn't realize she was holding. Sheriff Dale heard, but misunderstood.

"So you never saw this man." He was setting facts straight again.

"No." Maggie was grateful she could answer honestly. She wasn't sure she could have fooled him with a lie.

Sheriff Dale peered around the cabin again. "It's just you here."

Maggie could tell he had already decided it, based on his inspection. She turned to check the coffee.

She could feel Canon Dale's eyes studying her. When she turned back to him to confirm it, his eyes fell to the cell phone Maggie had set on the counter.

"Who's Cal?" He pointed to it with a nod.

"My son. In Franklin."

"You're from Franklin."

"I live in Nashville now. I came here to..."

"Recover."

Sheriff Dale looked down at the phone again. "I don't mean to act like I know your business, just seemed like you might have been through a recent..." He left the words hanging there.

Maggie rearranged the mugs on the counter again and wished the coffee would hurry up and perk. Finally she blurted, "Do I have 'divorce' stamped on my forehead? How do you know it was recent?" Had the sheriff run some kind of check on her car tags before coming in?

He looked apologetic again. "You have an unconscious habit of reaching to twist a..." Canon pointed "...non-existent ring on that left hand."

Maggie covered her left hand with her right. "Oh."

"Sorry." But he smiled when she looked at him and his eyes didn't really look sorry.

Maggie changed the subject. She didn't want to talk about *her*. "Do you often work through the night, Sheriff?"

Canon rubbed the back of his neck. "I feel bad about that. Couldn't sleep. Decided to check on Ollie Thompson. Been trying to get up here since the storm hit, but there were accidents. Then the prison break. Someone called in that they saw a man walking along the highway not far from here." He sighed. "I shouldn't have bothered you this early, but when I couldn't get Ollie to come to his door, I decided to drive down here to see if he had a renter. When I looked in..."

Maggie looked up when he hesitated. "I could see you on the couch and...considering the prison break and all...wanted to make sure you were okay."

Now Maggie was worried. "I called Mr. Thompson a couple of days ago and didn't get him. Do you think he's okay?"

The sheriff smiled sadly. "Chances are he is. Right as he can be. He's gettin' old and I worry about him."

Maggie's brow knit.

"He drinks sometimes," Canon explained. "When it snows."

"Did something happen?"

"Yes."

Maggie decided not to press the point when he didn't offer any more on the matter. She glanced through the kitchen cut-out at the empty bottle of Pinot Noir on her own dining table hoping the sheriff didn't think she had a drinking problem.

The coffee was ready. Maggie poured a cup and handed it to him. *Zeke was the last person to drink from this mug. Or was he? Had Zeke been real?*

Maggie pointed toward the dirty dishes in the dining room. She never was one to leave dirty dishes until morning. But she hadn't been herself last night...the last couple of nights. "Is it okay if I wash those?"

The sheriff nodded and gulped the coffee, his eyes fastened on her face.

She put a hand on his arm—his arms were thick indeed. "You don't have to rush through your coffee, Sheriff Dale."

His eyes went to her hand. "Canon."

"You must be tired."

The stool creaked as he leaned to watch her gather the dishes and carry them back to the kitchen. Turning on the faucet she filled the sink with soapy water. Her eyes fell on the knife block. The knives filled each hole as if they'd never been removed.

Had Zeke been nothing more than an invention of Maggie's mind? *But it was all so real...so vivid.* Maggie wanted proof she wasn't going crazy. But how could she look for evidence with the sheriff watching her every move?

*   *   *

Canon tried not to show his feelings. Surprise. Confusion. *Hope.*

In his dreams he'd seen a woman, but didn't know where she was. She was here. In the old Patterson cabin. He was looking at her.

Canon never got a clear look at her face in the dreams and couldn't really tell peering in at the window by the glow of the embers, but the hair was the give-away, that brown hair falling around her shoulders.

This was her, all right. When she opened the door it nearly stole his breath.

It wasn't like Canon hadn't seen his share of lovely women. A small town sheriff knows the people in town. That's his job. Nobody moved to Marston County without Canon knowing about it. He knew every house, every road, every truck, every car. He certainly knew the faces.

But Canon didn't know when he'd last laid his eyes on a woman so lovely.

It thrilled him to know she was alone in the cabin. And not in danger. The empty space on her finger was an unexpected bonus. He told her he was sorry about her divorce, but that was a lie. Canon wasn't a man who typically lied. But this whole thing had him rattled.

Now he felt himself releasing the tension. The dreaming, the snow, the car accidents, the report from Turney Center—Canon felt them seeping from off his shoulders.

He might not understand the dream or how it pulled him here, but here he was. And there she stood, looking cute in those socks and her flannel pajamas under the robe.

Looking like a woman.

12

According to Sol Stein, the fiction writer's job is to entertain—to create pleasure for the reader.

As Maggie washed last night's dinner dishes, she marveled at how strange yet calming it was to have the sheriff here, if the man sitting on her barstool was real this time. Canon Dale's presence certainly felt solid—comforting—especially with that gun fastened to his hip.

Maggie thought of Cal's gun. Where had Zeke put it? Was it back under the pillow in the bedroom? If so, did the sheriff see it in his search? Or had it ever been removed from under the bed in the first place? What about the first aid kit? Was it in the bathroom, or still in the trunk of the Subaru, never having really been needed?

What day is this? New Year's Eve.

When Canon finished his coffee, he stood.

"What happens now?" asked Maggie.

"I've got some paperwork in the car. Thought I'd go out there and leave you alone. When it gets daylight, I'd like to scout around."

Maggie looked at the clock. "It won't be daylight for nearly two hours."

"I'm slow at paperwork." Canon nodded toward the coffee pot. "If I get my thermos, can I have the rest of that coffee?"

She heard his stomach growl, long and low. "Why don't I cook you breakfast?"

Canon grimaced. "Mrs. Raines, I feel awful about waking you so early. I just...I had to be sure Rodriquez wasn't here. I could see there weren't any tracks leading up to the cabin, but...when I peered in and saw you on the couch, I...I had to know."

Maggie knew the sheriff would have checked on anyone, that was his job, but the thought that he cared for her well-being was a welcome one. "I don't mind cooking you breakfast. Really, I don't. I'm up now. You're obviously hungry."

"Well." That sheepish look of his was starting to grow on her. "I'm not fool enough to turn down a good meal."

"You haven't eaten it yet. It might not be good."

"Any woman who brings a stack of cookbooks on a get-away is a *cook*. Plus, I did open the fridge. Saw the homemade bread on the counter. If I'm a decent sheriff, your last cooked meal was a great smelling salmon with asparagus, two of my favorite things."

Maggie smiled. Her eyes kept sweeping the kitchen, the laundry, for any sign of Zeke. How could he be explained? Here was a seasoned officer—the county sheriff, no less—also looking for signs of a second person in the cabin, but no evidence had presented itself.

Maggie excused herself to the bathroom. She wanted to put up her hair and wash her face. Zeke had borrowed her toothpaste, her soap, used extras towels and hung them on the rack. *Where were those things now?* The first aid kit was not in the bathroom.

Under the guise of getting dressed, she stepped to the bedroom and closed the door. Lifting the matelassé coverlet she saw Cal's gun case still under the bed as if never opened. There was the Tylenol bottle in her purse. In the cedar chest her fuzzy socks sat rolled where she put them when she unpacked the day she arrived. She pulled them on, along with jeans and a long-sleeved t-shirt.

By the time she padded back to the kitchen, Canon sat snoring on the couch. Maggie didn't know how he could sleep sitting straight up, but was glad he allowed himself the luxury. Not wanting to disturb him, she worked quietly in the kitchen. A radio on his hip belt hummed with white noise periodically.

At 6:00 a voice spoke over his radio, "Sheriff? This is Amos."

Canon answered as though he'd never been asleep. "What've you got?" He'd apparently learned to wake faster than Maggie had.

"A third witness says he saw a man on the highway near Patterson Road just before the storm hit. Thought I should let you know."

"Nothing seems amiss at Thompson's. I checked there early this morning. No forced entry. Couldn't get him to come to the door, but it was early and you know how he is. I'll head back down there later."

"Where are you now?"

"Cabin down the road. Has a current tenant. Been here since before the storm. Hasn't seen anyone. Soon as it's light, I'll scour the area."

Technically, Maggie never said she hadn't seen anyone. The sheriff had not asked that specific question.

"Want company?" asked Amos.

"No. I'll holler if I need you. People are gettin' cabin fever. We'll get calls. Oh, and Amos."

"Yes, sir."

"Thanks for coming in. I know it's your day off."

"Sure thing, Boss."

Maggie heard the couch groan as Canon stood. A stack of banana sour cream pancakes sat under the warmer. She was just pulling a frittata from the oven when he appeared in the doorway.

"Mind if I use your restroom, Mrs. Raines?"

"Not at all. And call me Maggie."

He disappeared. Soon she heard water running. When Canon reappeared his eyes looked brighter, his footfalls on the floor more brisk.

Maggie wondered how many couches the sheriff had napped on. He took the dining chair across from hers and picked up his fork, eyeing the pancakes and frittata like he was looking on heaven itself.

"I didn't ask you what you like," she said.

"Do I strike you as a picky eater? I like everything." Then he commenced to prove it to her. Several mouthfuls in, he pointed with his fork. "You got those molasses at Anderson's." It appeared to be the sheriff's custom to state things as facts rather than questions.

He reached for the jar then poured some onto a pat of butter on his plate. Breaking off pieces of pancake, he used them to sop up the mixture. "I'm sorry if this is not proper manners. I love this stuff and I've never tasted it on anything like these pancakes." Canon smiled before stuffing a large bite in his mouth. When he got it chewed, he said, "An Amish community on Cane Creek in Perry County sells the sorghum to Anderson's. I try not to buy it, because I can't resist it."

His eyes looked straight at her, almost through her. Maggie got the feeling they always saw more than the recipients of his gaze really wanted them to. By the time they finished eating she was convinced she had only imagined Zeke. *And Zeke had been so lovely.*

What other explanation was there? Zeke looked like a fair-haired version of one of her teen idols, had blue eyes to Tom's brown, was taller, more fit, and in spite of frightening her, appeared so willing to see and love her for what she wanted to believe she was. Zeke washed the dishes. Did laundry. Told her she didn't need make-up, and that she ought to leave her hair down. These were things Tom Raines had never done or said.

Maybe Maggie had gotten the text from Cal, then let her imagination wander. The realization that she might have wanted a Zeke so badly that she made him up left Maggie feeling sad...empty...but she tried not to show it in front of her present live and watchful company.

***

Canon didn't mean to fall asleep on Maggie's sofa. But he was tired and it felt so good. Everything about this morning felt good, like he might still be dreaming. Listening to her pad softly through the cabin, going to the bedroom to dress, then waking to the smell of breakfast, sitting with someone at a table, sorghum to pour, felt like the old days. Rita had never failed to have sorghum on the table.

Flowers in a vase. Books beside the couch. A lot of water had passed under the bridge, but Canon still missed those things. This woman made a space so pleasant he nearly dropped his guard and told her about his dreams. But something stopped him.

He didn't really know Maggie Raines. He didn't want her to think he was crazy. It had been a long time since he'd felt so comfortable in a woman's presence. Canon didn't want to spoil it. Plus...he came here to do his job.

* * *

Maggie watched Canon push back from the table. The sky outside was lightening. He thanked her and stood to leave. Before putting his jacket on he checked his gun then pulled on his hat.

"Do you need gloves?" Maggie didn't know why she asked, she didn't have any gloves to fit him. Maybe she was stalling. She suddenly hated to see him go. It felt safe with Canon Dale there. Would Zeke reappear when Canon was gone? Did she want him to? Maggie wasn't sure.

Canon leveled his gaze at her. "I can't work my gun wearing gloves."

"Oh. Right." *A gun.*

Maggie wanted to ask if she could search the grounds with him, but she suspected he would tell her no. "You really think someone could be out there, having survived in this cold weather?"

On what seemed a highly diminishing chance Zeke had been real, she hated to think about him fleeing the cabin only to have the sheriff shoot him. She thought of her dream—red blood dripping from Zeke's chest onto the snow.

Canon shook his head. "I've learned never to say never. Noticed you had a case under the bed. What kind of handgun?"

"Colt .22. Belongs to Cal. He insisted I bring it."

"Cal's a good son, sounds like. You might want to keep it close 'til

I get back." He nodded to her. "Thank you for the fine breakfast, Mrs. Raines."

She gave him a look and he corrected himself. "Maggie." He smiled. "I don't know when I've had a finer one." He turned to open the door. "Or company to share it with."

Then Canon Dale was gone.

13

Twice in Act 2 there should be a plot twist, a major turning point, something the reader is not expecting. Often it surprises the writer, too.

Maggie sat on the couch staring at her computer, trying to write, but she couldn't concentrate. The dishes were washed, the cabin was tidied, and she'd searched all over for evidence Zeke had ever been there, but...nothing. She looked over at her cell phone, back in her possession, and thought of texting her children, but could think of nothing to say.

Hey. Thought there was an escaped convict in the cabin with me for a couple of days. Turns out it was only my imagination. I'm fine now. No need to worry.

The wail of a police siren coming up the road cut through her disheveled thoughts.

Maggie pulled on her coat and boots, reached for a hat and gloves, and watched at the window. When the car came into sight she stepped out on the porch. Canon's squad car, a silver Taurus with green lettering, was still parked near her Subaru.

A young man jumped out of a newly arrived SUV.

"What's happened?" she asked.

"Sheriff found a body in the woods. You the tenant?"

Maggie nodded and came down the steps zipping her coat to her chin as the man reached for a bag. "Can I go with you?"

He gave her a startled look. "Dead bodies aren't pleasant."

"I'd still like to come."

"You'll need to stay wide of the crime scene." The man looped the bag strap over his shoulder and clapped his hands together. "It's awful cold!"

Maggie tucked her hair into the cap and pulled on her gloves as she followed him past the cabin and into the woods behind it. In moments her toes felt numb inside the shearling boots she wore.

The deputy plucked a radio off his belt. "I told the tenant she could come. Hope you don't mind."

"I don't mind," came the deep timbre of Canon's reply.

A clearing surrounded the cabin, save for the few trees that dotted the yard—the large oak that covered the bedroom windows and the two mid-sized hickory trees in the front where the rick of wood was stacked. Otherwise the land was open and flat then began to slope uphill into a wooded area behind. Maggie stepped through the snow-blanketed landscape, following the young officer in front of her.

They climbed for several minutes then turned left following Canon's tracks. After what must have been a half mile, Maggie saw him coming toward them in the distance. The terrain had grown rough, ice-covered brush pulling at the fabric of their coats. Canon nodded to his deputy then reached a hand down to help Maggie up the next sharp rise. When all three stood on top of the ridge Canon pointed down.

A man lay sprawled in the ravine below.

Maggie's breath caught—she had seen Zeke falling in her dream.

"There's a deer path over here." Canon led the way. Maggie could see dainty tracks mixed in with his. "This is the best way down."

He turned every few steps to make sure Maggie and the officer behind him each had a solid foothold on the slippery descent. Long before they reached the bottom Maggie knew it wasn't Zeke. The clothes weren't his. This man wore prison garb. And his hair was too dark.

Maggie didn't realize how tightly she had been coiled until her shoulders relaxed. She stood back as the men spoke low and leaned over the body.

"Been here since the snow started," said Canon.

"Think he fell?" asked the deputy. Canon had called him Amos.

"I don't know. Get a picture of this." Canon pointed at the man's head. Amos pulled a camera from the bag and leaned in to get a closer shot. "Blunt force trauma. Something hit him. Paul can tell us more."

Maggie didn't know how they could tell anything. All she could see was a man frozen and stiff, with a bluish sheen all over, lying face down in the snow. The man was nearly covered, all but for a patch of his hatless hair.

Canon looked up at her. Maggie's face must have looked ashen because he asked, "You okay?"

She nodded, but in truth didn't feel well. Maggie had never seen a dead person like this. When her father died, medical staff were quick to attend to him. Maggie shouldn't have come traipsing out here. That was a mistake. But she wanted—*needed*—to see with her own eyes that it wasn't Zeke.

After Amos took several photos, he and Canon began dusting snow from around the man, getting him ready to turn over. Canon looked up at her again before they flipped him. Maggie turned away, focusing instead on the land around them and the steam of her breath hanging in the air. She rubbed her arms. She needed to keep moving.

The cold air made Maggie's vision sharper. She noticed how beautiful the ravine was, with rocks jutting out, with animal tracks here and there. Maggie recognized the deer tracks but none of the others. Squirrels? Rabbits? Maggie heard the men grunt behind her as they lifted and turned the body. It must have been heavy. Groans. Thuds. More snapping of pictures.

Canon was suddenly beside her. "Why don't I walk you back to the cabin? It'll take us a while to get the shots we're after, and I need to get a stretcher."

Maggie glanced back. She could see dark stains on the man's head now—what must have been days' old blood, a mass of mottled blue and black, covered by icy hair. By the time she and Canon reached the top of the ravine she was shaking all over, and not from the cold.

Zeke must not have been real—he couldn't have been real. But where had the thought of him come from? Had Cal really even texted about the prison break? As Maggie stepped numbly through the snow she pulled her cell phone from her pocket and pulled off her glove so she could punch in the code and scroll back through her messages.

Yes. There was Cal's text: *Keep your doors locked. There was a prison break not far from your cabin.*

Then her response: *I'll keep them locked, Cal. Thanks for loving me enough to let me know!* An exclamation point.

The phone slipped from Maggie's hands, dropping into the snow. She didn't text Cal that message. Canon, close beside her, picked up the phone, brushed off the ice, and handed it back to her with a pinched brow.

She clutched the phone again, avoiding the sheriff's probing eyes. There was Robbie's text the next morning: *You making it okay?* And her response: *Swimmingly.* Had Maggie ever used the word "swimmingly" before? Why wasn't Robbie suspicious? Why hadn't she questioned Maggie's use of an out-of-the-norm expression?

Great! Happy writing.

Maggie felt Canon looking over her shoulder. They were almost back to the clearing now. Canon had already read the messages, of course, but now he stepped in front of her with pinched brows. "I'm sure it's upsetting to know he was this close to your cabin."

"Upsetting?" Maggie choked. Or was it a sob? She stumbled through the snow past him into the clearing, then stopped and turned back to him, her face painfully cold, but her body now on fire under the down of her jacket.

"You're going to think I'm crazy, Sheriff. I was *not* alone for the past two days. The night that man in the ravine escaped from prison, a man came to my door. A *different* man. He was nearly frozen, curled in a heap. I pulled him inside by the fire. I helped him thaw out. Later when I tried to leave he wouldn't let me."

Canon put a hand to her elbow. "Did he hurt you?"

"That's just it. He was in my cabin for two days and he...he was *nice*. I liked him. He was good for me. He said the nicest things—things I wanted to hear, things I *needed* to hear. I've been so..."

Maggie's words got twisted like a logjam in her throat. *A dead man in the woods behind my cabin!* What must the sheriff think of her? She tried again. "This has been hard. I've never lived alone. But I have to now. Tom didn't give me a choice. He didn't ask how I felt about it."

The sheriff's forehead pinched again. "Your ex-husband's name is Tom."

Maggie nodded.

"I see."

"This man's leg was cut. I keep a first aid kit in the car, but it's not in the bathroom any more. And there *should* have been two plates on the dining table this morning. I don't know how to explain that."

"Slow down, Maggie. Start from the beginning. Tell me what happened. Every detail."

They were back to the cabin now, stepping onto the porch, stamping their feet. Maggie hadn't locked the door. The police were here, after all. All the danger was on the outside. *Or was it?*

"Please don't think I'm crazy."

*   *   *

Canon didn't think she was crazy. Hadn't he seen things *himself* in a dream that he couldn't explain? But he was the sheriff, sworn to uphold the law. And laws were supposed to be rooted in truth...on facts.

What Canon believed was *evidence*. He had a body and a body was evidence. But there weren't any bodies in that cabin but Maggie. No evidence at all to suggest anyone else had ever been there...no tracks in or out of the cabin.

Canon felt it best not to state this...for the present.

*   *   *

Maggie opened the cabin door and stepped inside where the fire was still going but dropping low. Canon took off his jacket and bent down to stack more logs on while Maggie removed her wrappings.

Then he stood. "I'm listening."

They sat at the dining table and Maggie walked him through the first night. "I went to the kitchen to heat soup, then started a warm bath for him." Her eyes landed on her computer. "Here!" She picked it up and flipped the screen open. "You can read about it. I started writing everything down. I'm a writer. I never told you that. I came here to work on a book."

Canon took the computer, his eyes combing over the words. Maggie saw them stop and bore into one spot on the screen. "His name was Zeke?"

"Yes. Short for Ezekiel." Maggie pointed to that line of dialog.

The sheriff got a strange look on his face and rubbed his jaw. "You ever been to Marston County before?"

"No."

"You've not done research on this place?"

"When I rented this cabin there was a short blurb online about the history of the man who built it. I was curious to know more. But that's all. Why?"

The sheriff closed the lid. "You mind riding down to Ollie's with me? I'd like to show you something."

Maggie pulled her boots and coat back on. As they left the cabin Canon plucked the radio from his belt. "Amos, I'll be a little longer getting that stretcher back down there. You okay?"

"Take your time, Boss. I'll go around the ridge and see if I find anything."

When Canon parked at Mr. Thompson's, he didn't go to the door as Maggie had expected. He motioned for her to follow him around the side of the house instead. In back, several yards behind a car shed, lay an old cemetery. Maggie had noticed it on her walks down to the cottage, but it was well off the road. She never thought to come closer and have a look. The sheriff walked out to the cemetery now and stopped near one of the graves, the one with the most modern headstone. He crouched down and scraped snow and ice until the words beneath them were revealed: *Ezekiel Thompson, beloved son.*

Maggie stared. She wasn't sure when her head started shaking but presently heard herself saying, "That's not possible. That's not...I mean..."

She felt the sheriff put an arm on her shoulder, but it spooked her. Maggie flinched and stepped away. "I don't know what's going on here!" Her voice was strange...shrill. The vocal cords—Maggie wanted to scream suddenly from all she knew about the vocal cords. But this...she didn't know anything about this.

Maggie didn't know anything about writing, or cabins, or dead bodies, or Ezekiel Thompson. She needed to go home. But where was that? The condo? The condo wasn't home. She didn't have a home. She didn't have a husband. She didn't have anybody who cared about her. No, that wasn't true. Robbie and Cal did. They still loved Maggie, but they had Mark and Yvette. *I am no longer anyone's top concern.*

Maggie shook worse than when she'd seen the body in the woods, worse than when Zeke was in the cabin.

No! Zeke was dead.

Maggie looked at the headstone again—at the dates. 1950-1986. Zeke had been dead for thirty years? Maggie thought of his outdated jacket and shoes, the Rick Springfield haircut. A strange noise gurgled from her throat. *Cursed vocal cords!*

The radio on Canon's hip crackled. He picked it up, his eyes never leaving Maggie's face. "You got something?"

"Yeah. Can you get back up here?"

"Coming."

Maggie's breath came in lurches, and from the look of the sheriff's face the look on hers was bad. "I'll be fine," she whispered, not sure she believed it.

Concern etched deep around Canon's eyes. Maggie wanted to fall into the pool she saw there, wanted to believe his care for her was real, not simply part of his regular duties. But she steeled against the thought. Knights on white horses were only to be found in fairy tales. Maybe that was why fiction had called to her so strongly. *Is that what Zeke was? A fairy tale? Fiction?*

Canon reached for her elbow. "I'd feel better if you weren't alone."

"She's not alone."

Maggie and the sheriff turned to see Mr. Thompson leaning on his cane. Neither of them had heard him come into the yard. "Saw your deputy go by earlier. He made a lot of racket. What's brought you out here this time, Canon?"

Canon scowled. "You didn't come to the door this mornin' when I knocked."

"Hadn't had my coffee yet." Mr. Thompson looked down to his old boots then over at the headstone. He repositioned his cane on the ground, seemingly unable to find a spot he liked.

"You had enough coffee now for me to leave Mrs. Raines with you?"

"'Course I have." Mr. Thompson waved Maggie to the house. "Come in out of this cold, Mrs. Raines."

Maggie pointed down to the headstone. "You lost your son? His name was Zeke?"

Mr. Thompson nodded.

Canon took Maggie's elbow and saw her to the front door of Mr. Thompson's cottage. She didn't pull away this time.

"I'll be back as quick as I can," he said low.

Maggie's breathing was nearly back to normal. Mr. Thompson felt like a friend. She didn't doubt that he was real. "I'll be fine," she told Canon again. And she almost believed it this time.

14

"I will put my Spirit in you and you will live." Ezekiel 37:14, NIV

Mr. Thompson's cottage was as outdated as Graceland's Jungle Room. It hadn't seen a woman's influence in a number of years.

"Irene died of cancer," he explained as Maggie followed him through the front room into the more lived-in den behind it. If Mr. Thompson was sleeping off a drunk, he didn't leave signs of it out in the open.

The old man picked up a frame from a side table and handed it to Maggie as he pointed toward two patched recliners. A middle-aged woman stared out through the glass. Sandy-colored hair, reminiscent of the seventies, not exactly a beehive, but stacked in stiffly sprayed Aqua Net. The collar of the woman's dress looked to be influenced by Audrey Hepburn or Jacqueline Kennedy.

"She was lovely," said Maggie. When she handed the brass frame back to him, Mr. Thompson picked up a second photo from the top of the TV cabinet.

"This is Zeke."

Maggie took the frame and stared down at the familiar face. *So it is.* But the young man in her hands was a younger Zeke than she had met. This was a graduating high school senior, hair to the top of his shoulders, in an ill-fitting coat and tie.

Mr. Thompson chuckled from where he leaned on his cane watching her. "That was my suit jacket. Too big for him. We never were well off. I been the caretaker for that cabin you're stayin' in since the year Zeke turned sixteen. That's when we first came to Marston County. Irene worked at the Levi factory. When she got the cancer, she had to quit. Lost our insurance."

Maggie was well familiar with the high cost of medical care. She had an appreciation for the steep price tag to the professionals who provided it. She also knew that for the average citizen—particularly one without insurance—it was a delicate balance to weigh the cost of treatments for something terminal against the good those treatments couldn't really guarantee.

"How long...I mean...what year did you lose her?"

Mr. Thompson motioned for Maggie to sit, which she did, still holding the picture of Zeke. He took the recliner beside her. "Eighty-six. She got the cancer right after Zeke's conviction in eighty-three, and died just before he broke out."

The old man suddenly seemed more stooped, more frail than on the day he showed Maggie the cabin. "A parent never imagines when their child is born they'll go to prison one day. Or die too young."

Maggie's mouth felt dry. "What happened?"

"Zeke married a local girl, Tandy Wilkins, right out of high school. Irene wanted him to go to college. That was the whole reason she worked. Nearly every dime was put back for his education. But that Tandy was a pretty girl—rough as all get out, rough family—but pretty. She turned his head. Irene and me begged him not to marry her, but it's hard to talk reason to a boy when a pretty girl has got into his head. Tandy was the reason he went to prison."

Mr. Thompson's jaw clenched. "Irene used to say there was no choice, after the choice to follow the Lord, as important as the choice of who one married." He looked around his humble cottage. "I guess she knew as well as anybody. Her own life wasn't raised much by marryin' me."

Maggie put a hand on his arm. "Her life was rich if you loved her."

Mr. Thompson's blue eyes watered—Zeke's eyes, but older. "Oh, I loved her. As well as I knew how. She deserved more, but...she put up with me. And I reckon she's earned her place among the angels because of it."

Maggie looked down at Zeke's high school picture again. "Your son had your eyes, Mr. Thompson."

"Please. Call me 'Ollie.' Enough of this 'Mr. Thompson' business."

Maggie grinned and handed him the photo. "He reminds me of Rick Springfield."

"The singer? On that soap opera?" Mr. Thompson chuckled, running a creased hand over his son's likeness. Maggie wondered how many times he'd held the picture and stared down with regret.

"That would have made Zeke smile. Irene cut his hair, even after he was married. And that's *exactly*"—Mr. Thompson pointed a crooked finger as he said this—"who he wanted it to look like. That soap opera singer." He chuckled again at the memory.

Maggie smiled. "I'm really sorry you lost your wife and son, Ollie."

Mr. Thompson sighed. "That's life, I reckon. We're all headed to the grave. I wouldn't have chosen to be the last one standin', but...I guess I'm glad it didn't have to be one of them."

He ran his hand over the frame again before hauling himself out of the recliner to set the picture back on the console. "Only good that come of him marryin' Tandy Wilkins was it gave us his college fund for treatments for Irene. But she wouldn't let me use it. We were savin' it for children they might have, but Zeke and Tandy never had no children. The Thompson name will end with me. I used the money on attorney fees instead. I reckon Irene don't hold it against me. Money always did run through my fingers."

Mr. Thompson folded himself back into the recliner. "I guess Canon told you how Zeke died."

Maggie shook her head. "No, he didn't."

"I found him dead on the porch of that cabin you're stayin' in. Not a scratch on him, but he was stiff. Paul said he froze to death. He was only wearin' a light jacket. Got out of jail somehow—Canon told me how—I don't recall right now. Just walked out, I think he said. I was still tore up about Irene and didn't know he ever come here. But the cabin key was gone from the shed out back and I found him down there two days later."

Maggie stared at Mr. Thompson. Time seemed to slow. *I didn't imagine Zeke. He was there.*

"The truth is, Mrs. Raines," Mr. Thompson continued, his already hoarse voice cracking. "I had too much to drink that night."

"Please." Maggie put a hand on his arm. "Call me Maggie. Enough of this 'Mrs. Raines' business."

His face relaxed then. "I knew I liked you the first minute I laid eyes on you."

Maggie squeezed his arm. "Same here."

Mr. Thompson patted her hand. "I hope you're gettin' along okay in this snow. I'm sorry I haven't been up to check on you."

Maggie thought of how Zeke's head had whipped around when she mentioned Mr. Thompson's name. As if he'd forgotten. Had Zeke never appeared to his father?

"I started drinking too much when I was a kid. Irene still married me. We grew up together. Made it hard to keep a job sometimes. I tried to quit. Did quit, for years when Zeke was young. I got this job and it provided us with a home. Zeke loved it out here. Hunted all over these woods. He was a real good boy, Maggie. Apple of his mother's eye. She taught him to read before he went to school, and he was smart. Boy, I *mean* smart! Top of his class. Teachers bragged on him. That was thanks to Irene, his smarts. He got those from her. She really could have been somethin'. Never did know how I caught her eye."

"Zeke was your only child?"

"Hmm?"

Maggie could see Mr. Thompson traveling in his mind. She felt bad to interrupt him.

"Oh, yes. Only child the Lord ever blessed us with."

Maggie had stirred enough emotion for the old man for one day. She stood.

Mr. Thompson looked up. "Canon never did say what brought him out here. It wasn't just to check on me."

"No. He..." Maggie hated to tell Mr. Thompson about the prison break. "He found a body in the woods behind the cabin. A Hispanic man he was looking for," she was quick to add.

"I see." Mr. Thompson thought for a minute, grasping his cane to rise. "How'd the man die?"

"I don't think they know yet. They were going to take the body to someone named Paul."

"Yeah, Paul. He'll know. That's the coroner."

Maggie started for the door. Cold as it was, she looked forward to walking back to the cabin, to being in the open air. "I'll let you get back to your day, Ollie."

He rose to his feet to see her off. "I hope you've had a good stay, Maggie. In spite of this business with the man Canon found. And knowing about me and my troubles."

"I have." She put her hand on the old man's arm again. "And we've all got troubles, don't we?"

Mr. Thompson's eyes were so like Zeke's it caused a knot in Maggie's stomach.

"You're a fine lady, Mrs. Raines. Maggie. I've tried to give you your space, so you could write. But I've enjoyed knowing you were in the cabin. You know I'm here if you need anything."

She didn't tell him he had failed to answer the only time she had called him. She didn't want to make Mr. Thompson feel any worse. *Or did I call him?* Maggie wasn't overly sure of any of the events from the past two days.

"You still planning to go home tomorrow?" he asked.

"Yes."

"I'm glad this unpleasantness hasn't driven you away."

"No. In fact..." The thought just occurred to her. "Would it be okay if I come back, Ollie?"

His countenance lifted. "All you have to do is say the word, Maggie. Deal directly with me, instead of going on the Internet. You'll always get first dibs with me."

"Thank you."

On impulse, Maggie hugged him. He didn't seem as startled this time. Then she walked out into the crisp golden day. As Maggie turned a corner on the snow-covered lane and the cabin came into sight with the sun reflecting on the windows, she suddenly knew why Zeke had come to her there.

Zeke wants me to tell his story.

15

If a story comes to you and takes root, you are the keeper of the tale. You may never know how it truly sprang to life, but now your job is to feed it. See what kind of fruit it bears.

Maggie's vision had never been more sharp. The snow glistened in the sun like a sea of diamonds. In her precarious new mental state...maybe *because* of her precarious new mental state...Maggie felt alive.

The closer she got to the porch of the cabin, the stronger she pictured a man curled in front of the door, until movement on the hill beyond drew her gaze. Canon and his deputy were coming down with the loaded stretcher.

Maggie stood and watched, then sat on the swing until the two men slid the body in the back of the SUV. She wondered how much money it cost to outfit a vehicle for a sheriff's line of work.

Canon arched his back like he was glad to be free of the load. Maggie remembered how heavy Zeke's stiff body had been when she pulled him in and dragged him toward the fire. As Amos drove away, Canon came toward her looking tired, lifting a boot up to the step.

As Maggie watched his breath roll out she thought of Zeke's breath on her hair as she undressed him. *Everlasting. Why the word 'everlasting,' Zeke?* She wished she'd thought to ask him. Would she ever see Zeke Thompson again?

Only on the pages. Maggie felt it in her bones.

Canon's deep voice brought her back to the moment. "How are you?"

"Full of thought."

The knit cap was back on his head. *Canon...one 'n' like a law, not a weapon.* Even so, Canon Dale looked as solid as the weapon.

He exhaled again, blowing more steam into the wind. The sun had melted some of the snow, but the temperature was still below freezing. "I'd like to get an official statement from you about all this."

Maggie offered a weak smile. "Even if I don't really know what 'all this' is?"

Canon nodded. Creases lined the corners of his eyes as he looked out toward the snow and squinted. "I've learned to trust the process. I still write the reports, even on things I don't understand. Sometimes in the writing things become more clear. You probably know that if you're a writer."

What did he mean by *if* ? Maggie knew she hadn't really earned the right to that title, but still had to fight the temptation to get her hackles up. "What's involved?"

He took a minute answering, a look of satisfaction crossing his features. "You riding back to the station with me. I'll try not to keep you any longer than I have to."

Resigned, Maggie went inside for her purse. Then she locked the cabin door.

As she climbed into the sheriff's car, her mind continued to try to make sense of things. Canon's car was clean...nice smell...man smell, of coffee, cinnamon gum, and something like polished steel. Maybe it was his gun cleaner—some chemical used in detective work. Or carpet cleaner used on the rugs of his floorboard.

As the car rolled past the snow-covered land, Maggie turned to study the sheriff as he drove. How did Canon Dale factor into this story?

He knew the curves of the county roads well, taking them at a careful pace, the only tracks his and the deputy's. Once he got out onto the highway he picked up speed, keeping his front tires in the two gray ruts glistening wet in the sun.

The police radio on the dash hummed. It all sounded like static to Maggie's untrained ears, but every now and then Canon would reach over and turn the volume up, listening. Then he'd turn it back down, she assumed out of respect for her. They didn't talk, but each time Maggie turned to watch the passing scenery she could feel him studying her.

Her mind rolled over what she'd learned from Mr. Thompson: Zeke as a teenager, roaming the woods around the cabin. Getting his head turned by Tandy Wilkins in high school. What did Tandy look like? Where was she now? Traditional church wedding? What was the timeline? Irene's sickness. A trial.

"Sheriff?" asked Maggie.

Canon had reached to turn up the volume on the regular radio, a country station to cover the static, but turned it back down again.

"Why was Zeke Thompson in prison?"

"Ollie didn't tell you?"

"No. He said it was because of Zeke's wife, Tandy, but he didn't say what it was."

Canon sat quietly a minute before answering, as if trying to decide if Maggie could handle the news. "Zeke was convicted of killing Tandy. And a man from Trenton, the man she was cheatin' with at the time."

Silence ballooned and filled the patrol car. *Zeke was a murderer?*

"He couldn't have," whispered Maggie.

"He did it. I was the first one on the scene."

I'd kill him if I thought it'd make you feel better, Maggie. But it wouldn't. Trust me.

Maggie thought of how she had pictured Tom dead in a coffin. *If I wrap my hands around his trachea—cut off his windpipe below his larynx—could I squeeze hard enough to shut him up? Forever?* In those initial moments after Tom had told her, Maggie thought he deserved to die for his betrayal...and Bethany.

As Canon turned the car and they entered town Maggie asked, "Just so I'm not caught off guard, there's not any chance you think *I* killed the man behind the cabin, is there?"

"Of course not." Canon scowled. "There's no evidence that points to that."

So he *could* have conceived of her as a killer if there had been evidence? This was not a comforting thought. "I suddenly feel like I'm being brought in for questioning. Is that the same thing as making a statement?"

"Not by my way of thinking." Canon could be as matter-of-fact as Zeke. "If I was bringing you in for questioning you'd be behind the cage in cuffs, and I'd card you the minute we got in the door."

The sheriff's uniform...his hip radio...the gun on his belt...now his words bouncing off the cage behind her head sent a chill tickling up Maggie's spine. If the sheriff thought she was guilty of something, he wouldn't be swayed by her charm...if Maggie had any to claim. So she didn't need to be thinking about how thick his arms were, or wonder if those creases around his eyes indicated potential feelings for her. The sheriff was just doing his job.

She decided not to ask what 'carding' meant. Fingerprints?

Maggie craned her head to peer through the hard plastic mesh separating the back seat from the front. Was Zeke cuffed and carded? What did squad cars look like in Marston County thirty years ago? Same mesh screens separating the back from the front? Was it always called a cage? Like for animals?

"I guess that makes me feel better," she muttered. Canon patted her arm above the wrist. She wondered if the sheriff had been taught this was a safe place to touch a woman. Non-threatening.

"This is just a statement for the report," he said.

We're both writers, me and the sheriff—he writes fact and I write fiction. What exactly was fact? And what exactly was fiction? If facts led to conclusions of truth, what did it mean when facts didn't add up?

Maggie could think of more than one life moment she couldn't explain, like two especially close calls in traffic. Both times she had been daydreaming. Both times she had her foot on the gas to pull into traffic and didn't see the trucks barreling down on her—one a black SUV, the other an eighteen wheeler on the interstate. Something she still couldn't explain moved her foot to the brake each time—mashed it to the floor and saved her life.

When she told Tom about each incident, he said, "Lucky you saw it in time. Lucky your instincts kicked in." But Maggie knew it wasn't her—*her* instincts never kicked in.

The facts she was about to share with the Marston County Sheriff wouldn't add up, either. Did it mean those facts weren't true? Had they never really happened? And if they had, how could she ever explain them?

Sometimes Maggie lost track of time. That was a true statement. But her pride didn't want her to admit it to Canon. Could that have happened at the cabin...with Zeke? Did Maggie lose track of time?

But her phone said today was Saturday. And how could her vision of Zeke look exactly like an older version of the picture in Mr. Thompson's cottage? How was that explained? That the man she spent the past two days with was the same man who froze to death on the steps of her cabin thirty years ago?

That first day she walked down to Mr. Thompson's before the snow started, hadn't they had a brief conversation on his porch? Had she seen into his den that day? To the picture on the console?

Maggie and Canon arrived at the station, a low-roofed, red brick building off the square.

When they stepped inside, no one else was there. "It *is* a holiday," mumbled Canon. "And Shirley has the weekends off."

Amos must still be at the coroner's. Maggie was glad. An audience of one and a voice recorder was more than she really wanted.

Canon showed Maggie into his office at the back of the station, dragging a chair in to sit beside his desk. He was at home—master of the ship—and set right into acting like it, hanging his coat on a hook by the door, straightening a stack of mail on the edge of his desk, starting a pot of coffee.

"You drink coffee all day?" Maggie hoped her voice sounded steady.

"Only on days I don't get enough sleep."

He took her coat and hung it next to his then poured two cups without asking, handed her one, and set the other on the desk before inching around her in the small office. He was respectful, and only lightly placed his hands on either side of her hips as he slid past, but Maggie felt them. Then she watched as he rolled his sleeves to his elbows, changed the setting on his phone to *record* and laid it face-up on the desk in front of her. He had nice forearms.

Guilt stabbed her. *So what if he has nice forearms?*

She looked away from Canon's arms and concentrated on his nameplate instead—block letters carved in wood—hoping the solidity of it would help bring her heart back into its regular rhythm. It wasn't every day a woman's statement was needed. It wasn't every day she got an up-close look at the dead.

Next Maggie's eyes landed on the phone he had laid in front of her. A Samsung. In a black case. On a brown desk. The desk was well-worn, the finish rubbed off the two corners nearest to her. Was it from guests having gripped each side with their hands during interrogations? Did Canon make everyone nervous...or just Maggie? Was it his title...or those forearms?

*   *   *

Canon watched Maggie inspect his office, noting how she avoided his eyes. He couldn't blame her. Tough day. But he had a hard time keeping his off her. Maggie Raines wore an elegance not often seen in Marston County, even in those worn jeans—the kind that hugged her curves and went down into her boots.

He marveled at the miracle that she was standing in front of him and wondered what she saw, wondered what she thought of him, hoping once again the cleaner he had used on the back seat of the cruiser had gotten Tim Drexler's stench out. It never occurred to him that the woman from his dreams would materialize and be the next one to ride in it.

Just before she sat down, he inched her chair toward his desk. He wanted her closer.

*　　*　　*

Not knowing what to do with her eyes in the close quarters of Canon's office, Maggie peered through the window looking out over the larger front office instead. She suspected Canon pulled her chair closer so he could pat her arm if she needed encouragement.

How do I know this about him already? She just knew.

"Nobody's going to listen to this recording but me," he said. "I want to be sure I get the facts straight when I write the report later. This lets me listen to you instead of taking notes."

Thoughtful of him. Or was this some kind of trick? Maggie couldn't think straight.

Canon's gaze was as calm as the hands folded in front of him. Had he always been this patient? Or had he learned it over time? Did that uniform affect him when he put it on, or did it only affect others when they observed him in it? What was it about a man in uniform?

No...it wasn't the uniform. Canon Dale simply had a way about him. He was obviously used to dealing with the traumatized.

Is that what I am?

*   *   *

Canon watched Maggie run a finger along her bottom lip, then chew on the finger as her eyes wandered around his office one more time before landing back on his. Then, looking self-conscious, she pulled her hand from her lips and laid it on the desk.

"Deep breath." His gaze never strayed from her eyes—the eyes of a doe caught in headlights. His chair creaked as he leaned forward and touched her arm, seeking to reassure her. "From the beginning. Day you arrived at the cabin."

"I arrived the day after Christmas. About noon." She stopped and cleared her throat.

"To be clear, this is the cabin on Patterson Road past Ollie Thompson's place." Canon needed that on the recording.

"Correct."

*   *   *

Maggie cleared her throat again, giving courage to her vocal cords. Everything about the sheriff was starched and crisp, strong and solid, including his voice. She tried not to let it intimidate her.

Ollie must be short for Oliver. Maggie studied Canon's eyes. Straight on. Unblinking. Brown like hers. *Zeke's eyes were blue. Does Canon have that in his files?*

She laid a hand on his arm above the wrist this time.

*   *   *

Canon looked down at Maggie's hand on his arm, thinking of his dream, the part where the dark-haired woman undressed him.

Do your job, Canon.

"It started with Tom," she said. "In August. That's what sent me to the cabin in the first place."

"Okay." Afraid of her touch but trying not to show it, he covered her hand with his own. "Start with Tom."

16

"Where, O death, is your victory? Where, O death, is your sting?" 1 Corinthians 15:55, NIV

When Maggie finished talking—telling Canon each detail exactly as she remembered it—he continued to stare at her. She heard the clock ticking on the wall behind him. In one slow but fluid motion he reached to stop the *record* button on his phone, raised his brows, and leaned back again causing his chair to creak.

"That's quite a story, Mrs. Raines."

"What happened to 'Maggie'?"

Canon's eyes flashed. "This mean you're going to call me 'Canon?'"

Was this the first time the sheriff had asked Maggie a direct question? And not worded his question as a statement?

Maggie looked away. She had already begun to think of him as Canon rather than Sheriff Dale. He studied her in silence so long she began to grow uncomfortable. What did he mean by *story*? Did he think she was making this up? All this detail?

Canon picked up his phone and turned it over absentmindedly. "Zeke Thompson died thirty years ago," he finally said.

"So how did he know about cell phones?" wondered Maggie. Now that she had gone through it again, laid it on the table for Canon, Maggie's mind was free to explore some of the particulars, and why it might have happened. She had been handed a gift. Zeke could unlock her way forward as a writer...free her to be who she was meant to be all along...liberate her from a captivity she had allowed herself to crawl into.

Turn the prism a quarter to the right, Maggie.

If Tom hadn't had the affair with Bethany, Maggie never would have gone to the cabin in the first place. She would never have met Zeke Thompson. *Can I do Zeke's story justice?*

She realized Canon was staring at her. Maggie longed for him to believe her, even as her mind raced through inconsistencies. She didn't need the sheriff to point them out to her. "He did act like he'd never heard of a 'text' before," she said. "But then he knew how to put a code in—he knew a code was needed."

"I didn't see any evidence there was anyone in that cabin but you."

"Or *computers*! How did he know the laptop was my computer? When did personal computers come out?" *He ate food! Borrowed my toothpaste. His leg bled. I bandaged it.*

Canon's hand was back on her arm above the wrist. "Forgive me for asking, Maggie, but is there any chance you dreamed this?"

His doubt punched a jarring hole in Maggie's musing. "He was *there*, Canon. It didn't feel like a dream."

"Neither did Dorothy's."

That stung. "But two days passed. How you do account for that?" She realized as she said it that Canon only had her word on the time. There was no one—nothing—to back her up. From all appearances Maggie had been alone in the cabin.

The sheriff rubbed his neck. It seemed an absentminded gesture, but absentmindedness didn't fit him any better than his nervous talking when he first met her.

"There was an empty bottle of wine on the counter," he said.

That stung, too. "I only had one glass at a time." Again, who could back her up on that? Or had it been two? Yes, last night she had two glasses, but Maggie chose not to correct herself.

"Are you a regular drinker?"

"No...I mean...what does 'regular' mean?"

"Daily."

"No, I don't drink daily." *Once or twice a month. Well...except for this week.*

"How does alcohol typically affect you?"

"I do not have an alcohol problem, Sheriff!"

"Is there any chance the lines blurred between fact and fiction, then?" Maggie's eyes flashed up at him. He looked a little embarrassed. "And I thought we agreed on 'Canon.'"

"I had one glass of wine before I fell asleep on the couch Wednesday night." *That* was a true statement, best of her recollection. "One glass of Chardonnay."

"So there were two bottles of wine."

Maggie clamped her mouth shut.

"You ever blacked out from drinking?"

"No!"

"And you never heard of Zeke Thompson before? It was a long time ago, Maggie. Isn't it possible you read it in the papers at the time, about the murders and conviction, saw his picture then and simply dreamed it?"

Maggie shook her head. She had been finding Canon Dale attractive in his brown uniform, with his satisfied and sheepish looks, but now she reconsidered. "Does that not seem like an incredible coincidence, Sheriff?" He gave her a look. "Canon."

"I don't know, Maggie, but isn't it worth asking the question? I'm on your side here. I don't *not* believe you. I'm just trying to find a plausible explanation!" Canon seemed as frustrated as her. "Could your subconscious mind have known you were at that same cabin? That, married with the glass of wine..."

The question, much as Maggie's better judgment tried to resist it, burrowed in and planted a seed of doubt. Oh, who was she kidding? She'd been doubting since she woke that morning. She'd been doubting for the past two days. Could she have dreamed it? Like Dorothy in *The Wizard of Oz*?

Was it possible she had awakened that first night, or the next morning, in some kind of writer's trance? Had she really only had one glass of wine? Or was it two? Did she sleep through a whole day? Is that what got her days off? Or had she gone straight to her computer and lost track of time that way? Did hours fly by without her knowing?

No...that was crazy! Maggie wasn't crazy. She knew what she had seen and heard. *Zeke's blood was red!*

Today was New Year's Eve. That meant two days had passed. And, by God, she did not use the word *swimmingly*! But the way Canon looked at her now, she knew better than to say so. He was not convinced.

Maggie's face flushed hot. Once again she was glad they were the only two in the office.

Canon reached for her arm above the wrist again. She almost jerked it away. But she knew this wasn't his fault. The sheriff was only doing his job. It was right for him to get the facts straight.

"Why don't we get a bite to eat, then ride back out to the cabin?" he suggested. "You can walk me through it again when we get out there. Step-by-step, just like you remember. Maybe it will lead us to something. I believe Shirley said The Local Café was going to be open for lunch today."

Maggie didn't answer. She didn't see the point of trying to eat, and she didn't see the point of rehashing the story. Canon obviously didn't believe her. It did sound crazy, even to her own ears.

She tried to focus on her jacket as the sheriff held it out to her. She knew she shouldn't be mad at Canon for acting like a sheriff. And he didn't have to believe her for Maggie to know what she had experienced. Zeke's presence in that cabin had *changed* her. It was kind. Tender.

Maggie numbly followed Canon to The Local Café and took a seat across from him.

Zeke's story was a blessing. While Maggie had questioned whether she should ever have gone to the cabin in the first place, going had been a blessing. And Zeke's story—whether Zeke's ghost had handed it to her or she'd pieced it all together from subliminal remembrances or a dream—Zeke's story was a gift for the unwrapping.

Noises filled the café around them, but none of the sounds really registered. *Trust in the gift, Maggie, and don't overthink it.* Wasn't that what Zeke would say? Isn't that what he had tried to teach her? What a person *believed* was the important part.

Blinders that had grown like cataracts over Maggie's eyes prior to Tom's betrayal—then persisted stubbornly through the withdrawing of his love, the storms of his confession, the bludgeoning of the sturdy pillars that had held her life together like a bedrock—the blinders were ripped away at last. All the facts were the same, but what she *believed* about them had changed.

As confused as Maggie felt, as crazy as she sounded, she knew she had it right now. *I see more clearly than I did.*

She wasn't sure what she ordered for lunch, but she was sure the waitress sized her up more than was normal. Was it because Maggie was a stranger? Or because she sat in the restaurant with the town's handsome sheriff? Did the waitress think Maggie was guilty of something?

Canon attempted to make small talk after the woman left. "So, twins. Do they favor?"

Maggie had spilled a lot of details about the last five months of her life back at his office. She pulled out her phone now to show him an obligatory photo so he could put faces with the names.

As she thumbed through a string of pictures from Thanksgiving she said, "That's Cal's fiancée, Yvette. And this is Mark, Robbie's boyfriend." Then she was into the pictures from last summer, the Fourth of July picnic. There was one of the twins. She held it out to show him. "They're fraternal, not identical."

"A boy and girl can't be identical." The sheriff was stating facts again.

"That's right. Most people don't know that, because they ask me all the time."

"Twins run in my family."

Maggie was going to ask him more about that, but as she brought the phone back she looked at the picture again, realizing for the first time that Bethany stood in the background, talking to Tom, who was smiling. Maggie turned her phone off.

Bethany was already pregnant by the Fourth of July picnic. Maggie had done the math. She suspected that's why Tom had pushed the divorce papers through so quickly. So his next child wouldn't be born while he was still married to Maggie.

Canon smiled. "Nice looking kids. They favor you."

Their food came and Maggie ate so she wouldn't have to talk, but her meat and three went down like cardboard. Canon wasn't wearing a wedding ring. She hadn't thought to notice that until he reached for his wallet to pay for lunch, insisting she put her purse away.

On the ride back to the cabin, Maggie's mind wouldn't stop swirling with the events of the day. *Tom...Zeke...Canon...the headstone...her future.*

She clamped the edge of her forefinger hard between her teeth to keep from crying, a sudden rush of emotion going straight to her eyes. Maggie was tired. Wrung out.

Had anyone told her prior to this day that ghosts or nightmares could prove a blessing, she never would have believed them. But now she realized it was true—they could—and, in spite of the hard bite to her flesh, she wept.

Maggie kept her face turned to the window, but presently felt a nudge at her elbow. Canon held out a small packet of tissues. She took them without speaking and turned away from him again.

All at once the squad car lurched right, then left. Canon was wheeling it around. "Saw something out of place back there. Hold on."

Maggie clutched the door handle as ice and snow spewed beneath Canon's tires. They careened dangerously close to a drop off on Maggie's side of the roadway. She inhaled and braced for impact, but Canon held it steady, steering the car back into the clear asphalt ruts. He pointed them toward a once-white building with no windows they just passed, on the opposite side of the road from where Maggie had her head turned. 'Ron-dee-vu' flashed on a sign with holes in the plastic.

As they neared the parking lot, Maggie saw a group of men. One was suddenly thrown to the ground, snow spraying up from the force of it. Now another man kicked him. Maggie's breath caught—this was worse than nearly going off the embankment.

Canon wheeled into the lot and threw the car into park. The tires slid, then caught. "Stay here! Don't get out." The command was barked—not open for debate. Then he was out of the car and running.

Maggie watched him swing a leg under the back of the man who was kicking, knocking him to the ground beside his victim. When the other two turned, he knocked them to the ground too, before Maggie could suck wind from the shock of it. Now his pistol was out, and he must have been telling the men to keep their hands where he could see them because they each held out their arms. Then they were picking themselves off the icy parking lot, slowly, keeping their eyes on Canon and hands where he could see them.

Everything had happened so fast. Maggie's mind raced to catch up. What if one of those men pulled a gun on Canon? She checked the glove box. Sure enough, there was a small pistol lying inside it. Maggie's fingers shook. She was afraid to take it in her hands.

With the hard cage behind her head, the crackle of the radio, and the cold steel of the gun in front of her, Maggie's respect for the sobriety of Canon's job suddenly soared.

She watched as Canon motioned the three men to the side of the building then put a hand down to help the one still on the ground. The four of them lined up. Canon was asking them questions and listening, but Maggie couldn't tell what they were saying. If they turned on him, Maggie would grab the gun and come to Canon's rescue. He told her to stay in the car, but surely this would be a justified exception. Maggie strained to keep her eye on them.

Canon looked over his shoulder at the squad car. Would he have taken them to the station were it not for her? Should Maggie get out and offer to wait at this questionable-looking bar while Canon took the men into custody? But what other men might be inside? Only a handful of cars were in the lot. Who came to a place like this on New Year's Eve?

Lonely people. That was who.

Canon kept the three attackers by the side of the building while the man they had beaten limped to his car and left. When the man's car was well out of sight, Canon motioned with his gun for the other three to go. He stood by and watched until each one disappeared down the road. Then he walked back to his squad car and opened the door, his eyes brushing over Maggie. "You okay?"

"Am *I* okay?" All Maggie had done was sit in the car. "Are *you* okay?"

Canon eyed the open glove box. He got in and reached across her knees to close it, suddenly grinning. "You were planning to come to my rescue." It wasn't a question.

"If necessary."

He cut his eyes over to her as he put the car into gear. "Did you not think I could handle it?"

Maggie didn't know how to answer. She was pretty sure by the way he asked the question—and the smirk on his face as he turned the car around—that Canon knew exactly what he could handle.

"I'm not used to fights in parking lots," Maggie mumbled as they turned off the highway onto Patterson Road.

"That was pretty mild."

Maggie was silent as they rode past Mr. Thompson's cottage. It was 3:15. The sun dipped low in the sky.

"I guess it's been a full day for you," said Canon.

"And for you." She watched the cabin come into view, then Canon was parking beside her Subaru.

"Walk me through it again."

How could he not be tired of this? Maggie was certainly tired of telling it. But she walked him through it again as they got out and made their way toward the steps. Maggie wondered if this was what law enforcement did—kept having victims go through their stories over and over, to see if they kept the facts consistent.

Just like a writer.

"He was right here." Maggie pointed to the porch. "Curled. Half frozen. I pulled him in, toward the fire. I went back in the kitchen to heat some tomato soup. We got him thawed out."

Canon's boots echoed on the wooden floors as he followed her through the cabin, inspecting again. "You said you doctored his leg, but there are no bandages anywhere."

"Hold on." Maggie grabbed her car keys and went back out to the Subaru. The first aid kit was undisturbed in the trunk. Inspecting its contents, she brought it back inside. "I can't explain it. I did, I doctored his leg. I used these. There should have been bloody bandages in the trash."

"But there aren't."

"Okay." Maggie threw the kit on the table and lifted her hands in defeat. "I guess a ghost cleans up after himself."

"The neat ones, anyway."

Was he smirking at her again? "You don't think he was really here."

This time the sheriff's look wasn't satisfied or sheepish, it was frustrated, causing the lines on either side of his eyes to crease again. "I can't find any evidence that he was, Maggie."

"What about the things I wrote?"

"From all appearances, that's just fiction."

She tried to keep the hurt from showing on her face, but knew she did a poor job of it.

"Sweetheart..." Canon held out his arms to her.

Maggie looked up sharply.

Canon stepped back, his ears turning scarlet. "My apologies. That was inappropriate. I didn't mean anything by it. Look," he lifted his hands. "I know I'm skatin' on thin ice here, and the last thing I want to do is upset you."

"I realize you're doing your job, Sheriff. But..." Maggie shook her head. She could feel tears welling up again, like in the car, before the bar fight. She didn't want to cry in front of him again. "I don't know what I'm supposed to *do* with all this. I think maybe I'm supposed to write Zeke's story. That's why he came to me. It was so clear when I was walking back to the cabin from Mr. Thompson's earlier. That's the only explanation. Or is it some *phenomenon* that happens when weather conditions are just right? I mean, he was so real, Canon. He was as real as you are now, standing there."

He *hugged* me, she almost said, but thought better of it. *I felt his arms around me.*

Canon balled his fists. Maggie would have loved for the sheriff to hug her, too, but she hardly knew him. *Of course that didn't keep me from curling up with Zeke Thompson on the red sofa.* Maggie's face flushed. Did the sheriff call all women 'sweetheart'?

A man in uniform was not only sexy, he seemed so safe.

But nothing about Canon Dale raised Maggie's natural defenses. She was simply tired.

Hadn't his ears turned red? She could only imagine what kind of scandals a small town sheriff was susceptible to—how careful a footing he must be required to keep.

Canon might be used to days that started at 4:30 by waking a woman inside a cabin, showing her a frozen gravesite, hauling her in for questioning, barking for her to stay in his squad car while he broke up a fight in a seedy bar's parking lot, but Maggie wasn't. Her emotions had run the gamut again, same as the night Zeke first showed up.

"Look, I hate to ask you this," said Canon, "even though I know what the evidence points to, but it's my job."

Maggie held her breath and braced for his question.

"Is there *any* chance Rodriquez was the man who came to your cabin?"

"No! That man in the ditch? I'd never seen him before."

"I needed to ask." Then, as if to himself, "He must have died in that ravine the same night he broke out of prison."

"Like Zeke."

Canon looked at Maggie sharply. "What did Ollie tell you about Zeke?"

"That he found him frozen on the steps of this cabin."

"When?"

"Two days after he escaped from prison. But he said it must have happened that same night."

Canon nodded. "Look, I know as well as anyone Zeke Thompson died thirty years ago, because *I* helped bury him. The ground was still frozen so hard when Ollie found him, he couldn't get a grave dug. Had his body under a tarp in his shed when I came asking questions the next day. I reported it quietly, kept it out of the papers, then came back out here and helped him dig the grave when the ground thawed the following Monday. Zeke broke out on a Monday."

I died on a Monday. That was a good opening line. Good possible book title, too. *Same night I broke out of prison.*

"I don't question how Zeke died," continued Canon. "He froze to death. But Rodriquez? I'm not convinced he froze to death."

"How did he end up in the ravine?"

Canon avoided her eyes. "I don't know. Amos and I didn't find any evidence to suggest anybody else was out there."

Maggie shivered suddenly. *You don't have to worry about that other guy.* "Is it possible he slipped and hit his head?"

"I guess anything is possible."

Maggie thought of the loud whack she heard the night Zeke showed up. How much time had passed between that whack and the pounding on her door? Enough time to kill a man then drag his body to the top of the ridge and throw it down a ravine?

"You don't think Zeke could have done it?" Maggie's voice was barely more than whisper.

Canon shook his head. "I don't know how I can write in my report that a man who's been dead for thirty years—a man *I helped bury*—was responsible."

Maggie searched his eyes. "But you don't think *I* did it?"

Canon shook his head again, his face softening. "No. I don't think you did it."

Maggie breathed a little easier. "Is it okay to ask you to let me know what you find out from the coroner?"

Canon nodded. "I should get your number. In case I need to ask you more questions."

Maggie recited it for him. He punched it in his phone. "How long will you be staying?" he asked.

"I leave tomorrow."

"Oh. Tomorrow." Canon studied his phone. "And home is Nashville."

"Yes. But Mr. Thompson said I could come back."

Canon looked up. "Yeah?"

Maggie nodded.

"Are you worried about being alone? Do you want me to... I can post a deputy outside. All night if you want."

"That's not necessary."

"You've got that .22."

"I'm not sure it works on ghosts."

Canon's sheepish look crept back. "Are you worried he'll come back?"

Maggie wanted Zeke to come back. She had questions for him.

"I've proven I can sleep pretty good on a couch," continued Canon.

Now Maggie's ears turned scarlet. Hadn't she fallen asleep beside Zeke on that same couch last night? Hadn't her body fit perfectly into each bend of his? What would Canon think of her if he knew that? She had left that detail out of her report.

"I appreciate the offer, but I'll be fine." Maggie tried to make light of it. "You're starting to sound like my daughter."

Canon scowled. He squeezed his knit cap in his hands and stepped toward the door. "Sorry this took so much of your day."

"It's alright."

"You're sure you'll be okay?"

Maggie nodded. Canon took a step back toward the kitchen. "Let me check this phone for you, make sure it's working."

She stopped him, putting a hand on his arm. "It's fine. And I have a cell phone."

"What about the fire? Can I build it back up for you?"

"Canon," Maggie said. He stopped and looked at her. "I'll be fine."

"Back door's locked?"

"I'll double-check it after you're gone."

"You trying to get rid of me?" he teased.

Canon really was a nice looking man. Who did he remind her of? Sean Connery, minus the Scottish accent, and minus the James Bond swagger. Canon was plenty sure of himself, but not cocky. There was a difference. Maggie wasn't sure it was possible for a man to be both sheepish and cocky.

"You trying to get a supper invitation?" she asked.

She almost wanted to ask him to stay and eat. But she didn't. Canon nodded and put his knit cap back on.

"Evenin' then, Maggie."

She watched him walk out to his car. He turned back once as if he'd forgotten something. Maggie almost stepped out to insist he come back in. But she wanted to be alone. It was a lot to process.

Maggie wanted to write her thoughts down.

17

"The job of the artist is always to deepen the mystery." Sir Francis Bacon

Canon drove away from the cabin feeling like a fraud. It wasn't as if he had lied to her, he simply didn't reveal everything he knew. Or did he know it?

That's just the thing.

His dreams had been real enough, but that didn't mean they could be explained. Could you really know something that defied explanation? What were the origins of a dream anyway?

Canon pictured Maggie sitting in his office attempting to do that very thing—explain something that defied logic. Why couldn't he have told her then?

Somehow he couldn't.

Canon had known plenty of law enforcement officers who used mediums—usually women who claimed they saw things in dreams, or visions. *What was the difference in a dream and a vision?* But Canon never thought he'd see the day when he turned to such measures to seek the truth of a thing. If a man knew what he was doing, if he knew where to find the evidence, no hocus-pocus was needed.

No...Canon was a practical man. At least, he tried to be. He'd seen too much foolish behavior to be otherwise. And as a practical man Canon had not been prepared for the dream...nor was he prepared for Maggie's testimony...nor was he prepared for Maggie. Was his years' long lack of sleep finally catching up with him?

Canon had been forced to swallow hard and look away from her eyes in his office...those jeans...that green t-shirt...her silent tears in his squad car.

What was he thinking when he called her 'sweetheart'? He'd actually *reached* for her! She had looked so confused...so lonely. Canon didn't want her to feel lonely. She wasn't in this alone—*he* was the one who had the dream, after all. And there was the body right where Canon knew it would be. Because of the *dream*.

The Taurus was back out on the highway now, the sun slipping behind the horizon. The stark brown trees that lined the road brought to mind how she'd looked coming up the hill that morning, steam rolling from her lips, her nose red from the cold. On the way back down the hill when she dropped the phone and started telling him about Zeke, Canon almost told her then. But a voice in his head said, *The time's not right. Just listen to what she's telling you. Gain her trust. That's the only way.*

Canon had been sheriff for twenty years—a job filled with long stretches of the ordinary—speeding tickets, domestic spats, the growing complexities of technology—interspersed with moments of high action calling for quick-thinking and calm. A shooting. A murder. That time a disgruntled teacher at the high school turned on the gas burners in the chemistry classroom planning to blow up the building. Canon was lucky to still be alive. Much of the credit went to logic. Caution. Luck. Or someone else keeping their wits long enough to call a problem in.

As he drove himself out to the farm, Canon replayed the scenes of the dream, sliding snippets of the day around, trying them this way and that, like fitting pieces into a puzzle.

He had seen the killer standing at the top of the hill. Had it been

Zeke Thompson? Canon never got a clean look at the man's face, not in his dream. He did remember seeing summer sneakers—impractical for the weather—matching Maggie's description of Zeke's footwear. Those shoes matched what Canon remembered, too. Zeke froze to death and was buried in a well-worn pair of Chuck Taylors. How could she have known that detail?

As Canon turned off the highway onto the gravel road his thoughts turned to the woman he'd seen bathing in his dream...to the flickering light of the candle in the window. He pictured Maggie as the woman now. No, that was wrong. Canon shouldn't be thinking that.

But he did. He thought of Maggie's smell, clean and fresh. Canon would have sworn that part of his pulse had quit working. All the nice women Shirley tried to fix him up with—that widow on Elm who used to bring him pies. *Nothing.* The widow finally married again and moved to Columbia. Canon's waistline was grateful.

How could a woman intoxicate him so fast, and after all this time? When Canon pressed his nose to the glass of the cabin's front window that morning and saw her lying so still on the couch, pain—actual *pain*—shot through him. He was pounding on the door before he knew it. Then she stood there in the doorway, the embodiment of his dream.

The single plate on the dining table had been such a relief.

Then she cooked him breakfast. Canon woke wondering if he'd died and gone to heaven. Why God would send an angel like that to Marston County, then send Canon straight to her door, he would never know. But now it was Canon's job not to run her off.

He had expected to find Rodriquez dead in the ravine. But that didn't mean he knew how to write the report. *Wait and see.* 'Wait and see' had proven an effective strategy on many a mystery prior.

As Canon pulled into his driveway, he picked up his radio and asked Amos to man the scanner. "Don't call me unless you find any more bodies." He was beat.

Thankfully, this time when Canon crawled into bed, it was a dreamless sleep that overtook him.

18

"I died on a Monday—same Monday I broke out of prison. My name was Ezekiel Thompson. Everybody called me Zeke. I killed three people, but only one from hatred."

As soon as Canon's tail lights disappeared around the bend, Maggie went straight to her computer. The notes she had so far were great. All salvageable. The story would be best in first person. She already knew the opening lines.

Maggie didn't look up from her computer until the wee hours of morning. No knocks on the door all night. She crawled under the mate-lassé coverlet and woke as dawn broke, grateful to witness the magic of the sun rising over the oak tree one more time. She remembered that it was New Year's Day. Peace lay over her like the blanket of snow outside.

All was silent. With no smells of perking coffee or frying bacon to greet her, Maggie dozed off again, then woke mid-morning and showered. It was hard to pack with her mind so full and racing. She kept stopping to go back to her computer.

Finally, she took the dish crate out to the Subaru, stepped back on the porch and turned the key in the lock.

"Thank you, Zeke," she whispered, running the toe of her boot across his spot on the porch. "I'll be back."

She stopped at Mr. Thompson's to give him the key.

"When were you thinkin' that next visit would be?"

Maggie had already checked her calendar. "Last week of January?"

"I'll need to look at the AirBib notes." Mr. Thompson shuffled toward the den and Maggie followed him, smiling at his mispronunciation, picking up the framed picture of Zeke to study one more time.

"Nobody else has asked for it," he said a few minutes later. "I'll put you down."

"Does the cabin stay rented out frequently?" asked Maggie.

The old man shook his head. "Folks hardly ever come in the winter months."

Maggie wondered if Zeke had ever visited other tenants. "Has anyone ever said anything about..."

"Noises?" Mr. Thompson squinted, searching her face. "When that oak tree drops its acorns in the fall, folks complain about the noise. And I know the squirrels run across the roof sometimes. They do that here, too."

Maggie decided not to press the point. She didn't want to ask Mr. Thompson outright if anyone else had reported seeing his son's ghost in the cabin. "I'll pay the deposit online when I get home."

She set down the frame, kissed Mr. Thompson on the cheek, and drove down the lane. It took her longer than it should have to get home. She kept pulling over to write down another thought.

*   *   *

Maggie cooked dinner for Cal and Robbie at the condo. No Yvette. No Mark. Just Cal and Robbie. Cal's favorite: Spinach ricotta pasta and tiramisu. As they moved to the sofa in the living room, dessert coffees in hand, Robbie said, "I want to hear more about your week at the cabin, Mom. You've hardly said two words about it."

"Yeah. Why so secretive?" asked Cal.

"She's working on a book." Robbie nudged Cal with her elbow. "Writers get all secretive about their stories."

"But not with us. You'll tell us. Right, Mom?"

Maggie took a deep breath, feeling suddenly shy. She'd rehearsed for this moment all week.

"Oh, my gosh." Robbie clamped a hand over her mouth then pulled it away. "You met someone!"

Cal looked at his sister. "Where did that come from?"

"Look at her!" Robbie pointed. Maggie felt her face burn. "*Mom!* Why haven't you said anything? Who is it?"

"Robbie, slow down," scolded Maggie. "It's not what you think."

"Tell, tell!" said Cal.

Maggie sized up her son and daughter, Robbie sitting on the opposite end of the sofa, Cal sitting on the floor with his head next to his sister's knees. "You know, just because I'm single again doesn't mean the two of you can treat me like I'm a teenager."

"Are you *acting* like a teenager?" Cal's eyes twinkled. "Are your hormones getting the better of you, Mom?"

Maggie threw a pillow at him. "I'm not going to tell you anything if you're going to act like that."

"We'll behave, won't we Cal?" Robbie smacked her brother's shoulder. "We want to hear. Every detail."

Maggie took a deep breath. She knew before she started, as much as she'd rehearsed this moment, that she would fall short on describing the new lightness of heart she'd felt since getting home.

"It was a great cabin. Very rustic. Big stone fireplace, lots of windows, just like in the pictures. Sweet, old caretaker named Mr. Thompson down the road, who, as it happens, lost a son several years ago."

When Maggie paused, Cal waved his hand for her to go on. "So, what's the story? And...is the sweet, old man the one who has you blushing?"

Maggie laughed. "No. I guess that would be the handsome sheriff who came by the cabin looking for the prison escapee that *you*," she pointed to Cal, "texted me about."

"Aha!" Robbie clapped her hands. "A handsome sheriff." She winked down at Cal. "That's nice. Continue."

"So...all of these events got mixed into a kind of stew in my mind, and you know...even my own recent experiences seem to have worked their way into the mix, and...I think I might be on to something."

"When can we read it?" asked Robbie.

Maggie froze. "I don't really have anything yet except a jumble of notes and a loose idea. I need to go back and do some more research."

"To the cabin?" asked Cal.

"When?" said Robbie.

"Last week of January. I need to go back to Canon's office and—"

Cal raised a hand to stop her. "I'm sorry. Who is Canon?"

"The handsome sheriff." Robbie nodded smugly, knowing she was right and enjoying it. "I like it that you're on a first-name basis."

Cal grinned up at Robbie. "I see where this is tracking."

Maggie shook her head as they snickered. "How can it not bother you to think about me being interested in another man? Doesn't it bother you that your father is with Bethany?"

"Mom." Robbie shook her head. "Those are not the same things."

"We want to see you happy," said Cal. "You deserve that."

"Well, don't act like I've got something going on with the sheriff. I *don't*! The ink is hardly dry on my divorce papers."

Maggie didn't tell them Canon nearly hugged her, or how much she'd wanted him to. Nor did she tell them he had occupied nearly as many of her thoughts the past week as Ezekiel Thompson. And she'd only been around Canon one day. Still...ready to admit it to her children or not...the Marston County sheriff had gotten under Maggie's skin...or in her heart...something. And Maggie didn't know what to do with that so soon after Tom's severance of their thirty-year marriage.

Maggie and Tom's divorce was so lightning fast, in part, because Maggie didn't contest anything. Why contest? Tom was as generous as she had expected him to be. "The sheriff came by the cabin looking for information on the escaped prisoner, is all. Then he found him dead in the woods after it got daylight."

"Wait—there was a *dead guy* in the woods?" Cal leaned forward.

"Yes! If you two would be serious for a minute, I was trying to tell you how I met the sheriff, who, as it happens, knows a lot about this story with the caretaker's son because he was the first one on the scene when Zeke killed his wife."

"Zeke was the caretaker's son?"

"He killed his *wife*?" Robbie leaned forward now, too. "Is this a murder mystery?"

Maggie raised a finger. "He was *convicted* of killing his wife."

"You don't think he did it?" asked Robbie.

"Does the *sheriff* think he didn't do it?" said Cal.

Maggie hadn't decided yet what to do with the actual moment of the killings. Were they murders? That was yet to be explored. And she couldn't tell Robbie and Cal she had actually met Zeke. It was her job as a mother to protect her children from truths they couldn't handle. In the same way that it was her job as a writer to sift through fact and fiction to find what was plausible for the reader.

"I haven't decided on my final version of the story," Maggie said honestly. "But I'd like to learn more about it. So I'm going back the last week of January."

Cal nodded. "Spoken like a woman who has made up her mind."

"Yes." Maggie stood and held out her hand for his empty cup. "Now hand that over. It's time to wash the dishes."

19

A writer pries open a lot of lids seeking truth for a story. Sometimes she closes them fast, knowing these are the contents that need to be brought to light, but sorry to be the one given the job.

Maggie had just finished peeling carrots for beef stew when she heard a cruiser coming up the gravel road.

Canon's hand was in the air for a knock when she opened the door of the cabin. Yes...a younger Sean Connery...who spoke Tennessee Southern. She had thought about the Marston County sheriff more than she cared to admit in the month she'd been away. Zeke's presence was vapory, but Canon's was real. This made the sheriff more frightening.

"Hello, Canon." The afternoon was sunlit behind him. Maggie had only arrived a couple of hours ago.

Canon grinned, looking sheepish. "Ollie said you were back. Thought I'd come check on you." His nose caught the air. "I've interrupted your supper."

"I'm still working on it—beef stew. Won't you join me?"

He shook his head. "I couldn't."

"Why not?"

"You probably only made enough for one."

"None of my recipes go that low." Maggie stepped aside. "Please, come in."

Canon followed her into the living room and removed his coat. "Well...I remember what a good cook you are."

Maggie went back to the kitchen to mix up cheesy cornbread. When Canon followed her in and sat on the red stool, she slid a cutting board, a grater and two peeled carrots toward him on the counter. It pleased her to have someone to cook for...someone to cook with. "You have to work for your supper. My aunt taught me to put grated carrots in the cornbread. She said, 'slip vegetables in whenever you can, Maggie.' Robbie and Cal never seemed to mind carrots and peppers in the cornbread as long as it had plenty of cheese."

Canon made quick work of the carrots and raked them into the batter bowl. Then he reached for the green bell pepper, deftly chopped it, and raked that in, too. The sheriff had obviously done his share of cutting vegetables. "What else?"

"You're not in uniform." Maggie had noticed the moment she opened the door. Jeans and an untucked flannel shirt instead. He looked good in blue.

"It's Sunday."

"You came to check on me on your day off?"

That sheepish look again. "And at dinner time, too. I'm subtle like that." Then, changing the subject, "You had any other visitors?"

Now it was Maggie's turn to look sheepish. "You're my first, this trip, other than Mr. Thompson with the key."

Canon nodded and looked out the window, but Maggie felt his eyes on her while she finished the cornbread batter and poured it into the hot skillet. He was quick to reach to open the oven door for her when she got ready to slip the heavy iron pan inside.

"Thank you." Maggie straightened, conscious of his nearness, remembering how his hands had lightly brushed her hips when he slid past her in his office that day.

"Least I could do." His gaze lingered on her lips.

As Maggie turned to stir the stew, Canon stepped back to the doorway to the living room and glanced around the cabin. She wondered if it was simply wired in him to do constant surveillance on his surroundings. At least he wasn't wearing his hip radio...or his gun.

"Who commandeers the ship on Sundays?" she asked.

"We rotate on the weekends: me, Amos, and Becky. Amos is there today, and Becky's on call."

"You have a female deputy? I'm proud to hear that."

"Oh, yes. She's better than Amos, but don't tell him I said so. I'm trying to toughen him up, that's why I let him drive the Explorer. Becky, she's naturally tough. Say," he stepped back into the kitchen. "I didn't mean to interrupt your writing."

Maggie's laptop lay open on the dining room table, along with several papers.

"It's okay. I had already stopped to cook dinner. But can I ask you questions while we eat? I can chalk it up to research that way."

"Ask away." Canon picked up a bottle of Merlot from the counter. "Are we having this?"

"Only if you let me prove to you I don't pass out from one glass of wine."

He smirked. "I don't remember accusing you of that."

"No, but you did ask how wine affects me."

Canon reached for the corkscrew to open it while Maggie set out the glasses. "I'll make a note of my observations, even though it's my day off."

An hour later, the sun had set and Maggie still had half a glass. She was too busy scribbling notes to drink it, and didn't trust herself to get too relaxed with Canon in the room.

"So you were a deputy when Zeke was arrested?"

"Yes."

"And you responded to the call?"

He nodded.

"What do you remember? Wait—back up. What did you know about him and Tandy Wilkins *prior* to the call?"

Maggie had jotted pages of questions in her spiral notebook over the past month and had so much to ask, she hardly knew where to begin. It was greatly to her benefit Canon had stopped by. She had trouble containing her excitement.

Canon swirled his wine, seeming to enjoy her enthusiasm, watching her with a measure of amusement. "Everybody knew Tandy cheated on Zeke. It's a small town. No secrets. There's a dozen folks you could ask about it."

Maggie readied her pen. "Who?"

"Dot Jenkins at the library has her ear to the ground better than anybody. She's old enough to remember. Make sure you've got plenty of time if you go see her, though. She's a talker."

Dot Jenkins, librarian, talker.

"Who else? Any of Tandy's family still in Marston?"

"Her sister, Rynell. You already met her. She waited on us at the café that day."

"That was Tandy's sister?"

Canon nodded.

"Why didn't you say anything?"

His eyebrows raised innocently. "I just did."

Maggie smiled. "Alright."

Rynell, Tandy's sister, waitress at The Local Cafe.

"Who else?"

"Brad Bybee is the newspaper editor. He'd remember the story. And they called June Hargrove to testify as a character witness in Zeke's trial. She was his teacher, close to the family. She's principal at the high school now."

Brad Bybee, news editor.
June Hargrove, high school principal, Zeke's teacher.

"What did Zeke and Tandy do? Where did they work?"

"Zeke worked at the factory. His supervisor was a character witness, too, but he's dead now. And the plant shut down five years ago. They'll have old records somewhere in the courthouse. I'll ask Shirley to check into it when she's back on Monday. I'll see if she can get you a copy of the trial transcript, too, if you like."

Shirley, sheriff's office receptionist, will check court records—HR and trial.

"Thank you. What about Tandy?"

"Tandy never worked that I know of. I doubt she could have kept a job. She had a drug problem."

"Oh." Maggie's pen stilled. "Did Zeke have a drug problem?"

"Not that I'm aware of. 'Course it's been a long time, but I've seen it over and over. One spouse takes on all the responsibility. Sometimes it's a kid living with an addict parent. They work hard bringing money in the front door, and the one at home shovels it out the back faster than they can haul it in. It happens too often in small counties like this one. I imagine it happens everywhere. Something eventually gives. Responsible party can't take it any more, or the addict overdoses or does something to get themselves jailed. We try to dry them out, and as soon as they're released, most of them are right back at it again." Canon looked up, his eyes apologetic. "That probably sounds pessimistic. I don't mean for it to be. This job makes you a realist."

Maggie twisted the pen in her hands. "I know if I work on telling this story it's going to have some darkness, Canon. Murder...adultery...drugs... I don't like thinking about all that, and I certainly don't want to sensationalize it, or try to capitalize in any way on someone else's pain."

"Of course not."

"It's important to me that you know that. I'm trying to work my courage up to ask Mr. Thompson about this before I get too far down the rabbit hole. I wouldn't want him to think that was my goal."

Canon put his hand over hers. "You don't come across that way, Maggie."

Relief washed over her. "Thank you for saying that."

Canon pulled his hand back. She immediately missed its warmth.

"But..." How could Maggie explain this so he would understand? "I'm looking for the shafts of light, Canon. That's what I want to do with the story. I came to this cabin needing hope, and I found it. I found it in getting a glimpse of Zeke. Regardless of whether I dreamed him or he was really here, he convinced me I was going to be okay. And that's what I want to do for him in return. Use his story to offer anyone who might be walking a dark path, a ray of hope...a shaft of light. Does that make sense?"

Canon was suddenly staring at her in a way that made Maggie's heart knock. His look was warmer than his touch had been. It was nice to see him in plain clothes. He was softer, more approachable. The words had tumbled out easier with him now than they had with Maggie's own children. Canon was the only one who knew about Zeke, whether he believed her or not.

Canon picked up his glass. "Should we move to the couch to continue this interrogation?"

Maggie smiled. "This is a change for you, I guess, to be on the other side of the questions."

As he stood, Canon said, "If a pretty lady wants to ask me questions after fattening me up, I can't say I mind."

Canon thought she was pretty? *That was nice.* Maggie suddenly wished she'd left her hair down. She always pulled it up into a loose knot when she was cooking.

She picked up her notebook, her pen and her glass, and followed him over. Canon sat in Zeke's spot, Maggie in hers, both of them stretching their legs to the fire on the ottoman. Before putting his feet up, Canon pulled his boots off and set them to the side.

"I hope this is okay," he said, when he caught her gaze again. "I wouldn't want to get dirt on your furniture."

Maggie resisted the urge to remind him that this wasn't really her cabin. It wasn't her furniture. Canon wore navy Gold Toe socks, same kind Maggie used to buy for Tom. She thought of Zeke in her blue and white striped fuzzies. "It's nice to see you more relaxed." Maggie poised her pen again. "Tell me about that day."

"Night," he corrected, getting the facts straight again. "I don't want to minimize what you said. I think you tell that to Ollie Thompson, exactly what you told me, and you'll have his full support."

"You do?" Canon's words washed over Maggie and loosened her tongue. "Here I've jumped feet first into trying to put into words a life and a series of events I don't know anything about—it's really none of my business—and yet I feel so strongly that I'm supposed to do it. I confess it's given me a focus and energy I needed, but I don't want this to be a selfish endeavor, Canon. I want this story to be the kind of gift it's been to me."

"How has it been a gift?"

Maggie looked around the room. What was it about this cabin? Something spiritual hung over the rafters. "I don't know how to explain it, any more than I know how to explain what happened here before you showed up. Or *after* you showed up."

Canon grinned. "I'm part of the story?"

Maggie laughed. "Maybe."

He grew serious. "I'm sorry for what you've been through...with your marriage."

Maggie looked down. She didn't want to talk about that.

Canon seemed to sense it. "So you want to know about that night?"

Maggie nodded and got her notebook ready.

20

"Even though I walk through the darkest valley, I will fear no evil, for you are with me; your rod and your staff, they comfort me." Psalm 23:4, NIV

"I was out on Treetop Ridge when the call came in." Canon picked up his wine glass, swirled it, and stared down into the burgundy liquid. "Now remember, this is thirty years ago. I know as well as anyone how memories can twist in the mind a little over time. But I remember Zeke made the call himself."

"He called to report the…"

"Murders. Killings. Shootings. Don't get me started on the differences. He called from the house right after it happened."

Maggie tried to imagine the scene.

"I always liked Zeke Thompson. He was older than me. I was twenty-four at the time, had only been a deputy two years, not long out of college."

Suddenly curious, Maggie asked, "Where'd you go to college?"

"Vanderbilt. Class of '82. Criminal Justice Program."

"I went to Vanderbilt! But I didn't start until '85."

"I knew it!" Canon's eyes flashed in the firelight. That smirk again. "Sorority girl."

Maggie shook her head. "Never had time. I met Tom my freshman year. He was a senior, headed to medical school. My parents didn't see the point in me finishing my education, and I didn't question their judgment on it. One of my life's regrets."

Canon nodded. "We've all got some of those."

Maggie watched his eyes cloud over and wondered what regrets Canon lived with.

"So Zeke made the call," she said.

"He said, 'There's been a shooting.' Gave the address. He and Tandy lived out on Mill Creek. That's all he said, that there'd been a shooting. I headed over there, and called it in to my dad who headed over there. My father was the sheriff before me. I don't guess I told you that."

Another surprise! "Did he retire?"

Canon shook his head. "Shootin' at a robbery at the Interstate exit. Anyway..." He shook his head again, as if to swat the painful memory away. "I got there a few minutes ahead of Dad. Zeke was sittin' on the porch steps, covered in blood.

"I said, 'What's happened?' and he said, 'Tandy shot the man from Trenton, then tried to shoot herself. She didn't have the strength, and asked me to do it for her. He beat her.' Zeke's voice broke then, I remember. 'He beat her real bad, Canon.'

"'Anyone else in the house?' I asked.

"'No.'

"'When did it happen?'

"'Right before I called you,' he said.

"He looked so lost. I got him up and brought him in with me so I could check the house. Roughest crime scene I'd ever witnessed up to that point. Scenes like that have a way of staying with you.

"Man from Trenton was dead on the floor in the bedroom. Tandy was up on the bed, blood everywhere. Zeke said the man beat her bad, and he did. That was pretty evident. She wasn't wearing much, and her body was twisted up, arms and legs splayed at odd angles.

"About that time, my father got there. Told me to cuff Zeke and put him in the car, which I did, but I felt bad about it."

Maggie thought of the men at the Ron-dee-vu roadside bar last month. Canon didn't seem bothered to break up their fight and send them on their way. But those men were all belligerent. Sounded like Zeke was contrite. Was that why Canon felt bad about it? Because Ezekiel Thompson didn't seem like a killer?

Canon stopped to rub his forehead. Maggie wondered at the disturbing sights he'd seen over the years and how many times he'd been conflicted by what his job required. It was odd to think how this gray-templed man at the end of her couch now was younger when these events happened than the mid-thirties Zeke that Maggie had met.

She laid down her notepad and found herself reaching for his shoulder. "Canon?" When he looked up there was sadness in his eyes. "Why don't we stop there for tonight?"

"You said you knew it was a dark story."

"I know." Maggie nodded. "So I'm probably going to have to take it slow."

Canon's eyes scanned the room. Was it surveillance he was always doing, or did dark memories haunt him? *Did Canon Dale see ghosts, too?*

"I shouldn't be sharing these darker details with you staying out here alone," he said suddenly. "I should have thought about that before getting too far into the—"

"Don't be silly. I asked you to."

Canon stared at her so long Maggie grew uncomfortable. Could he not find the words he was looking for?

"I should go." He finished the last sip of his wine and stood. "I've taken enough of your evening. You weren't expecting company."

Maggie smiled inwardly at the understatement that was. But neither Zeke nor Canon had proven an interruption. Together, they were jump-starting her heart again.

She sought to put a final upbeat note on the conversation by saying, "I'm glad you stopped by," but she still felt the cloud that settled over the room.

Canon pulled his boots on, then stood and reached for his coat. "Come by the office in the next day or two and I'll let you read the reports if you want."

"I'd like that."

Before he went out, he whispered, "Lock your doors."

*   *   *

On Tuesday, after two uneventful nights, Maggie drove to town and parked at the sheriff's office. The weather was cold and cloudy, but no snow was in the forecast.

A stocky woman looked up when Maggie opened the door.

"Hello," said Maggie.

The woman scrunched her nose. "You're not that writer, are you?"

Maggie swallowed as a young brunette at a side desk in a deputy's uniform stuck out her hand. "Becky Renco. You must be Maggie Raines."

"Do I have a writer's look about me?" asked Maggie, taking Becky's hand.

Becky gave her three hard pumps, holding the last one midway in the air. "You were in one of the pictures Amos took of the crime scene on Patterson Road." She spoke at a clip as fast and strong as her handshake.

"Oh." Becky turned her hand loose and sat back down. "I thought it must be a small town indeed if I was the only stranger to come through in a while."

"Well..." Shirley Weems, the receptionist in plain clothes who hadn't identified herself but whose nameplate sat on the corner of her desk, had a slower drawl. Her words came out as thick as Becky's came out thin. "Lord knows, we don't get a lot of strangers in this office."

Shirley and Becky cut their eyes at one another. Maggie felt she was missing some piece of information they were privy to. Had Canon told them Maggie claimed a ghost was in her cabin?

"Sheriff Dale said I wasn't considered a suspect." Maggie wanted to be sure they knew that.

Both women guffawed. "Of course not," said Becky. "Amos takes pictures of everything, that's all. He loves that new camera."

Shirley looked over her shoulder at Canon's office window. He was on the phone, with his back turned.

"I'm working on a book idea," said Maggie.

"So we heard." Shirley eyed her, taking in Maggie's hair, hoop earrings, black North Face jacket, tan corduroys and black leather boots.

Maggie had thought she looked stylish—European, even—until she fell under Shirley's eye. Now she seemed inappropriately dressed and pulled at the ends of her cashmere scarf. She glanced through the glass at Canon again, wishing he would hurry up and get off the phone. These women made her feel more antsy than when Canon brought her in for questioning.

"Sheriff Dale said I could come by and look through the Zeke Thompson case files." It seemed wrong, somehow, to refer to him as Canon in front of them.

"We've been expecting you," said Becky pertly. Her gaze was admiring. Why was Shirley's so critical? "Canon said you'd come by."

"It'll take a few days to get the records from the courthouse," drawled Shirley, whose hair was cropped bluntly beneath her ears. No one had likely ever accused Shirley Weems of being a style maven.

Maggie smiled at her again, wanting to win her over all the same. "I appreciate you doing that."

Silence swelled then as Shirley nodded, her eyes fixating on Maggie's scarf. Maggie wondered what to say next. Thankfully, she heard Canon's voice come through the open door of his office. "Alright then, Paul."

All three women looked toward the window as Canon turned to face the glass, setting his office phone in its cradle. He must have seen Maggie the minute she'd come into the station, before he turned his back, because Canon didn't look surprised now as he stared at her. A ghost of a smile crossed his lips.

From Maggie's peripheral view she saw Becky and Shirley exchange glances again.

"You've got a visitor, Canon!" Shirley called.

Canon stepped to the doorway. "You come to see those case files?"

Maggie's heart skipped a beat to see him back in uniform. "If this is an okay time."

"Of course!" He waved her in, refusing to meet the looks of the two women he worked with.

Maggie felt their stares as she went into Canon's office. Three file folders sat ready on the corner of his desk.

"I'd like to keep them in the office, if you don't mind. You're welcome to sit there." He nodded toward his chair as he reached for his coat. "I need to run down to the hospital a minute. Can I bring you a coffee on my way back? Shirley made a pot this morning, but it's weak." He looked over his shoulder at Shirley, who was watching them through the glass and dropped his voice. "Don't tell her I said that. She's sensitive about her coffee."

Maggie smiled, she hoped not too broadly, as she inched past him then around the desk. It was strange to be behind the old behemoth and look out over the office from Canon's point of view. She laid down her notebook and pen. "No, I'm fine. Any rules I need to know about? Anything off limits?"

Canon shook his head. "I reread the reports this morning. They're pretty straightforward—one on each of the slain, one on Zeke that includes some trial notes. Took some pictures out. The rougher ones. You don't want to see those." He was making statements again. It wasn't easy to question Canon's judgment. "I know you have a healthy imagination," he went on. "There's plenty of detail in the reports."

Was he smirking at her again? Feeling protective? Or both?

As he went out the door, Maggie said, "I'm going by the newspaper office next. Do you have a problem with me seeing pictures that were in the paper?"

"No." This was in his matter-of-fact voice. "Those were mild enough for public view."

Maggie stared at him.

He started to go again, but stopped. Maggie must have had a strange look on her face.

"What?" he asked.

"I'm just wondering what kind of images you have burned into your mind."

He shook his head darkly. "You don't want to know."

As Maggie watched him nod a good-bye to the two women in the office and go out the front door, she couldn't help but feel she'd done Canon a disservice with their conversation on Sunday night. The cloud that formed over them then seemed to have followed him.

21

Thoreau said the regularity of the news, in his case a daily stroll to the village to hear the gossip, was "as refreshing in its way as the rustling of leaves and peeping of frogs."

The Marston County Times was located in a nondescript building next to the Caroline Baker hardware store on a sloped side street off Main. A balding man with thick glasses looked up from a table behind the counter spread with papers: *The Washington Post*, *The Wall Street Journal*, the Nashville *Tennessean*, *The Atlanta Journal-Constitution* and *The Commercial Appeal* out of Memphis were a few Maggie recognized.

He came to the front counter and stuck out a hand. "Brad Bybee. What can I do for you?"

"I've just come from the sheriff's office. I'm working on a book."

Those words—like the idea—sounded good in Maggie's ears. But they were frightening, too, like pulling a long-held secret from a box with several locks. What if she failed in her mission? What would she be then? Nothing more than a scorned woman with an unfinished degree who couldn't really make it as a writer.

The man's eyebrows raised with interest. He leaned an elbow on the counter, his demeanor now conspiratorial. "You're a writer?" That made them kindred spirits.

"This will be my first book," Maggie confessed.

That tidbit didn't appear to diminish the man's admiration. "What's it about?"

Ah...the million-dollar question...the one Maggie was sure to be asked every time she had the courage to tell someone she was working on a book. She'd read about pitches and log lines—had written this one out and practiced it in her mind—but this would be the first time she said it aloud. "It's about a man who was convicted of killing his wife and whether he was really guilty of her murder."

Brad Bybee looked genuinely interested, which Maggie took as a hopeful sign. "Like *Shawshank Redemption*?"

"A different angle," said Maggie, heartened by Bybee's comparison. She leaned in from the other side of the counter. "Last month I rented a cabin in Marston and met a gentleman named Oliver—"

Bybee snapped his fingers. "Thompson. The old caretaker of the Patterson cabin." His eyes lit up. "Your story about his son, Zeke?" He was quick to add, "He did kill his wife."

"Yes. But I wonder if he was really guilty of her *murder*."

Bybee's brows lifted, then his forefinger. "I see where you're going." He nodded as if to say he and Maggie were both writers. It was their job to question these things.

"I want to tell the Ezekiel Thompson story." That was probably all Maggie needed say here in Marston County.

Bybee pulled back and looked at her appreciatively before leaning in again. "That there *is* an interesting story. *Sad* story. You know, I been covering every event that's happened in this county that was newsworthy—and frankly an awful lot of events that aren't—for the last thirty years, and *that one* was memorable. In part, because I had just come to Marston to run this paper weeks before it happened. Thompson killed his wife and that other man—the man from..."

Bybee snapped his fingers three times looking for it, then snapped harder when he found it. "Trenton! What was Thompson's wife's name?"

"Tandy Wilkins."

"That's right!" He snapped his fingers again. "The Wilkinses." Bybee got a knowing look that said there'd been more Wilkins stories over the years. "Then his escape, a few years after that, was big news. And that tragic death." Bybee wagged his head. His glasses were so large on his face, and his nose so angled down, he reminded Maggie of an owl. "Poor old man."

He leaned both elbows on the counter this time. "Word was, the son froze to death and his father found him." Bybee dropped his voice another notch, though he and Maggie appeared to be the only two in the news office. "Canon asked me not to put any official notice of the son's death in the paper, but..." Bybee glanced over the black frames of his spectacles, "...word got around. You don't have to put a story in the paper in this town for folks to know."

News would travel fast in a small town, and speculations even faster. Maggie really needed to talk to Ollie. She didn't want him to hear from someone else that she was doing a story on Zeke before he heard it from her. Canon, Shirley, Becky, Amos and now Brad Bybee all knew.

Maggie hoped she could convince Brad Bybee to keep her secret if he was willing to keep Canon's all these years. "I haven't talked to Mr. Thompson about this yet. I'd like to get a handle on what happened first."

Bybee nodded. "You've come to the right place, then." He waved her back behind the counter, toward a large open room behind it.

"Forgive the mess." The space was indeed cluttered. Papers from the past weeks, months, years, covered every table top and each corner of the floor. "Now I came in the summer of '82, that would make his trial..."

"February of '83," said Maggie.

Bybee snapped his fingers. "The eighties are in that south corner."

He pointed, stepped in that direction, and was soon pulling papers from a stack. "We're just a bi-weekly paper, so that's a hundred and four issues a year, fifty-two weeks in a year. That makes it a little easier to find things. The murders happened...yep...August of 1982! Here it is."

He pulled out one, two, three—Maggie lost count of the issues.

"Looks like the trial started in February like you said." Bybee was into the stack beside it now. "It was always front page news, of course. That makes it easier to find. There will be some repetition of the facts, but I'll include each issue in case there's new information. How long was he in before he escaped?"

"Almost four years. It was in December of—"

The snap of Bybee's fingers again. "Eighty-six." He thumbed until he found the desired papers and started pulling issues again. "Just walked right out, if I'm remembering right. Turney had a skeleton crew that night."

Maggie stared at the growing stack, marveling at the richness of the opportunity to learn more. *First the sheriff's case files, now this. Court reports still coming.* Her head was reeling.

Bybee pointed at the papers. "You're welcome to take those with you, if you promise to bring them back. One of these days I'm going to get all this online. But it's not that day yet. We put the new issues online, of course." Bybee looked around the cluttered room. "I'm sure I have a box around here somewhere you could put these in."

Maggie couldn't believe her luck. "I promise to take good care of these and get them back to you by the end of the week."

Bybee waved a hand. Maggie was grateful he didn't snap his fingers. "Take your time! No rush. Not a lot of folks coming in here wanting to read news from the eighties."

Maggie piled the papers in the box he offered and started to lift it when she had a sudden thought. "Mr. Bybee, there's another news item I'm curious about. It doesn't have anything to do with the Zeke Thompson story, but do you remember an interstate exit stand-off about twenty years ago?"

"The one that killed Sheriff Dale?"

Maggie suddenly felt like a snoop, there was no other name for it. An astute, finger snapping man like Brad Bybee was going to see right through her. "Sheriff Dale mentioned it briefly in passing, and I hated to pry, but was curious to know what happened exactly."

Bybee had already moved to another stack of papers—the nineties, evidently—and began thumbing through the headlines. "Here it is." He pulled out three issues. "You want the trial on that one, too, or just the event, itself?"

"Just the event."

"These three should cover it, then." He pointed. "That second one includes a nice insert on the Dale family. They have a long history in the county. Dickson County deputies finally found the man who shot Sheriff Dale—the senior Dale, Canon and Shirley's father."

"Shirley?"

Bybee pointed in the direction of the sheriff's office. "Shirley Weems. She was a Dale before she married."

Shirley was Canon's sister? Of course...she had his same coloring and solid build.

*   *   *

Maggie didn't get to the stack of eighties papers until Wednesday. She spent the rest of Tuesday poring over, then pondering, the articles in the three papers from 1996.

Robbie and Cal had been six years old as '96 came to a close. The day, month and year were seared into Maggie's mind because the twins got the flu, one right after the other.

Cal came down with it first, two days before he was supposed to be Jack Horner in the kindergarten play. While Tom took a rare day off early to take Robbie to play her part in the Mother Goose production—Little Miss Muffet—Maggie sat rocking Cal in the La-Z-Boy. She remembered protecting his hot, fevered ears from his sister's peels as Robbie practiced her screaming run from the spider—over and over through the living room, Maggie's own head throbbing—while Tom seemed to take forever to change his clothes.

The same day Cal's fever broke and he crawled down from her lap, Robbie came crawling into it. Then, as Robbie's fever broke after nearly two weeks of continual rocking in the La-Z-Boy, the flu finally claimed Maggie. She hadn't quite recovered when Tom's parents arrived from Michigan. It was the only time Tom's parents ever drove down to stay with them.

Maggie could still feel the criticism in their eyes for the condition of the house and how unprepared Maggie seemed for the holiday and their arrival. She actually overheard Tom's mother say, when Tom made some effort to defend her, "It's not as if she didn't know we were coming, Tom. Christmas has been on the calendar all year."

And that was Maggie's memory of December, '96. She had felt so sorry for herself...thought she had it so rough. But Canon—and Shirley, she realized now—felt the bite of that bitter week on the calendar harder than she did.

The same day as the nursery rhyme play, and at nearly the same hour, three men on a crime spree that started in the southern tip of South Carolina and curved its way northward through Georgia then Alabama stopped at a gas station off Interstate-40 at the Marston County exit in Middle Tennessee. They shot and killed the older gentleman who only worked on Fridays, and took two customers hostage who happened to be inside the Handy-Mart.

A trucker pulling up to the gas station heard the shots and called it in on his radio. From his high vantage point inside the truck, he could see the waving guns and terrified patrons inside.

Sheriff Dale was on the scene within moments. Maggie pictured an older version of Canon throwing his patrol car into park, opening his driver's side door, planting a large boot on the concrete, his blue eyes taking it all in, his hand reaching for the radio to give more details and call for back-up.

Other truckers, a few of them armed, also having heard the "10-31" on the airwaves began to peel off at the exit and pull into the asphalt lot.

When one over-eager trucker ran up to Sheriff Dale's patrol car from behind, brandishing his pistol, the sheriff barked, "Drop to the ground! Drop to the ground now! Hands where I can see 'em!"

Maggie could easily imagine that part, the memory of Canon barking his order to her, *Stay here! Don't get out*, when he squealed into the parking lot at the Ron-dee-vu on New Year's Eve.

With screams coming from inside the Handy-Mart and truckers blaring their horns and yelling to let the sheriff know the guy on the ground was trying to help, Sheriff Dale exposed the right side of his neck from behind the bullet proof glass of his patrol car door as a fugitive inside the station shot.

The bullet cut through the sheriff's carotid artery.

When his son, Deputy Canon Dale, pulled into the station only moments later, his father was already slumped over the seat of his patrol car, his lifeless hand having let go of the radio.

Maggie was as familiar with the carotid arteries that lined either side of a neck—the major vessels that took blood to the brain—as any ex-wife of a throat specialist could be. It would have taken a body less than two minutes to die with a wound like that, with no one there to stop the bleeding.

The truckers and hostages likely sat as stunned as she did now with her eyes glued to Brad Bybee's words in the twenty-year-old newsprint, tears streaming down her cheeks for a man she never knew.

> Deputy Canon Dale, the sheriff's son, was the first to arrive after Sheriff Dale was shot. Two of the fugitives inside the station were killed and one of the hostages wounded when the incensed truckers who witnessed the shooting joined the deputy and ensuing shots were fired. The fugitive who shot

Sheriff Dale fled out a back door and into a wooded area behind the station. Dickson County Sheriff's deputies apprehended him three days later.

Maggie's eyes scanned through the rest of Bybee's first article but there was no more mention of Canon...how he felt...whether it was he who cradled his father's body and laid it on the ground until the ambulance...or hearse...arrived.

Maggie only took one journalism course in her short college career. She knew a reporter's job was to record the facts—only the facts—but this was the very reason newspaper articles frustrated her. They never included enough information to help the reader stand in the hero's shoes...see what he saw...feel what he felt.

No criticism intended toward Brad Bybee personally.

From the special section on the Dale family in the next issue Maggie learned more. Bybee must have been a history-lover, because this was where he really shone.

There was a whole page of black and white photos: Buchanan Dale, who was shot and killed. Buchanan with his family, when Canon and Shirley were teenagers. Canon was nice-looking then, too, both he and Shirley thinner. A photo of the sheriff's office crew, with Canon as a younger man, no graying at his temples. Pictures of Canon's grandparents. Great-grandparents.

The Dale family has the longest line of law enforcement service in Marston County's history.

The pictures began with a grainy photograph of the first Thomas Buchanan Dale, born in 1837, who fought for the South in the Civil War. He returned to the family farm in Marston County after his parents both died "as casualties of the conflict." Maggie wondered what that meant. This first Dale, known as Buck, married late in life and fathered his only son, called Tom, at the age of sixty-two.

Tom Dale, born in 1899, became the first Marston County sheriff in

1934, the same year his son, Buchanan, was born. Then that son, Canon's father and the third namesake, became sheriff when Tom died prematurely in a tragic house fire in 1967—the same house the first Buck Dale returned to after the war. Buchanan rebuilt on the family farm, and continued his father's legacy as sheriff until the tragic stand-off at I-40 Interstate Exit 159.

By the time Maggie went to bed that night, pictures of the four generations of Dale men—all looking like they could have shared genetics with Sean Connery—were seared into her mind. It took a test of her will over the next several days to leave the nineties papers lying to the side so she could focus on the tragedy that sent her to the news office in the first place.

This was Zeke's story, after all. Maggie needed to concentrate on it. She didn't know if it was the cabin or the county, in general, but stories suddenly seemed to call from all directions and every decade.

Maggie spent the next day immersed in Brad Bybee's articles from the 1980s about Tandy Wilkins' murder and the subsequent Ezekiel Thompson trial and conviction, taking notes as fast as she could write them.

*   *   *

On Friday morning Maggie resisted the urge to bake Canon something—a cake, some muffins, a pie. *Why do I want to bake him something?* Because she'd learned that twenty years ago he had lost his father in the line of duty? And Canon had arrived only moments too late to stop the bleeding?

Maggie felt she ought to acknowledge what she knew. But what would Canon read into it if she did? The sheriff was a scrutinizer. He was likely to probe into why Maggie played the role of a busybody. Why would Maggie poke her nose into a past Canon obviously didn't enjoy talking about? She wasn't writing a book about *his* family, after all. And hadn't a cloud settled over him the last time Maggie pried open his memories?

Canon had been a great help to her. He didn't consider her a suspect in the death of a man found behind her cabin, and he didn't act like she was completely crazy for telling him a ghost had spent two days with her. Maggie didn't want to betray Canon's trust. Betrayal was the last weapon she wanted to wield on anyone, knowingly or otherwise. So Maggie made banana bread for Brad Bybee instead. His articles, after all, provided her with the newly inscribed reams in her notebook.

"You're an excellent writer, Mr. Bybee," she said, setting the cardboard box on his counter. He was the sole human in the office again. "Are you the only one who works here?"

He nodded. "Maybeline was helping out, but she had back surgery."

"Who's Maybeline?"

"Old woman who lives across the street. She used to come in here and sit at the counter while I was out covering stories."

"When did she have back surgery?"

Bybee cocked his head to think. "Eleven years ago."

Maggie bit her lip to keep from smiling and pulled his wrapped banana bread from the box.

"What's this?" Bybee's eyes lit up behind his round frame glasses.

"I wanted to show my appreciation for you letting me borrow the papers."

Bybee's mouth dropped open, reminding Maggie once again of an owl. It was the crook of his nose under the tortoise frame lenses.

"It's homemade?"

Maggie nodded. "Banana bread. I hope you're not allergic to nuts."

Brad Bybee shook his head and looked at her as if seeing Maggie for the first time. "The whole thing's for me?"

"Why, yes! Take it home to your family."

"I don't have a family," he mumbled, putting his hands around the Saran Wrap, peeling a corner of it back, smelling. "Oh, my. That was mighty nice of you, Ms. Raines." He smiled shyly. "And it was nice of you to say I was a good writer. That means a lot to me coming from you. I guess you're the real deal. I've always to wanted to write a book, but can't imagine taking on such a long project."

Maggie looked past him into the room with stacks and stacks of papers. Hadn't Brad Bybee written all those articles? It was enough to fill a library.

When Maggie came out of the newspaper office, she looked down the street toward the sheriff's office feeling a powerful pull to stop in and say hello. But after that, what? *I read about your family, all the tragedy. I'm sorry.*

She couldn't say that. Was she looking for a reason to see him again? Hadn't she told Robbie and Cal only weeks ago that the ink was barely dry on her divorce papers? The last thing she needed was to put her heart in jeopardy so soon after getting it shattered. Maggie was already disappointed Canon hadn't found a reason to come back out to check on her at the cabin. Didn't he have her phone number? Why hadn't he used it? Mightn't Maggie look desperate if she showed up at his office again? Shirley and Becky would have another chance to exchange their glances. Maggie already read the case file. Shirley might have those court documents ready by now...that could be Maggie's excuse.

Oh, what was wrong with her? No, she would wait until Shirley—or Canon—called to tell her the court reports were in the office before stopping back in. Or maybe Canon would bring them out to the cabin...unless he was avoiding her because she had opened old wounds. All the more reason not to tell him she had read about his father's death.

Maggie got back in the Subaru and pointed it down the highway toward the cabin. But her heart went out to Canon as the sheriff's office sign grew smaller in her rearview mirror. A great grandfather who fought in the Civil War...a grandfather who died in a tragic house fire...and a father killed in an interstate stand-off.

Canon Dale was becoming as interesting to her as Ezekiel Thompson.

*   *   *

No one from the sheriff's office called the rest of that day. So on Saturday morning Maggie packed her bags and drove back to Nashville.

"When you coming again?" asked Ollie when she took him the key.

"I'm not sure," she said, honestly. Maggie wanted to ask Mr. Thompson if it was okay to tell his son's story, but lost her nerve. She needed some time to go sit with the new information she'd gathered. "Soon, though."

"Don't let it be too long," he wheezed. "I'm an old man."

22

In The Artist's Way, Julia Cameron recommends morning pages. Three, free-flowing, unedited pages. Get the toxins out of you and onto the paper—fear, worry—all that stands in the way of the story.

The first week of March the weather turned unseasonably warm. Maggie awakened on Friday morning filled with a desire for fresh herbs in the condo kitchen. Back at her and Tom's house—try as she might, it was hard to wash that beginning phrase from her head—she had had quite a nice herb garden off the back patio.

Clearing a spot in the sunniest part of her new condo's kitchen, she filled terra cotta pots with soil and stacked them on a plant stand she found at the local nursery. The stand had five arms that swung out at varying heights that now held basil, cilantro, rosemary, thyme and chives. She wanted to add sage and mint, but would have to get more pots for those. This led to another trip to the local nursery. The condo was in a high rise building and to Maggie's regret, had no terrace or balcony. But…it was only temporary, she kept telling herself…until she figured out exactly what she wanted her next life's chapter to be.

Maggie was on the elevator bringing up the last load from her car and missed the phone call from the Marston County Sheriff's Office. She saw the notice on her cell phone when she set down the bags. Shirley had left a message letting her know the court reports were in their office if she happened to be back in Marston any time soon and wanted to come by and get them.

After listening to the message twice, Maggie stared at the phone on the counter as she washed dirt from her hands, disappointed Canon's deep voice hadn't left the message instead.

She missed him. Maggie wasn't missing Zeke—she'd continued to spend hours with him while working on his story—but she missed the stocky sheriff with his graying temples. Before she could talk herself out of it, she called Mr. Thompson to ask if the cabin was available.

*   *   *

Maggie's iPhone promised another cold spell before the end of the week, so she packed her winter jacket and boots, and the dish crate, then drove to the cabin.

She arrived at noon for the same drill with Mr. Thompson. Big fire going in the fireplace. "I know it's not as cold as it has been, but thought that fire would be cheerful. 'Course I'm cold-natured. And the doctor's got me on blood thinner. It's good to see you again, Maggie. If I didn't know better, I'd say there's more color in your cheeks."

Maggie smiled. Not only had the writing of the past month done her soul good, she had made a bold decision and plunged ahead before she lost her nerve. "I'd like to cook supper for you and Sheriff Dale one night while I'm here this time. Would that be okay, Ollie?"

He seemed taken aback. "Why, of course it'd be okay."

"What did Irene used to cook for you that you miss the most?"

He thought for a minute. "Oh, my...she was a good cook, that's for sure. Just simple stuff, from the garden mostly. But there *was* this lemon cake. That was Irene's specialty. With real lemons. And layers. She used to cut 'em with a thread, after puttin' 'em in the freezer. You ever heard of anything like that?"

"I'll see what I can do. How does Wednesday evening sound?"

"Sounds mighty fine to me. And Canon's coming?"

"I haven't asked him yet."

Maggie was nervous about seeing Canon. Once again, she had spent far too much time thinking about him between her visits to the cabin. Valentine's Day had come and gone in February. Cal and Robbie came by with flowers and chocolate, thinking she would be sad, thinking she would miss the boxed roses Tom sent to the house each year.

But Maggie didn't miss Tom's roses. She found herself thinking more about Canon Dale than Tom Raines on Valentine's Day, and the way the stocky sheriff stared at her lips in the kitchen that last time she ate with him...and again just before he went out the door.

Maggie couldn't believe she was letting herself get feelings for a man in another town—a *sheriff*, no less—in a dangerous line of work, when all she had intended to do was get away and clear her head, then try to write another man's story. Somehow Zeke and Canon had gotten linked inside her heart.

"Well..." wheezed Mr. Thompson, bringing Maggie back to the moment. "I can't see Canon turnin' down an offer like that. What time?"

"Six?"

"Sounds good." Ollie grinned like an eighty-five-year-old schoolboy.

After his green pickup rattled back down the lane, Maggie unpacked the groceries she brought, then revised her list to include more farm vegetables and the ingredients needed for a lemon chiffon cake.

When Maggie drove to town, she swung by the sheriff's office on the chance this was Canon's weekend. It wasn't. Amos sat behind the front desk instead. He stood up too quickly when she came inside, knocking his iPad off the desk. Maggie could see he was playing solitaire.

"Hello, Mrs. Raines."

Maggie hadn't realized that Amos was a red-head. He had worn a hat when she first met him. She had noted the freckles dotting the bridge of his nose that cold day, but they were more pronounced with his hair showing.

"You remember me?" she asked.

"Of course!" Amos looked back at Canon's office and grinned. "How could I forget you?"

Maggie put out her hand. Amos brushed his off on his shirt before shaking it. "Shirley made you a copy of the court proceedings." He looked for the large envelope on her desk. "Here it is. She said you could take it and keep it since it's a copy."

"Thank you." Maggie looked inside the envelope. There was a copy of Zeke's work evaluations, too. Shirley was efficient. Maggie followed Amos's gaze through the glass to the empty sheriff's office. "Sheriff Dale must not be working this weekend."

"No, he's out at the farm." Amos looked uncertain. "You need him? I can call."

"No, don't do that." Maggie waved a hand. "But can I leave a note on his desk?"

"Sure. Oh, sure! Or you can text him. It'd be faster."

Maggie smiled. "I'll just leave the note. He'll be in tomorrow morning?"

"Unless somethin' happens before then. Been a quiet weekend so far."

Maggie stepped back into the sheriff's office and found a blank notepad and pen.

I'd like to cook you and Ollie supper at the cabin if you're free Wednesday at 6:00. Maggie.

No, she didn't like that. One of her college English teachers said never start a letter with the word "I."

She tore the page off, wadded it and threw it in the waste can.

Supper? Wednesday? Cabin? Ollie coming, too. 6:00. Maggie.

No, that was too cavalier. She tore it off and tried again.

Are you free for supper Wednesday at the cabin at 6:00? I've invited Ollie Thompson, too. Maggie Raines.

Maggie didn't want Canon to think she was inviting him on a date. It wasn't like *that*. It was just... Canon was really the only person she'd gotten to know in town. If she was to get Ollie's permission to work on Zeke's story, Canon could provide moral support. That was all.

On her way out she asked Amos, "Where can I buy a spool of thread?"

Amos opened his mouth, then closed it, frowning. "Let's see...Mrs. Herbert's dress shop has fabric. I reckon they'd have thread. But she's not open on Sunday."

Maggie looked out the front window. Marston was as much a ghost town as it had been on New Year's Eve. "Looks like I'll be making another trip to town then. Thank you, Amos."

"Yes, ma'am. Mrs. Herbert's dress shop is off Main past the flower shop, on the corner of Elm and Maple." He followed her to the door and pointed.

"Perfect!" Maggie might pick up some flowers for the table, too. "And where's the library, Amos?"

"It's off Main, too. You go down Elm and turn on Maple. It's the last house on Maple Street. Well...used to be a house." He pointed again. "Real nice library. Blue with white trim, and a big wraparound porch.

There's a sign in the front says Marston County Library. In fact, Canon made the sign. He does that sort of thing. Likes to work with wood. Made the sign for the flower shop, too. Well, and *our* sign."

Amos and Maggie stepped out to look at the sign on the front of the building: "Sheriff's Office" in red block letters shaped like Old West script on a tan background, with a silver badge in the middle. Maggie had first noticed it on New Year's Day, then again when she visited in late January. The sign was quaint…fitting.

"He painted the badge and everything?"

"Oh, yeah." Amos was evidently used to the sheriff's side talents and bored quickly from looking at the sign. He turned back and pointed toward the library again. "Ladies around here are always having socials and meetin's at the library. Canon said you were a writer, so I guess you like libraries."

Canon talked to Amos about me?

Maggie pulled her gaze from the sign. She was here in Marston to find out more about Zeke's life, not Canon's. She'd already pried into Canon's life more than she should have.

"I do like libraries." Maggie put out her hand. "Thank you, Amos."

"Yes, ma'am."

*   *   *

As Maggie lay with the matelassé coverlet pulled up to her chin watching the sun rise next morning, her phone buzzed. She reached to see.

Supper sounds great Wednesday. What can I bring?

So…Canon did keep her number. In case he had follow-up questions about the investigation. Which he hadn't, obviously.

Just you.

She added his contact information to her directory.

Canon with one "n." Dale. Marston County Sheriff. And in the notes: *lives on a farm and makes wooden signs.*

Maggie set the phone back on the nightstand thinking Canon was finished when it buzzed again. This time it was a picture of her wadded notes from the trash smoothed out on his desk.

What was wrong with these?

Maggie cringed, then decided he was flirting with her.

Perfectionistic tendencies with words. Should have thought to remove my evidence. Forgot you were the sheriff.

His quick reply:

Wish I could forget sometimes.

Oh, no...that cloud again. Maggie had a deeper appreciation for it now. As she panicked, wondering how to respond, he sent a final text:

Looking forward to it.

She breathed a sigh of relief.

See you then.

And then Maggie turned off her phone and reached for her journal so she could begin the task of what she had truly returned to the cabin for—not to text-flirt with the handsome sheriff, or to cause him consternation, but to write her New York Times bestselling novel about the ghost she cozied up to on the *red sofa in front of the crackling fire...only months after being rejected by her husband of thirty years.*

Julia Cameron's morning pages had become a habit, providing some solace to Maggie in her new life as a writer.

Yes, Maggie had sunk to low and desperate levels, fantasizing about each new man who entered her life. Was that UPS man looking at her lips? Did the bank teller brush her hand on purpose when he handed over those twenty dollar bills? Or was Maggie's imagination simply getting the best of her?

Was this what it meant to be a writer—the curse of it? To weep with those who didn't ask you to? And to fall in love with each protagonist, real or imagined? Did Maggie really want to expose her heart to this kind of life?

Of course she did. Imagined heroes were safe enough. It was the real heroes, especially those in uniform, best kept at bay.

Hold the real heroes at a safe distance, Maggie—a long, long, long, double-arm's length away.

*   *   *

Canon was the first to arrive. When Maggie opened the door, her heart thumping in her chest, he held out a 5-gallon bucket filled with daffodils.

"These are from my farm."

There was his standard sheepish grin. *So much for keeping real heroes at a safe distance.*

Maggie thought of the red roses that had come in stiff boxes every year. It was hard not to compare them to this bucket filled with yellow blossoms...cut by these man's own hands...from his yard. How fortunate that Maggie had forgotten to get fresh flowers at the shop in town the day before.

"Did you bring them all?" she asked.

"No. This?" Canon scowled. "Hardly made a dent."

Maggie took the bucket as he came inside, thinking how a sea of

186 - LEANNE W. SMITH

daffodils really put her little herb garden back at the condo to shame. Canon was in plain clothes again, jeans paired with a polo shirt this time. Green. Short-sleeved, with his strong arms showing. And he had a penchant for boots. These were ostrich.

"You'll want something to put them in that looks better than that bucket," Canon said.

She went to look for some Mason jars. It was going to take several. Maggie had never seen such buttercups! The blooms were big golden saucers. She put the largest grouping on the dining table—already set with three places and the lemon cake—after taking smaller arrangements back to the bedroom and bath, and she still had a fourth vase-full for the kitchen counter—an arrangement for every room in the cabin, and they'd likely stay beautiful all week.

Canon watched her set out the flowers. "Amos said you got the envelope with the court reports."

"I did! Thank you."

"I hope they're helpful."

"They will be. I've only glanced at them." Maggie looked away from Canon's probing eyes, feeling self-conscious. Was he wearing cologne or was that only great-smelling aftershave? Canon's good smell and the flowers had her feeling nervous. Maggie was relieved at the sound of Mr. Thompson's truck coming up the road. Canon turned to open the door.

"My goodness," the old man wheezed as he came in, "Where'd all these flowers come from?"

"Canon brought them."

Mr. Thompson's eyes got big again when he went to the table and pointed a crooked shaking finger. "Is that a lemon cake?"

"It might not be as good as Irene's," Maggie cautioned.

"It's ever bit as pretty."

To Maggie's pleasure, the men raved over the food, a burgundy roast with potatoes and carrots, with green beans and sweet potato rolls. She hadn't cooked for anyone new in a while. It was important to her to have their approval. When she cut and served the cake, Ollie commented on the flowers again.

Canon pointed at the old man with his fork. "You never have been out to my place."

"No. I don't get out much these days."

Maggie let Mr. Thompson get several bites into the cake—a warm smile on his lips as he closed his eyes and savored each mouthful—before taking a deep breath and plunging into her question.

"Ollie." He opened his eyes and looked at her. "You know I'm a writer."

"How's your book coming?"

"It's starting to take shape." Maggie looked to Canon for support. He smiled back at her. "I never have told you what it's about."

"Well, whatever it is, I was going to ask you if it would be available in large print. I don't see as good as I used to."

Maggie looked at Canon again. He winked encouragement. "If I'm able to sell it to a publisher, I'll ask for that."

"Is it based on a real story?" asked Mr. Thompson.

"Yes."

"Any chance it has to do with events around these parts? Here in Marston County?"

Maggie nodded. Ollie looked at the lemon cake and back to Maggie. "Any chance it has to do with Zeke?"

Yes...it was as if something spiritual hung over the rafters of this cabin. Maggie had felt a growing connection with Mr. Thompson in the few short months she'd known him. He must have felt it, too. She leaned toward him. "Is that okay? If I try to tell your son's story?"

The old man put a hand to his chest and opened his mouth, but nothing came out for a minute. Ollie's vocal cords had apparently seized up. The old blue eyes watering, he finally wheezed out, "Why, that'd be more than okay, Maggie. I confess I was hopin' you might. I have a feelin' you could tell his story real fine."

Maggie went on to share with him what she'd shared with Canon on her last visit—that she wouldn't seek to be sensational—that she might not get all the facts just right—but that she wanted to use Zeke's story to offer a shaft of light to others.

Ollie listened and nodded, smiling intermittently. When she finished he dabbed his eyes with his napkin. "That all sounds good. Mighty good." He blinked across the table at Canon. "Listen, I don't have the kind of stamina you young folks have. This fine meal..." Mr. Thompson waved his hand over the table, "and this fine news has me wore out all of a sudden. I hope you'll forgive me if I take my leave."

"Can I send the rest of the cake with you?" asked Maggie.

"I'd love a piece or two, but send some with Canon there. He's a strappin' man!"

Maggie went to the kitchen to fix a plate of leftovers to send with him, along with a generous portion of the cake. She handed the foil-covered plates to Canon who carried them out to the old green pickup for him.

As Maggie stood in the doorway, the sun inching toward the horizon in the distance, she overheard Canon say to Ollie, "I told her you'd be pleased."

"Oh, I am, Canon. I am. She's a good one, that Maggie. I reckon you can see that. If you don't get over your own demons and set your cap for her, I'm goin' to."

Maggie hid behind the door when Canon glanced back at the cabin, not wanting him to know she eavesdropped. She couldn't hear what he muttered to Mr. Thompson as he helped the old man into the truck and swung the creaky door closed.

She was clearing the dishes as Canon came back inside. He stepped to the dining table to help her. Maggie went to the kitchen to run the soapy water. The cabin didn't have an automatic dishwasher.

As Canon brought the last armload in and set them on the counter, he said, "You're a blessing to that old man. How long will you be here this time?"

"Through Saturday."

"You coming back in April?" Canon leaned his back to the counter beside her. "I notice you're on a four to five-week pattern."

Maggie enjoyed the feel of the porcelain plates in her hands. She was glad the cabin didn't have a dishwasher. Everything about this place felt more tangible—more sensory—than it did back at the condo. On her first trip back in late January, she'd had trouble sleeping. Every sound in the night woke her. She'd even called out Zeke's name once, thinking she heard someone walking. Then she realized it was one of the oak limbs knocking overhead.

"Thought I might," said Maggie.

"The cherry trees bloom in mid-April. It's something to see on Main Street. We have a Cherry Blossom Festival."

"Really?"

"Oh, yes. And you haven't lived until you've had a cherry pie from Mabel Stevens' booth at the festival."

Maggie laughed. Was he looking at her lips again?

"It'd be my honor to buy you one," Canon said. "Least I could do, to pay you back for all the fine meals you've cooked me."

Maggie looked back down at the suds on her hands and reached to the other side of the sink to rinse the plate. "One pie is going to balance things?" She let the water run off.

Canon took the plate from her hand, setting it in the drainer. When he turned back to her his eyes danced. "Are you doubtin' the pie?"

Maggie laughed and reached for another plate.

"Truth is," he admitted, "I was trying to work up the courage to ask you out to my farm. But I don't trust my cooking next to yours."

"I've seen you chop a mean pepper."

"How 'bout this." Canon took the next plate from her hands to set in the drainer. "After the Festival, I'll rig you a pole and we'll see if you can catch us a couple of rainbow trout from the pond. If you can do that, I'll cook 'em for you. I'm pretty good at rainbow trout. With peppers on the side."

Maggie handed him the silverware she'd just rinsed, her fingers momentarily getting tangled up in his. A swarm of butterflies gathered in her stomach. When her hands were free, she reached into the sink, pulled the plug and let the water out. "It's a date."

Canon had stepped toward the living room door after putting the flatware in the sink, but turned back now. "You would consider it that?"

Maggie's face flushed as she finished drying her wet hands on the dishtowel. "I was just...using an expression. Not if you..."

He reached for her hand as she laid the towel on the counter, bringing it up to his lips.

"Forgive me, Maggie, for not being smoother. I've not had a lot of practice. But I would like to consider it a date. If you're on board with that."

So much for holding Canon Dale at a long, long, long double arm's length away. Maggie's hand flashed with heat as he let it go. Unexpected tears rushed to her eyes. Canon was quick to notice and take a step back. "Did I—"

"No." Maggie shook her head, angry at her body's sudden betrayal of her emotions. She hadn't been touched that tenderly in a while.

The loneliness of divorce had been a shock to Maggie. At first, she thought it was the unfortunate timing, coming so soon on the heels of empty nesting. But Zeke's brief presence in the cabin—his prediction that she was not destined to be alone—lit a spark of hope in her. She wanted to be loved again. But she was afraid of it not being real...solid...standing the test of whatever time she had.

"No, it's not a date?" Canon asked.

"No. I mean, yes. A date is fine. It's just...I've been trying not to like you, Canon." Heat rushed up her neckline. "And I'm not doing a good job of it."

Canon's brow knotted. "Am I offensive?"

"No. You're perfectly wonderful. Just...unexpected."

"*I'm* unexpected, after you had a ghost in the cabin?"

Did that mean he really did believe her? Or was he poking fun at Maggie?

"I'm so recently divorced, Canon. I feel like damaged goods. And when you figure that out, you'll be gone." There, Maggie said it. And she immediately wished she could reel it back in. Tears sprang to her eyes faster than she could blink them away.

Maggie suddenly wanted Canon to leave. What was she even doing here in this cabin, in this remote little county? And why was she following a story that wasn't hers? Why was she spending so much time and effort on something that might prove to be a total waste of time?

Maggie didn't have an agent. She didn't have a publisher. There was no guarantee anyone would ever buy or read her story.

What is wrong with me?

Wasn't Maggie fine a moment ago? Bantering with Canon playfully? Where did this sudden flow of emotion come from? Were mid-life hormones hijacking her best intentions?

Canon stared at her, apparently as dumbfounded as she was.

"I feel really guilty for even *considering* being with—I mean, *dating*—another man." Maggie kept digging the hole of her shame deeper. "I haven't kissed anyone but Tom for the last thirty years. I don't know how it works anymore."

"We can fix that."

Canon was definitely eyeing her lips this time. He didn't try to hide it. But he didn't reach to take her in his arms like Maggie half-braced and half-hoped for. He looked down at her with a pinched brow instead. "Don't ever say you're damaged goods, Maggie. Nothing could be farther from the truth."

Canon stepped to the living room and reached for his jacket. Before he went out he said, "I didn't mean to upset you. I hope you'll come have that pie with me in April." Then he added, low, "Lock your doors."

23

When your heart lies in shards around your feet you think you'll never breathe normally again. Then one day, you feel the vital organ pumping. Like the soar of a hawk's wings lifting in the air.

Canon drove away from the cabin feeling like a fraud again. Today was Wednesday, March eighth. Canon hadn't seen Maggie since Tuesday, January thirty-first. That was five weeks and a day for a man who counted.

Five weeks and a day.

How long did he have to wait to make Maggie Raines a part of his daily life? Or would she ever want to be?

On her last visit to his office, he'd only interacted with her briefly. He'd just gotten Paul Wilkins on the line when he saw the front door to the office swing open, framing Maggie with sunshine. Her hair was almost auburn when the light hit it like that.

Canon had turned his back to compose himself, so great was the thrill that shot through him. Shirley would read him like a book. She would see how Canon felt about Maggie, then she'd pester him about it in that sisterly way she had.

He had almost driven out to the cabin again before Maggie left in January, but had already dropped by once that week. Twice felt like he was being too obvious...too aggressive. So he had stopped at Ollie's cottage instead. Checked on the old man.

"Mrs. Raines is back in the cabin," Ollie had said, nodding his head down the road.

"Oh, yeah?" Canon thought he was fairly nonchalant about it, but he hadn't fooled the old man any more than he would have fooled Shirley.

Ollie's eyes had twinkled, catching him in his false play at ignorance. "I saw you go by on Sunday. Saw you leave, too...late that night."

Canon looked down at his watch then, knowing that he had already revealed more than he meant to. "I better get back to the station. Shirley needed a report I had."

"You're not going to drive down and say 'hello' to Maggie?"

"Naw. I just came to check on you."

Ollie laughed. "It's not even snowing."

On Friday, Canon had stood in front of the big plate glass window at the bank talking to Fred Hinson after giving his annual safety tips presentation to the employees when he saw Maggie's car go by. She parked at Brad Bybee's. Canon hurried back to the station, trying not to look like he was hurrying, thinking she'd stop by before she left town. But she didn't.

Shirley and Becky both asked him later that day what he was in such a god-awful mood for. That was five weeks and a day ago. And now he'd made her cry.

Canon felt awful. He wouldn't have called it a date. He didn't want to scare her off. Maybe he shouldn't have invited her at all. She'd feel worse if she knew how the festival got started. Canon hadn't told Maggie he was ever married. He wasn't sure how she'd feel about that. But that was a long time ago. Sometimes his marriage to Rita felt no more real than the recurring dream he'd had about Maggie. He often wondered if it ever really happened.

Maggie called herself 'damaged goods.' That term made Canon want to hit something. If he ever got hold of the man who ever planted that idea in her head, he'd pistol-whip him. And Canon didn't care who got it on video. It'd be worth the risk of a public scandal to sink his fist into the man who ever made Maggie Raines doubt her value.

*   *   *

The day after Maggie's dinner with Canon and Ollie she was filled with insecurity. Canon obviously hadn't meant for his invitation to be viewed as a date—*she* was the one who planted that idea—*she* was the one who called it that. And what was Maggie *thinking* when she mentioned kissing?

Surely Canon would be relieved now if she called and said 'no' to his invitation to go to the festival. Or texted. Texting would be easier. That's how young people did it these days, wasn't it? That way you didn't have to look them in the eye.

Now that Maggie had revealed her insecurities to Canon, he likely wouldn't mind if she slunk back to Nashville never to appear in the county again.

She left the dining room where she was writing and headed to the bedroom to get her phone. She would text Canon this instant, get it over with. A sudden rustle and *thunk* behind her caused her to jump, thinking Zeke was back.

The court report envelope lay on the floor. She must have knocked it from its perch at the edge of the dining table, brushing against it in her rush to put herself out of her own misery.

Maggie picked up the report, thick with the papers inside. She had not yet read through it.

Instead of getting her phone, Maggie sat on the couch and began reading the pages.

Marston County vs. Ezekiel Thompson.

Charges were brought by the district attorney's office for two murders in the first degree. Zeke was represented by a lawyer named Hardy. Zeke was willing to plead guilty, but from what Maggie could gather it wasn't what Hardy had recommended so it went to trial.

A jury, rather than a single judge, deliberated seven hours before coming back with their ruling: guilty of two counts, but on reduced charges of manslaughter, for the killing of Tandy and a man named George Iontha.

The next two days passed in a blink as Maggie got back on her computer comparing notes from the court report to notes she had taken from reading Canon's files and the newspapers from the eighties.

*   *   *

Maggie sat across from Robbie in the hipster coffee house again, clutching a Cuban. The caramel espresso in her glass was a soothing fragrance—an aromatic comfort—even before she brought it to her lips.

"Canon asked me to go to the Cherry Blossom Festival with him in April," Maggie blurted out, thinking Robbie wasn't really paying attention.

Robbie looked up from her phone. Maggie could see she was reading a text from Cal, but couldn't see what it said. "When in April?"

"The fifteenth."

Robbie's eyebrows raised as she put the phone back in her purse. This conversation had evidently grown more interesting than whatever her brother was doing right now.

"What are you going to wear?" Robbie demanded to know.

Maggie shook her head. "I don't think I'm going."

"Why would you *not*?"

"Why would I?"

Robbie leaned in, looking at her mother as if Maggie had lost her mind. "Because a handsome sheriff asked you to, Mom!"

"But, Robbie, it's too..."

"*Soon?* Nonsense. *Scary?* Yes, I know." Robbie grew serious. "I was texting Cal that Mark asked me to marry him last night."

"Robbie!" Maggie reached for her daughter's hand—the left hand—but there was no ring.

"I told him 'no.'"

"Why, sweetheart? I thought you loved Mark?"

Robbie's purse began to vibrate. She started to ignore it, then reconsidered. "Let me tell Cal I'm with you. I'll call him later." She grabbed the phone, punched in her message, then dropped it back in her purse. "I *do* love Mark...I think I do." Then Robbie shook her head. "I'm not sure anymore. Look, I hate to admit this to you, but this thing with you and Dad...I guess it's affected me more than I realized. I wanted to get Cal's take on how he's doing."

Maggie didn't know what to say. *Ripple effects.* Robbie had always been the more serious of the twins. She took things to heart—deeply so—where Cal had the ability to laugh things off.

"All that therapy, huh?" said Robbie.

"Two days with a ghost in a cabin did me more good than—" Maggie stopped when Robbie looked up at her sharply.

"*Ghost?* What do you mean?"

Maggie looked down at the caramel swirl of her Cuban. "I shouldn't have called it a ghost. I meant the idea for the story that I got back in December."

"You gave me a fright for a minute."

"That must sound crazy, to get so caught up in a story you feel like you're spending time with ghosts. Wonder what Therapist Jim would say to that?" Maggie laughed, trying to make it sound natural.

"I've always thought writers were a little crazy," Robbie admitted.

"You think I'm crazy?"

"I think you're *dreamy*. Aren't you the one always losing track of time?"

Maggie didn't answer.

"And now you're talking about ghosts."

Maggie didn't answer that either.

Robbie sighed. "We didn't break up, exactly. But Mark is hurt I didn't give an immediate yes."

"Did he have a ring and everything?"

Robbie nodded. "Bended knee, all that. And, oh! Mom. The *ring*. It's gorgeous. There's no telling what he spent on it."

Maggie knew her daughter well enough to know a big ring wasn't her goal, but she was an accountant. Robbie always considered the cost.

"Mark is good to you, Robbie." He was right for her, too. If he hadn't been, Maggie would have been the loudest one cheering her daughter's hesitation.

"I know." Robbie looked so miserable it broke Maggie's heart. She didn't mean to add to her daughter's discomfort by pointing out the obvious. "If Mark had proposed to me eight months ago before all this happened, I wouldn't have thought twice about it. From the first few months we dated we've been talking marriage. But his timing really sucked. I've been pulling away lately, and I think he got scared."

"So how'd you leave it?"

"I asked for a couple of weeks to think about it."

"Why don't you come with me to the cabin? I'll call Mr. Thompson and see if it's available."

Robbie cocked her head at her mother. "I thought you weren't going to the Cherry Blossom Festival."

"Well, not for *that*—to be with you! I'd love to show the cabin to you."

"There's no way I could get off work right now, Mom. It's the middle of tax season. The only reason I got this lunch hour is because I've worked the last three weekends."

"You couldn't get off for one night? What if we went up next Saturday, the eighth. It's the weekend before the festival, but you could see the cabin and the town, then you could come home Sunday, and I might stay the following week."

"And go to the festival with the handsome sheriff on the fifteenth?"

"His name is Canon," said Maggie.

"Maybe I can." Robbie thought for a minute. "I'll have to work the following weekend for sure, but I think I could go for one night on the eighth. I would love to experience this cabin you've talked about so much." Then Robbie got a glint in her eye. "But I'll only go on one condition."

"What?"

"I want to meet him—the handsome sheriff."

Maggie shrugged her shoulders and avoided Robbie's gaze. "I do know where his office is." She had his number, too.

*　　*　　*

Robbie only got a 24-hour window—from Sunday to Monday—but it was enough. She worked until 3:30 on Sunday afternoon, then followed Maggie to the cabin. As soon as she parked, she leapt from her Jeep exclaiming, "Oh my gosh, Mom! Look at this place."

"You would hardly look at the pictures before I came here."

"I'm looking now." She crooned over the fire Mr. Thompson had going in the fireplace, the furniture, the claw foot tub and large shower, the matelassé coverlet. "This would make a great honeymoon cabin."

"Are you thinking of recommending it to Cal and Yvette?"

"*Eew!* I don't want to think about them here. I'm thinking of it for me and Mark."

Maggie smiled knowing it had been a good idea to bring her daughter here. Robbie was like a kid again, wanting to experience everything the cabin had to offer—the swing, the rockers, the red couch and ottoman, the bath. "How soon before we can walk down the dirt road? Where'd the sheriff find the body? What are you cooking for supper?"

That night, after two slices of Maggie's Margherita pizza and three sugar cookies, a calmer Robbie lay side-by-side with her mother looking up at the stars through the windows in the ceiling of the bedroom. She lay so still and quiet Maggie thought she'd gone to sleep. But then Robbie said low, "I still don't like thinking about you out here all alone."

Maggie had wondered all afternoon if she should tell Robbie about Zeke. But how could she? Robbie's mind was practical, like Canon Dale's. Telling her about Zeke would only cause Robbie to worry about her more than she already did. So instead she said, "I'll never be alone as a writer, Robbie."

Robbie propped up on an elbow, probably so she could better lecture her mother in the moonlight. "Fictional characters are no substitute for the real thing, Mom."

"Maybe. But you can make them whatever you want them to be, which is giving me a nice sense of control I confess I've enjoyed. Well...except when the characters surprise me."

"I've heard writers say that and I've never understood it. Aren't you the one writing the story?"

Maggie thought for a minute before answering. "I don't think I'm writing it so much as I'm listening. That's why it helps to come out here. I hear the words stronger here."

"Fewer distractions?"

Canon was something of a distraction, but Maggie felt it best not to say so. "Yes."

Robbie nodded, seemingly satisfied...for the moment. She lay back down and turned her head to the stars. Soon her breathing let Maggie know she was asleep. Maggie listened to the rhythmic rise and fall, thinking how it was her favorite sound in all the world.

24

If a story idea comes floating down the aisle and jumps inside your empty head (like J.K. Rowling says a boy wizard did for her), be the fertile mind most willing to water it.

The next morning Maggie was excited to show Robbie the town she was growing so fond of. They stopped at the sheriff's office first. Maggie handed Shirley a basket of pumpkin muffins and a card when they walked in.

"What's all this?" Shirley wore her customary scowl.

Maggie smiled sweetly. She was determined to win this woman over. "My way of saying 'thank you' for all you've done to help me."

Shirley had the same sheepish look as Canon's. She glanced over at Becky, who looked back with a bouncy grin. Once again the women seemed to pass secrets across the aisle.

Canon's office was empty. Maggie tried to keep the disappointment from her voice as she introduced Robbie.

"We heard you had twins, a boy and a girl," Shirley drawled. She stood and held out her hand. "Nice to meet you, Robbie."

"It's short for Robyn," Maggie felt the need to explain. "Calvin and Robyn."

"Nice names," Becky quipped, offering her hand to Robbie next.

"Canon's not here," said Shirley.

"He's at the library, though," Becky was quick to add. "Helping Dot change a flat."

Shirley offered more detail. "Dot Jenkins had a flat yesterday. He fixed it for her and went back over this mornin' to change it out with the spare."

"Amos told me about the library," said Maggie.

Becky turned to Robbie. "It's a real nice library. If you head over there now, you might catch him."

"He'd like to meet Robbie, I'm sure." Maggie thought Shirley's tone held a note of reluctance. She wished the women a good day and led Robbie from the office. When the door closed, Robbie squeezed her arm, "This is more serious than I thought."

"What do you mean?"

"Word of the sheriff's admiration is obviously out. By the way, how many cherry trees are in this town?"

They'd come up to Main and the trees were a show indeed.

"Wow." Maggie had noticed, of course, that there were a lot of cherry trees planted around the square, but now with the branches covered in their spring foliage bursting with blooms, she saw there were more than she had realized. Her eyes rolled from corner to corner, counting at least twenty of varying heights and widths. More were hidden by the white Colonial courthouse that sat in the middle.

"What a lovely town!" exclaimed Robbie. They'd come down a side street to the sheriff's office on Hickory and this was Robbie's first clear view of the square.

Maggie hooked her arm in her daughter's feeling smug about the jewel she'd discovered.

"I told you. A virtual Mayberry."

"And the sheriff is out changing a tire."

Maggie laughed and walked Robbie down Elm, then Maple, in the direction of the library.

"No wonder they have a festival," said Robbie. "You have to come. And I want lots of pictures." When her eye landed on a blue wooden sign at the end of the sidewalk announcing the Marston County Library in curved white lettering, Robbie's jaw fell open. "Oh, Mom."

The house the sign pointed to could have made the cover of *Southern Living*. In fact, it had...twice. Maggie and Robbie stood and admired the blue house and white shutters, the window boxes bursting with purple and yellow pansies, the large willow tree draping over the brick walkway that led to a wide white porch lined with upholstered wicker furniture. It was the kind of porch one dreamed of lounging on to sip tea, read a book, or visit with friends.

When they opened the front door, a gray-haired woman looked up from a desk in the foyer and rose quickly to greet them.

"Dorothy Jenkins, ladies. Marston County Librarian. How can I help you?"

Maggie put out her hand. "My name is Maggie Raines."

"The *writer*?"

Robbie looked at her mom as if to say, you have become known.

Dorothy Jenkins, who'd evidently come of age in the sixties and locked in there with her hairstyle and polka dot dress, leaned in for a closer look at Robbie. "You *have* to be related."

"My daughter, Robbie, Mrs. Jenkins."

"I see it! Please, call me *Dot*." Then Dot latched on to Maggie like an old friend, taking her by the arm. "You have *got* to tell some of the stories of this town, Maggie. We've been needing a writer like *you* to come along."

First Brad Bybee, now Dot Jenkins. Neither had read one word Maggie had ever written.

Dot, an earnest woman with a penchant for word emphasis, was a bit of a close talker. Maggie breathed easier when she let go of her arm and latched on to Robbie's. "This house dates back to the Civil War. It's *that* old. Woman who lived here then lost it to a *banking* couple. That couple nearly ruined it, but then a couple bought it *after* them, who only had one son, who *sadly* was killed in the second World War. It was *his* widow put up all this wallpaper you see now. Some of her furniture is still here. That side table." She pointed.

"Oh, and see this *hearth*? That man killed in the war? His picture hung here a *long* time, until his widow remarried. His *daughter* had the house after that. She never did marry. She was a real *industrious* woman, though. The hardware store is named for her. Caroline Baker. She only died a couple of years ago. Sad. *Alzheimer's.* But before she got *too* bad she said she wanted this house *preserved. Loved* books."

Dot Jenkins let go of Robbie's arm so she could lift her hands with the joy of this pronouncement. "Had a *big* collection of books. You would have liked her, being a *book* person." Dot gave Maggie a knowing smile, then waved them forward.

"Her most *prized* books are in this room, the *Caroline Baker* Room. This other room over here is the *tea* room."

The tea room was filled with a collection of small white clothed tables and white painted chairs. A narrow table sat in the middle of the room with a profusion of forsythia in the center.

"Is that not the *prettiest* forsythia on the *main* table you ever saw? We set the food on the main table and serve *buffet* style. Canon, that's the sheriff, keeps us in those—*flowers*, that is. Brings flowers for the library every Friday morning in *season*. He takes flowers by the nursing home, too. A lot of people don't know that."

Dot's voice dropped then like she was telling a secret. "He's a *good* one, that Canon. Changed my tire yesterday. I didn't know who else to call. Canon'll always come when you need him. No matter what for. Even on a *Sunday*."

Maggie opened her mouth to ask where Canon might be, but Dot pointed up a white staircase and kept talking, a well-practiced tour guide. "Those were the family's bedrooms up *there*." She waved Maggie and Robbie toward the next door opening. "Of course, Canon's had a lot of time on his hands since his wife died. That was *so* tragic. Now *there's* a sad story."

Maggie and Robbie turned to look at one another in the narrow hallway. When Dot realized she'd lost her audience, she finally stopped talking and turned.

"Canon was married?" asked Maggie.

"Why, yes! You didn't know? 'Course it was so long ago. To Rita. She had red hair. *Prettiest* red hair you ever saw. Kept it *curled*. She's the one planted all those flowers at the farm. That's what got the cherry trees started."

"The cherry trees in town?" asked Robbie.

"Why, yes! Rita Dale is the whole reason we *have* the festival. Canon's the master of ceremonies. He plants a new cherry tree every year in her *honor*."

Canon had struck Maggie as a lifelong bachelor. She'd never considered whether he had ever been married. Why had the newspaper article about Canon's family made no mention of him having a former wife?

"When did she die?" asked Maggie.

Dot leaned in, clutching Maggie's arm again, talking painfully close. "This will be festival number *thirty*. There's been some discussion about how many more the square can *hold*."

Robbie cleared her throat. "Tell me, Mrs. Jenkins, is it customary for the sheriff to bring someone with him to the festival?"

"Bring someone with him? What do you mean?" The older woman turned to Robbie, but kept her hold on Maggie's arm.

"A date," said Robbie, refusing to meet her mother's stare.

"*Canon?*" Dot's hands gripped tighter. "Well, *Lord*, no. Many a woman has set her cap for him, but my *word*. I reckon it near broke his heart to lose Rita. He's been the town's most *eligible* bachelor ever since. I guess he'll die a bachelor. Sad, too, he's such a *good* man."

"We heard he was here." Robbie finally looked at her mother. "Changing out your tire."

Dot nodded. "He was, but he got a call on that *hip* radio he carries. Right before ya'll got here."

Meeting a woman like Dot Jenkins was like hitting the mother lode for a writer, but Maggie was suddenly overstimulated. "Mrs. Jenkins we need to be going, but could I come back later to ask you some questions about the Zeke Thompson trial?"

"Why, certainly! *Zeke Thompson.*" Dot's voice dropped low again. "Now *that's* a sad story."

Before she could start telling them more about it, Maggie said, "Tomorrow? At ten?"

"Oh. Well, let's see, the education committee has a *luncheon* every Tuesday at *noon.* You mind if we make it *nine-thirty*?"

"That's perfect," said Maggie.

"I look forward to it!" Mrs. Jenkins finally let her arm go so she could lift her hands with the joyful prospect of Tuesday. Then she saw them to the door. One could tell Dot Jenkins was a stickler for southern hospitality.

Maggie and Robbie were silent as they came back down the walk under the swaying branches of the willow and headed toward the town square. Robbie was the first to speak "You do realize how significant this is?"

Maggie didn't answer. She wasn't ready to admit to Robbie all that she was feeling. Surprised...and a little betrayed to think Canon hadn't told her. But why should he? What was she to him? What were they to one another? Part of her was elated, the other part terrified.

"There's a cute dress shop I want to show you, Robbie. Next to the flower shop on Main."

"Don't think we're not talking about this, Mom."

Maggie was in the lead and turned the corner from Elm to Main. She stopped. There stood Canon, a block away, talking to an older gentleman in front of the bank. Maggie did an about-face to go back down

Elm as the gentleman turned to leave. Canon noticed her, his shoulders suddenly lifting. "Maggie!"

Robbie took her mother's arm and turned her back around. Canon came toward them, his eyes quick to note the similarities. "This has to be your daughter."

"Robbie," said Maggie, "this is Canon Dale."

He put out a burly hand. Robbie pumped it, smiling too big. "Sheriff Dale. I've heard so much."

Canon looked at Maggie again. "Yeah? You look exactly like the picture your mom showed me."

"Thank you for protecting Mother from escaped felons in the night."

Maggie wondered if Robbie had rehearsed that line.

"She didn't really need protecting."

"All the same. It makes me feel better to know you've been a..." Robbie's eyes cut back to her mother, "...steady presence on her visits to the county."

As Maggie could have predicted, it brought on Canon's sheepish look. "Well...it's been my pleasure." He turned to Maggie. "You in town for the festival?"

"She is," answered Robbie.

Maggie mashed the toe of Robbie's shoe to let her know she didn't need her help to have this conversation. "I was considering it," added Maggie, for clarification.

But how could she say 'no' knowing she might be the first woman Canon had asked to a festival that started because of his deceased wife? Was Canon seriously interested in Maggie? Or was he just being nice, being a good man like Dot Jenkins said he was, hospitable and making a visitor to the town feel welcome?

Maggie's wasn't trying to play naïve or coy. But this was new territory, and trust of late was hard for her. She never expected to have feelings for someone so soon after feeling the jerk of a rug. She didn't want to repeat mistakes she may have made.

"What time and where should she meet you?" Robbie sounded more like a parent than a daughter, ignoring Maggie's "considering it" comment.

"I could pick you up at the cabin that morning, about ten. Are you coming, too?" He looked at Robbie. "We'd love to have you."

See? Maggie wanted to say to Robbie. *You're invited, too. It's not just me.*

"That is so kind of you, but I have to get back to work. Later this afternoon, actually. I do wish I could keep my eye on the two of you."

Maggie swatted Robbie's arm. "Since when did you become a *comedienne*? That's Cal's job."

"We are twins." Robbie smiled at Canon. "You know what they say...twins think alike sometimes."

It was time to end this conversation. Robbie was having too much fun. Maggie pulled her arm. "It was nice to see you again, Canon. Robbie and I were headed to the dress shop."

"We're free for lunch," said Robbie.

"Oh, yeah?" Canon took the bait. "You like burgers?"

Robbie grinned. "You know, I haven't had a good burger in a long time."

That's because Robbie was more of a kale and quinoa salad girl.

"Pete's, down on the corner, has some awfully good burgers. And hand cut fries."

Robbie looked at Maggie. "Shall we, Mom?"

Maggie offered Canon a look of apology for her daughter's aggressiveness, but he smiled as if he were looking forward to being scrutinized over lunch. "I need to run by the station." He looked at his watch. It was eleven. "Meet you there in half an hour?"

"We'll be there," declared Robbie.

As he left, Maggie pulled her daughter into the dress shop. "*Robbie!*"

But rather than taking her scolding, Robbie's eye landed on a blue summer dress. "Oh, Mom." She reached for it, holding it up to Maggie. "Try this on. Teal brings out your eyes."

As Maggie stood looking at herself in the dressing room mirror moments later, noting how the teal dress did, in fact, bring out the brown of her eyes, Robbie whispered from the other side of the curtain, "I like him."

When Maggie slid the drape to the side, Robbie nodded resolutely. "That's what you're wearing to the Cherry Blossom Festival."

"Why do you like him?" asked Maggie.

"I don't know exactly. Ask me again after lunch."

"Please don't overdo it, Robbie."

Robbie raised her shoulders innocently. "When have I ever overdone it?"

Maggie pulled the curtain again and took one last look at herself in the mirror. She hadn't bought a new dress in what...seven months? But should she really show so much of her arms? April weather could go either way—cool or warm. The dress was sleeveless, a soft knit blend that swept the tops of her knees. The skirt hung straight, not too flouncy—she didn't want something that would lift in the wind. And it had pockets. Maggie liked pockets.

"You don't think this style's too young for me?" she asked Robbie.

"Mom...you're getting the dress."

Maggie had packed a pair of shoes that would look cute with it.

25

One day you find yourself dancing in the kitchen and you know you're going to be alright. Every day won't be for dancing, but those few that are? Those few are all you need.

"Here's why I like him." Robbie propped her feet on the dash as Maggie drove them back to the cabin after having burgers and hand cut fries at Pete's. "He's not bad-looking...for a middle-aged guy."

No, he wasn't.

"And it looks like he might not go bald."

Maggie cut her eyes sarcastically over at her daughter. "The most important thing to consider in a man, after all."

"But he could use someone to cook healthier meals for him than that grease pit we just ate in."

"You acted like you enjoyed your burger!"

"All for you, Mom."

Robbie grew serious again. "No, you know my real favorite thing? Besides the idea of a guy who keeps the flowers going that his deceased wife of thirty years planted? Who has waited that long to ask someone of his own volition to the Cherry Blossom Festival?"

"He makes signs, too," said Maggie. "Those cute signs you kept seeing around town? Canon made those."

Robbie's brows raised. "He's not short on admirable features."

"But admirable features alone are not enough reason to give your heart to someone. You want to believe it's the right person for you." Maggie felt the need to say this. It was her job, as mother, to be sensible.

Robbie gave her a look. "Which is the whole reason I'm here in Marston County with you this weekend."

"Mark is right for you, Sweetheart." Maggie felt the need to say this, too. Because it was also her job, as mother, to point out blind spots her daughter might be having—gently, of course.

"And I saw how that man back there in the burger joint was looking at you, Mom. He's scared to death of you. Do you know that?"

Maggie scrunched a doubting nose at Robbie. "Canon? He's not scared of anything." She decided not to tell Robbie she'd seen Canon whip three younger men into acting nicer.

"He's scared of you. He's scared you're going to break his heart. But he seems willing to take the chance."

"Look who's talking."

"I know."

Robbie moved her feet from the dash and hugged her knees up to her on the seat. "But I didn't get cold feet because I'm scared Mark will break *my* heart. I'm scared I might break *his*." Robbie's voice dropped to barely audible. "I don't want to have an unfaithful gene in me, and do him wrong. He doesn't deserve that."

Maggie saw a tear slide down Robbie's cheek.

"Nobody has a crystal ball, Robbie. None of us get guaranteed outcomes for our lives."

"I know. You have to be willing to be vulnerable. Thank you, Brene Brown. But back to the sheriff. I like the way everybody in this town *talks* about him, and *acts* around him. You can hear the respect in their voices." Robbie looked out the window at the passing farmlands. "He doesn't strike me as a guy who would ever do a woman wrong."

Neither did your father, Maggie started to say, but decided to keep it to herself. Robbie was being protective and Maggie couldn't fault her for that. She felt every bit as protective of Robbie, too, and knew as well as anyone she could promise no absolutes about her daughter's future with Mark. Or any other man.

"Dad's going bald," Robbie mumbled, after a bit. Maggie didn't say anything. Robbie moved her feet back up to the dash. "They're having a girl. Did you know that? Bethany's a week past her due date."

"No, I didn't know it was a girl."

"Cal and I are going to have a sister—half sister. How weird is that?"

Maggie's mind traveled back to the day the twins were born. "I hope it goes okay for them."

Robbie turned to her, her eyes glistening. "I'm proud of you, Mom."

"Where did that come from?"

"You saying that—being able to say that."

"I'm not mad at her or your father anymore, Robbie. I'm really not. I realized that my first week in the cabin. And I don't want you or Cal to be. We should all want the best for them. Yes, it hurts to feel betrayed. I'm not going to pretend it doesn't. You know better. But, I don't know... This journey I've been on, as bumpy as it started, it's a good journey. I'm grateful for it."

Maggie took her right hand off the steering wheel so she could set it on Robbie's. Robbie latched on and gripped Maggie's hand tight.

"I want to get where you are, Mom. I don't want to be afraid of the future. I don't want to be afraid to love Mark. In fact," Robbie was openly crying now, "I like this cabin of yours and this quaint little town so much, what would you think if we had our wedding here?"

Robbie had taken on a tougher exterior since Tom's betrayal. She must have felt the need, as oldest, to protect her mother. It was nice to see her soft again...tender...willing to be vulnerable.

"In Marston County?" asked Maggie.

"Yes!" Robbie's eyes were lit up now. "The more I think about it, the more I love the idea. At first I thought we could get married at the cabin. Ever since I pulled into the yard and parked, I've been imagining the place decorated with flowers in my mind. But I'd rather save it for the honeymoon getaway. Today, seeing the way all those cherry trees are about to pop on Main Street...that quaint little library down Maple. What if we got married at the courthouse and had our reception at the library? I don't want a big wedding. I'd like to keep it small. And I think Mark would love the idea. Don't you?"

Maggie smiled over at her. "I was hoping some of the clarity I'd gotten out here would rub off on you."

"I don't understand how in less than a day, but it has."

Robbie let go of her mother's hand and blew her nose. "To think I didn't want you to come out here. I really pooed on it back in December. But there's something special about this place, Mom."

"You hear all those stories Dot Jenkins was telling at the library?"

"I know, right? Writer's dream-talk. Do you think she wears polka-dots because her name is Dot?"

"You think?"

Robbie nodded at her. "I predict that's her thing. You pay attention at the festival. I want to know what Dot Jenkins was wearing."

"How can you not love a woman like that? I should have taken you by to meet Brad Bybee, he's the editor of the newspaper. And you didn't get to meet Amos. That's the other deputy. He has a shock of red hair and Opie freckles." Maggie soaked up the view rolling past. "I can't believe I'm so drawn to this place. You know I picked the Marston County cabin because of the online story about the man who built it for his bride in the 1850s. It seemed like a place that would generate stories. And it has all those amazing windows, but at night it can be a little creepy. I'm learning to be grateful for the hard things, though...the on-the-surface frightening things...and embrace the promise of the light that comes over the hills the next morning."

"That sunrise is magical," agreed Robbie.

Maggie had been tempted to let Robbie sleep in that morning in the bed beside her. Watching her children sleep was something she treasured now that she didn't get to experience it often. But she had nudged Robbie awake so she could watch with her as the sun rose and sent the shafts of light down through the branches of the oak tree.

When Maggie parked the Subaru back at the cabin and they got out, she put her arm through Robbie's. "Let's walk down to Mr. Thompson's. I want you to hear about Zeke before you go."

*   *   *

Robbie stared down at the old photograph. "Your son was handsome, Mr. Thompson."

Ollie reached for the frame and put it back on the television console where it regularly gathered dust. "He was a good boy. I hate he married that girl, but...we've all got our crosses to bear."

After Maggie and Robbie said good-bye to Mr. Thompson and walked with their arms linked back down the dirt road to the cabin, Robbie pumped Maggie with questions.

"So how did you learn about his son? Did he tell you about him when you rented the cabin?"

Maggie cast around for the right response, not wanting to lie to Robbie. "It's hard to pinpoint the exact moment." *Not really. Third night.* "Canon was the one who showed me his gravesite, behind Mr. Thompson's cottage, when he came to search the property. Then Mr. Thompson told me his son froze to death on the steps of the cabin. That's the moment I knew I wanted to tell his story."

"It's so tragic, to think he was right outside of Mr. Thompson's house and Mr. Thompson didn't know it. How are you going to balance fact and fiction on it? I mean, you're a fiction writer."

"I'm still grappling with that. Do you know who Truman Capote was?"

"Wasn't there a movie about him?"

"With Phillip Seymour Hoffman. Capote wrote a book called *In Cold Blood* based on this crime spree two men went on in the late '50s where they killed a family in Kansas. It went unsolved for a few months. Long story short, it created a new genre, which I find fascinating on this topic of fact and fiction.

"At the time, Capote claimed the book was all true—that he'd been accurate in giving a true story the flair of fiction. But in the final analysis...this is *me* talking, you know I don't have a Ph.D. on this topic...it's not possible to even report the news journalistically without bias and spin.

"A writer cannot separate who she is, at her core, from the story she is telling. I'm only beginning to try to tell Zeke's story, but almost from the first moment I could feel that it was a story about *me* as much as about *him*."

"How so?"

"I guess it comes down to this balance I told you about before, between crafting the story and listening for it. Michelangelo said he simply released the statue in the marble. He chiseled until he set it free—the image that begged to live all along.

"In thinking about why this particular story might beg to be set free, I keep going back to something Canon said about the difference in murder, killing and shooting. What constituted the definition of each.

"After reading the court reports and the police files, I think Zeke *did* kill his wife. But I don't think he made that choice in hate, like he had every right to. I think he made it in love—a displaced love, maybe. But love all the same."

Before Robbie could say anything, Maggie continued. "Or maybe that's just what I want to believe. But that is one of the great lessons of my experience at this cabin—what *I* believe matters, Robbie. It matters for *me*, if nobody else.

"When your father told me about Bethany, I had a choice. We always have a choice when someone hurts us. Most of us choose to lash out in an effort to protect ourselves. And I guess the more hurt we are—the more backed into a corner we feel—the more we lash out.

"I was so mad at your father that day I could have killed him. I thought about it. I imagined taking my hands and reaching for his throat and making him stop talking because he was shattering my heart, threatening everything that felt secure to me. But what if your father's choices, that look on the surface like he was being selfish, were ultimately an act of love that set me free? Maybe he didn't deliver his actions out of love for *me*, but why can't I chose to accept them as such?

"Glass shards falling all around me, threatening to make me bleed out...but when it was over, the door on a cage I didn't even know I was *in* was open, and I was free to walk out. Into a new life of my own making.

"And Robbie! It's the life I wanted all along. But I never had the courage to pursue it before. I lost writing along the way. I hid behind your father's money and your and Cal's schedules."

Whether he had intended to or not, Tom had given Maggie the hard gifts of freedom and self-sufficiency.

"Zeke made a choice of love and was thrown into prison for it, and yet...I wonder if he didn't finally feel free once he got there."

Zeke said as much.

"Then why would he escape?" asked Robbie.

"That's a piece I'm still working on." What Maggie wouldn't give to have Zeke back for an hour so she could ask him!

"Maybe he wanted to see his father," said Robbie. "Didn't you say his mother had just died?"

"And Zeke wasn't there for the funeral. I'm sure he felt guilty about that."

"So he came to the cottage and Mr. Thompson was drinking," continued Robbie.

Maggie took her daughter's interest as a great sign. If she could hook Robbie, the hard-to-convince accountant, on the value and merits of Zeke Thompson's story, there was hope she might hook readers, too.

Robbie continued through her audit of facts. "So Mr. Thompson didn't hear him. Zeke got the key to the cabin from the shed and came down here." Maggie and Robbie were back to the cabin now. "And he what...dropped the key?"

"Mr. Thompson said he looked everywhere for the key. It was gone from the shed, but never put in the lock."

"You could say he had a hole in his pocket," suggested Robbie.

"That's one idea."

"So he falls on the porch and dies. Mr. Thompson finds him."

"Two days later. I read about what happens to a body when it freezes to death. It doesn't take as long as you might think—scary, actually. First the extremities go numb as your heartbeat goes up. Then your heart and other organs begin to slow. You get as disoriented as if you'd been drinking. Near the end it starts to feel like you're burning up. Some people pull their clothes off. A lot of them burrow down into the snow in the body's last-ditch effort to protect itself."

This part of Maggie's research was difficult, like first reading through the case files in Canon's office. But if Maggie wanted readers to feel transported, she had to go there first. She didn't like watching Zeke die on the porch, knowing the sun rose and set twice before his father found him, or hearing Mr. Thompson's wail when he rolled the stiff, curled bundle over and saw that it was his son...his only son.

Robbie took a deep breath, perhaps seeing it also. "So Mr. Thompson takes Zeke back to the cottage..."

"And tries to bury him, but he can't dig the hole because the ground is frozen so hard. Canon comes and discovers the body in the shed. When the ground is thawed a week later, he comes back and helps Ollie dig the hole. And he tries to keep the secret. I guess that explains their bond."

Robbie shook her head. "I don't think that's all of it."

"Then what?"

"They both lost a wife."

26

Anne Lamott said first drafts are excrement. (She used a different word.) The trick is editing—trying to shape the pile into something more pleasing.

Maggie sat in Canon's squeaky chair on Tuesday afternoon behind the large desk reading the reports again about the night Tandy Wilkins died. Canon was out on calls, but Shirley told her she was welcome to sit at his desk to read the reports as many times as she wanted. The muffins seemed to have softened her a bit.

Maggie read, stopped to scribble notes on her pad, read some more, wiped tears from her eyes, then scribbled more notes. Her heart kept breaking for Zeke as she sought to crawl into his mind—have his thoughts—feel his pain.

She had spent two hours at the library earlier that morning getting an earful from Dot Jenkins about all she knew about Zeke, his rocky marriage with Tandy, and the fateful night that led to him being behind bars—same night Maggie theorized his chains were finally broken. And yes, Dot was wearing polka-dots again—white on a navy cardigan.

Facts and visuals filled Maggie's head.

Zeke drove a green '78 Camaro. It was pictured in the yard in a photograph taken the day after the murders. Canon didn't mind her seeing that one.

The house on Mill Creek was a humble brick ranch, no shrubs in the yard.

The files included reports and statements from his supervisor and co-workers at the Levi factory. High marks on his performance reviews. Everybody liked him. Supervisor Frank said he wished there were two of him...co-workers liked working with him...he was reliable...covered other people's shifts when they ran late...volunteered for overtime to make extra money.

When the ladies from the education committee had started coming into the library at 11:30 for their regular Tuesday luncheon, Dot waved a regal black woman over. "Maggie, this is the principal at the *high school*, June Hargrove. She had Zeke in *class*." Dot latched onto June's arm, and June took it in stride, looking like she'd had her arm latched by Dot *many* times before. "Tell Maggie what a good boy Zeke Thompson was, June, while I go get the pimento cheese sandwiches."

Then June Hargrove, tall, with salt and pepper hair and a warm smile, proceeded to tell Maggie what a good student Zeke had been. "He was put in my homeroom class when the Thompsons came here. Middle of the school year. Zeke was shy. But what a good writer! I remember. A good reader, too. The best students always are."

"Did you ever have Tandy Wilkins in class, Mrs. Hargrove? What kind of student was she?"

"Tandy was in that same class—sophomores. Oh, you knew it if Tandy was in the room. She had a way of drawing attention. And she was older, of course. Held back her freshman year. She lorded her street smarts over the other students. Most of them looked up to her, but for all the wrong reasons. She was worldly from a young age, if you know what I mean.

"Zeke, on the other hand, was quiet. Other students hardly knew he was there at all. I knew, of course, when I started seeing the kind of work he was capable of. I told his parents he could qualify for some nice scholarships, and he seemed interested his junior year. But by the time he and Tandy were seniors, he said he wasn't going to college and wouldn't apply for them."

"Were Zeke and Tandy friends from the beginning?"

June shook her head. "I don't think so. It surprised everybody when they started going together their senior year. I don't believe anybody saw that coming. It really upset his parents. Irene Thompson was a lovely person—a dear friend. We knew each other from way back, from the time that we were children. I feel so sorry for Ollie. He's had his share of heartache."

"I saw in the court report you testified at Zeke's trial."

"I've testified in lots of cases involving my students." June had a thoughtful wisdom about her, a certain grace, poise. Her voice was low, but carried authority. If Maggie had lived in Marston, she would want to know June Hargrove better.

June shook her head. "I don't think there's a person in this town blamed Zeke for what happened. Most of us felt sorry for him. Then it surprised everyone again he would break out of prison. He wasn't the type. You expected him to serve his time and get out early for good behavior. Then he just vanished. A rumor went around that Ollie found him dead, but...I don't know...sometimes puts me in mind of that movie...what was it? Stephen King wrote it."

"*Shawshank Redemption?*"

"That's it! You know how that main character goes to Mexico when he escapes from prison?" June nodded thoughtfully. "I wonder if Zeke did something like that, and his father started the rumor that he died so the law would quit looking for him. Some people speculated on that theory. I guess we'll never really know." June turned to Maggie then. "What do you think happened to him?"

Maggie smiled. Yes, she liked June Hargrove. It was easy to picture this woman in front of a classroom of students.

"I write fiction," said Maggie.

June smiled. "You can take liberties then."

Maggie thanked June for her time as the ladies of the education committee began to seat themselves around the room.

"Won't you join us, Mrs. Raines?" asked Dot Jenkins.

But Maggie declined. She had much to ponder, and a sudden desire to read back through the police files to see if she'd missed anything. She had nearly collected all the information readily available to her. Now Maggie needed to knuckle down and write the story.

So she walked back to Canon's office, and here she found herself, trying to drown out the hum of Amos' and Shirley's voices and the static of the radio in the main office, sitting behind Canon's desk reading through notes scribbled in his sharp, angular handwriting.

And the story began to come.

I drove home in the Camaro after a long day at the factory, stopping for take-out at the fish place on '47 between work and home because Tandy doesn't like to cook. I asked Hazel, behind the counter, if I could use the phone to see if Tandy wanted that night's special—catfish with a Cajun sauce—but she never picked up.

As the phone rang I wondered if she was out on the porch, or had gotten high again with the last of my check and was sitting on the frayed couch in the living room staring at the wall. I'd found her that way lots of times. I knew she had to be at the house—her Pinto was still at the shop after she drank too much at the Ron-dee-vu Road House last month and wrecked on the way back home.

Bob, at the factory, said he saw her there before the wreck and that she'd cozied up to a man at the bar who kept buying her longnecks. And when she sobered up, she swore to me that was all it was—the man had bought her drinks. She hadn't gone out back with him to his truck in the parking lot like Bob the liar reported. She didn't know why Bob would tell such tales on her.

I'm not a total fool. I knew pretty quick I'd made a foolish choice in Tandy. But she was my wife and I held out hope for her.

Plus, I remembered well the pain in my parents' eyes when they begged me not to rush into marriage. Like a stubborn, desperate man searching hard for self-respect, I kept thinking I could turn the sinking ship around.

I never told them Tandy was pregnant when we married. Or that she had an abortion two months later. When I demanded to know why, I'll never forget the words she flung back at me. "You should be glad, Zeke. It wasn't yours anyway."

I guess you could say things spiraled down from there.

My fate seemed sealed. I was to be Hosea rather than my namesake in the Bible. I was to learn the lesson well of a man longing for one kind of relationship, but who gets another—a flawed thing instead, that turns out to be so much less than it was intended for.

Shame clung to me pretty hard by the time I drove home with those catfish specials in the passenger seat of my Camaro.

Even driving home that night, I sensed the end was near. No dark road you ever walk down keeps winding on forever. I was tired...more tired than I'd ever been.

I thought back to that first fateful moment, that first clear crack in my future, when Tandy said, "You should be glad, Zeke. It wasn't yours anyway."

Two months into our marriage.

Tandy never was mine. Never would be. She was a rolling stone that could not gather moss. I don't reckon any man was ever meant to hold her. That was the oh-so-hard-to-resist appeal to me in the beginning—to think the mysterious, exotic Tandy Wilkins might love an ordinary guy like me.

I was seventeen, an easy target, when Tandy first turned her green eyes in my direction. By eighteen she was showing me things in the back of my daddy's pick-up I hadn't even thought to dream of. At nineteen, I was married.

When she spit those words at me, when we were still living in that trailer on Patterson down the road from Mom and Dad—You should be glad, Zeke. It *wasn't yours anyway—I packed to leave. Nineteen or not, I'd had all I wanted. Back seat fantasies or not, I didn't sign on for treatment like that.*

But Tandy cried and begged me not to. She broke down and told me about the abuses she'd suffered at the hands of her relatives. I felt sorry for her. I thought I could save her from all that—be the medicine for her broken soul, if I only tried hard enough, was patient enough.

I decided to give it another try, but only after getting her promise she'd be faithful from there on out.

Of course that didn't last.

I think I knew even then—that night she cried and I stopped packing to leave—she wouldn't be.

A cheated-on man like me, after a while, starts to build a blind eye. Either that, or something screws up so tight in his gut that it unfurls one night in a bar when he's trying to get his wife into the Camaro and get her home before she spews her sick out.

The smell of Tandy's sick became the fragrance of my life—a smell I could never quite wash from the seats of my Camaro.

Maggie set her pen down and closed the file, wondering what her true balance of fact and fiction was in her early drafts of scribbled notes.

There was nothing about Zeke's death in the file except a small notation Canon had written on a piece of paper and stuck in the back of the last folder. It was dated a week after Zeke's escape from prison.

Ollie Thompson found his son, Ezekiel Thompson, frozen on the property (cabin down the road) two days after Zeke's escape from Turney Center. Buried him in the old Patterson family cemetery behind his house. I, Canon Dale, saw the body and the grave and can verify it was Zeke.

Case closed.

27

"Prison is where I finally became free." Former student in the LIFE Program at Tennessee Prison for Women

Maggie was in town again. She wanted to look some things up on the Internet and sat at a table in the café to work on the wi-fi. She looked back over her scribbled notes—notes from talking to Dot Jenkins and June Hargrove, re-reading the case files and the newspaper articles, interspersed with her own random thoughts and conclusions, which might or might not be accurate.

She felt like she'd gotten a sense of who Zeke was and the basic events of what happened that night, but she didn't know how to best lay out the pieces. What was Zeke thinking when he came in and found Tandy with another man?

Maggie felt like she was undressing Zeke all over again by lifting the lid on the jar of his life. But...hadn't Zeke invited her to? Once again she pictured the word 'everlasting' on his chest.

Writing required a lot of thinking time...for Maggie, at least. She scribbled intermittent thoughts in her journal.

Walt Whitman said the powerful play of humanity goes on and that we each have an opportunity to contribute a verse.

Maggie held the power to resurrect Zeke's verse, let it live again, stretch out longer, like a radio signal sending waves into the unknown future. But she battled equal parts doubt and fear. Doubt in her ability to do the story—and Zeke and Mr. Thompson—justice; fear in pouring so much of her soul into a thing that might not interest others. She had to figure out how to make a living, financially. If the book didn't bring some income, she had lost time that might have been better spent going back to school, brushing up on her technical skills, networking for a more regular job.

Who knew what any book, like any life, was really meant to do once it was written and offered to the public? Maggie only knew that if she didn't write Zeke's story, nobody else was likely to. But a steadier job might have been easier, and the rewards for the labor more predictable.

The Apostle Paul said he kicked against the goads—the prods used to steer oxen. It was like he was saying, I don't know if I want the burden you are handing to me, LORD. I don't know if I believe it's really a gift in disguise. At least...I think that's what he meant.

Maggie felt the same way about writing. Why did she feel called to do this in the first place? It was too hard! She didn't come looking for this story. She had come to the cabin in Marston thinking she would make up a fictitious story about a guy named Micah Patterson. She had no way of knowing Zeke Thompson would appear.

Why? Why me, Zeke? What if I don't have the heart to tell your story?

What if I get the tone—the facts—the spirit of you and what you were trying to teach me all confused?

Maggie knew from personal experience how bad it felt to imagine the scene—your spouse offering himself to another—but to actually walk in on it? To see with your very eyes? How could Zeke not have been filled with rage in that moment? How could he not have picked up that gun and shot Tandy with it?

Maggie looked up and noticed a woman staring at her, the same woman who glared at her the first time Maggie had come to the café with Canon in January.

The woman walked over to her table. "I heard you were asking questions about Zeke Thompson."

"Are you Rynell?"

The woman's eyes flit around the restaurant as she nodded. "Tandy's sister." When her eyes came back to Maggie, a sheen covered them. "She weren't no saint. I know that. She did him wrong."

Maggie pushed a side chair out with her foot as an invitation.

"I cain't. I'm supposed to be workin.' I saw you from the kitchen and thought that was you."

"Can I meet you after work?"

Rynell looked around the restaurant again, as if deciding. The woman couldn't have been much older than Maggie, and had once been attractive. Now smoker's lines creased her face. Her hair, pulled in a tight ponytail, had been processed quite a bit.

Maggie had seen pictures of Tandy at this point. Everyone described her as beautiful, and she was. But the same sadness in the back of Tandy's eyes in the pictures was in this woman's, too.

"I get off at six," she said.

"Coffee shop on the corner okay?"

"Sure."

When Rynell walked into the coffee shop at six sharp, she sat across from Maggie and got right to it, as if she'd been sitting on information that had haunted her for years...like she'd tried to work the puzzle in her head and was pretty sure she held the final missing piece in her hands, she only needed to lay it on the table.

"I think Zeke was telling the truth. I think Tandy killed that man from Trenton."

No one ever referred to the murdered man by his name. Maybe because 'George' seemed too straight-laced a name for a man who sold heroin and had affairs with married women. Plus 'Iontha' was hard to pronounce. Everyone who ever mentioned him called him "the man from Trenton." Maggie thought that made a great title—at the least, a chapter header in the book.

"Zeke was the biggest reader I ever saw. That's all he ever wanted for his birthday or Christmas—books. Before he went to prison, Dot Jenkins told me he checked out two or three books ever' week. Not many men around here even go to the library—it's where the snooty women all go for meetin's—the high and mighty educated folk that run this town."

Rynell searched in her bag, pulled out a box of Marlboros and tapped one out. This was a no-smoking coffee shop—she glanced at the sign on the door—then she simply held it in her hand, perhaps for security.

"I cain't get my head around a reader like that killin' no one. That just don't go together. Plus, he knew she was cheatin' on him. She'd been doin' it for years. And you know why I think he didn't leave her? He *knew* she couldn't make it on her own. She would've taken up with someone like that man from Trenton and been livin' with him, and Zeke feared she'd end up dead."

Rynell clutched the cigarette a little tighter in her fingers. "Didn't make no difference in the end. And Zeke was the one paid for it."

She was quiet then. Maggie thought that was all she had wanted to say. "I really appreciate that you were willing to share that with me, Rynell." But there was more.

"I heard you were working on a book, to tell Zeke's story. I guess you'll make Tandy look bad. She was bad, but...she was my sister."

"What was she like, as a sister?"

The woman rolled her eyes. "She was a couple years older than me. Every boy in Marston County was in love with her, and her mean and self-centered as a rattlesnake! We all knew it at home, but she was sweet as honey at school. She knew how to make men love her...and boys before that.

"They teach in church that a wild child like Tandy won't get no self-respect, and that may be true, but she holds a certain power over the men. Tandy could have married anybody. I don't know why she had to go and ruin somebody's life like Zeke Thompson's.

"She ran with this one boy...what was his name? Oh, I forget...on the football team. He left Marston County right after high school. It wasn't long after that she took up with Zeke. Zeke was a year younger than her, a year older'n me. Didn't stand a chance."

Maggie looked closer at Rynell. Had this woman had feelings for Zeke? It was hard for Maggie to wrap her head around the idea. This woman seemed so aged and Zeke forever young. Tandy, too, was preserved at thirty-four, the age she was when she died.

"Tandy wasn't all bad," Rynell went on to say. "We had some good times, I guess. I wore her hand-me-downs. Tandy was real good at sewing—most people don't know that. She could have worked at the factory."

"What about Zeke? What do you remember about him?"

"Zeke?" The woman's eyes grew soft. "Lord, he looked like Leif Garrett. I had a poster of Leif Garrett on my wall from *Seventeen* magazine. He was real smart, too. I had a class with him when I was a freshman. He was new to Marston. They moved back here—his mother grew up here. He was quiet, but nice.

"He was one of those boys that nobody paid much attention to until he got to be a senior, and by then all the girls had noticed him. Here in Marston it was the football players that swaggered the most in the hallways. And Zeke...he wasn't an athlete. But he was nice-lookin'. And smart, except for the stupid choice to marry Tandy. That was an irony.

"He could have been a lawyer...a doctor...anything he wanted to be."

Maggie nodded. Yes, Rynell must have had feelings for Zeke. She wondered how much it had hurt Rynell to watch Zeke's life spiral from the sidelines.

"Were you friends? You and Zeke?"

Rynell looked startled, as if Maggie might be seeing too much, and was quick to shake her head. "I sat next to him in science class, that's all. And when we had to dissect a frog, he did all the work, so I wouldn't have to."

There was so much more Maggie wanted to ask her. Like, what did you dream of being when you were a girl? Did you marry? Have a family? Did the same demons that haunted Tandy, haunt you? Why did you choose to be different? Waitressing was a hard job, but Rynell was doing it.

Rynell tapped out her Marlboro, even though it had never been lit, and grabbed her handbag. "I was just curious about your project."

She stood to go, then turned.

"His teeth were real white, but a little crooked. And he told me one time he didn't have any feelin' in his left arm, so of course I scratched it all year when he wasn't lookin' to try to catch him in the lie. Then he told me the last day of school he really did have feelin' in that arm. I don't guess any of that matters, but it happened."

*   *   *

After Rynell told her about Zeke's love for reading, Maggie stopped back by the library to see if she could find out what kind of books Zeke checked out.

"We updated all the cards in 2000," said Mrs. Jenkins. "Went to a *scanning* system. Took me *months* to pull all those old cards out. I was going to keep them, I'm like that you know, a *historian*. Drives my husband *crazy*, but we had a summer *intern* two years ago, and when I went on vacation for a week, I came back and she had pitched those cards out with the *trash*. Didn't even *ask* me!"

"I thought it was worth a try." Maggie turned to go when she noticed the vase of fresh flowers again. "How did Canon's wife die, Dot?" Dot

Jenkins was the best source of information Maggie had found in Marston.

"*Brain* aneurysm." Dot's voice dropped low. "Canon found her in the garden. I wonder if that's not why he's kept those flowers going all these years. They're really *something* to see. From what I understand he's added to it *every* year."

Maggie studied the forsythia. She had thought death might be kinder than divorce, but maybe she was wrong. Death was so permanent. She wondered if death was as hard to forgive as betrayal.

"Canon brings me flowers all spring and summer. Those come in last *Friday*—well you were here on Monday, I told you that. He had asked me if we had the new *Stephen King* novel. He *loves* Stephen King."

"Sheriff Dale is a reader?"

"My word, *is* he? I can't keep him in books. He's *very* fond of those Jack Ryan stories. He's read *all* of those. A lot of mysteries. Oh! *Westerns.* That man is *crazy* for westerns. I believe he's read every Louis L'Amour book ever *was.*"

When Maggie reached inside her purse for her keys, Dot smacked her hands together and said, "I thought of a title for your book. 'The Murder of Tandy Wilkins.' What do you think?" Her voice dropped again. "She never *did* take Zeke's last name."

Maggie nodded. "Has a nice ring to it." Only problem was, Maggie didn't believe it was murder.

"That *would* make a good title, wouldn't it?" Dot went on. "'Course, what do *I* know? I just line the books up; I don't *write* them. I wish I *could* write them, because this town is *full* of stories. I guess every town is. Why, even this *house* has a story. I told you that one. I guess *every* town is rich with stories. And you know how folks *are* when they're telling stories. They go right to the *juice.* We hear *all* the juice here in the library. But sometimes I worry we're not writing enough of it down. So it's a good *thing,* you're doing. Let me know when the time comes. We'll do a *book* signing."

Maggie took her leave then. The pressure to finish Zeke's story was mounting.

* * *

Before she left town Maggie went to see Paul Wilkins, the doctor who served as coroner. His was the last name on her list of people to interview. Paul was a distant relative to Tandy and Rynell. His office was in the small county hospital. Maggie was catching him between his rounds, but he didn't rush his time with her. He remembered the events well.

"My grandmother married Jack Wilkins after Tandy's grandmother died. There's a lot of Wilkinses, but two sets. Jack Wilkins had fifteen children total. So we were related, but not close. Her people were a lot rougher than mine. Still, because of the family connection, I remember the details. Plus, we don't have a lot of killings like that in Marston.

"Tandy was beat up bad. I told Canon there wasn't any way Zeke could have done it, because his hands weren't bruised. That other man's were. But Zeke had gunpowder on him and that was enough to convince the jury. They brought in people from two counties over, to try to get a fair trail, but Zeke's lawyer was young, fresh out of law school. And he didn't know some of those Wayne County people knew Tandy's family."

A woman walked in with a file folder and laid it on Dr. Wilkins' desk. She nodded at Maggie and left. Everyone at the hospital, like everyone Maggie had met so far in Marston, was friendly and relaxed...welcoming...seemingly curious about her, the writer come to town to unearth a story that happened long ago.

"Was Tandy paralyzed by her injuries?" she asked.

"Yes. Spinal cord was damaged under the neck, up under the first vertebrae."

"But she didn't die from the beating she'd received."

"No. The gunshot killed her. And from all the evidence, Zeke did pull the trigger."

"What about the other man?"

"The man from Trenton? He died from two gunshots, one to the head and one to the upper chest that entered the right aorta and punctured a lung. One to the head entered over the right ear, straight to the brain. It's the one that killed him. He would have likely bled to death from the first one, but was leaned over from it when the second one hit him in the head."

Paul pointed to his body to show her. He was a lean, ruddy cheeked man in his sixties. Maggie was impressed with his memory of detail. His account perfectly matched the police and trial reports.

"Could Tandy have been the one who shot him, considering her injuries?"

"It's plausible. Zeke's lawyer tried to argue it that way. All I know is that the same person fired both those shots, in quick succession. Could have been Zeke, could have been Tandy. But the jury didn't believe it could have been Tandy seeing as how she was beat up and paralyzed."

"What about you? Do you think she could have done it?"

He gave a rueful smile. "I know for a fact she was mean enough to do it. If you're asking whether she could have physically held a gun and shot it with that damaged vertebrae, I don't know. And that's what I told the jury. She had gunpowder on her. I think she had use of her arms and hands until Zeke lifted her head, but I couldn't prove it then and I can't now. It's just that...Zeke Thompson wasn't the type to lie.

"I mean, if you're ever going to lie, it would be to save yourself from going to prison. But that's just it. Zeke pled guilty. He said he didn't mind going to prison. Seemed resigned to it. So why would he lie about that? About lifting her head and that being what severed the damaged cord?

"Zeke testified that he shot Tandy because she lacked the strength to turn the gun around and use it on herself. That takes a different set of muscles in the hand. It would have been easier for her to point it straight than to turn it back around. Zeke said it fell out of her hand and she couldn't get it back up and pointed right."

Maggie thanked Paul Wilkins for his time. As she walked back out to the parking lot she mulled over what he said.

The facts seemed pretty cut and dry—all but for the question of Zeke's true motive.

28

We fall, we get up. We lose, but we gain something in return. We love, in spite of the risk. So much of life is conquering fear to reach the gifts that lie on the other side.

Maggie cried while writing the scene.

As I came down the Mill Creek highway, I saw a red Chevy pickup with a Trenton County license plate sitting in our gravel drive. From the minute I parked the Camaro and opened the door, I could hear loud arguing coming from the house. It sounded like furniture being thrown against the wall of the back bedroom.

I ran for the side porch steps, but that door was locked, so I ran around to the front of the house. That door stood open.

As I came down the hall, two quick shots were fired. Then I was in the doorway of the bedroom. A man I didn't recognize—a man with black hair and John Travolta sideburns—was pinned to the wall by the force of the bullets, blood pouring from his chest and a hole over his right ear. I watched his body slide to the floor, red streaks and spatters staining the cream colored paint—Navajo White—a $9.99 special from Baker Hardware.

It was like walking in on a bad movie.

Tandy lay on the bed in her panties and blue t-shirt, as blood-spattered as the man, her legs splayed at odd angles. A stainless revolver was on the mattress beside her right hand. She didn't raise up when I entered or when the man from Trenton slid down.

I went to her, up on my knees on the bed. "Tandy."

I tried to lift her head but she screamed—a tragic, weak-kitten scream. "Don't!"

But it was too late. Somewhere deep down in me I knew in that moment that my lift of her head severed a cord already damaged. Paul Wilkins, Tandy's distant cousin, would confirm that later at the trial. But I didn't take time to think about it then.

"Tandy." She was like a stranger to me. All we'd been through...all the years...but in that moment it seemed I'd never known the broken body of the woman twisted beneath me.

She cut her eyes up and whispered, "Finish me."

"What do you mean?" I asked, but I knew. I knew exactly what she wanted me to do, and I knew I'd cave and do it like the coward I'd grown into, but I shook my head no.

"Finish me, Zeke," she insisted. "I can't move my legs. My hands now neither."

"Are you sure?" I lifted her arms. She didn't protest. They were limp as overcooked pasta. "Let me call an ambulance, Tandy. Let me get you some help."

"No!" she squeaked again. "Please. Finish me. Don't make me live like this, like Daisy Jenkins in a wheelchair."

Daisy Jenkins was a girl we went to school with, the niece of Dorothy Jenkins at the library. When Daisy was eight years old, she dove headfirst into a shallow pool at the Country Club. Daisy finished high school in a wheelchair. Daisy Jenkins had never been asked out. No man from Trenton had ever looked twice at her.

"I can't do that, Tandy."

"The hell you can't!"

She got foul-mouthed then. Called me things I'd been called before. "What kind of man lets his wife do such awful things to him and live? Finish me!" *Then she went from cussing to crying.* "Please, Zeke. As a final act of mercy. I beg you."

I looked down at her, my heart breaking. I started to leave, to get the phone.

"Don't leave me, Zeke!" *I'd never heard a more piteous cry coming from her throat, worse than that night two months into our marriage.*

"Put the gun in my hand if you can't do it. Please! Put the gun in my hand."

I stared down at the gun on the mattress—a Smith & Wesson, what they called a .38 Special, stainless steel, evidently the man from Trenton's because I never owned a handgun, only rifles—then lifted it and set it carefully into her hand.

It was heavy. Tandy tried to pull the trigger, but couldn't. Tears rolled over her cheeks. She twisted her face and shook her head, sobbing in frustration. Her head seemed to be the only thing she could operate.

"Don't make me endure this, Zeke. Don't! Please. Don't punish me by making me endure it."

When I wouldn't look at her she said it again. "Please, Zeke." *Then she added,* "You were better at loving than I was. I know that. You were better at everything."

I looked down at her and remember feeling tired...so tired.

"I did you wrong, Zeke. I know it and I'm sorry. I hate myself for the way I've treated you. Let me make it right. Let me go. I want it to be over."

I wanted it to be over, too.

"Won't you help me?" *she begged.*

I'd seen Tandy cry lots of times, but not like this, never like this.

The psalms David wrote say God is pleased with a contrite spirit and a bro-

ken heart. If that was true, I knew I ought to be in good standing with God, but I'd never known Tandy to be.

Not 'til now.

A voice whispered in me this was Tandy's best shot. If she went now, while she was begging, she might stand a chance, like that thief on the cross who knew he could never make it on his own. Maybe the Lord still made last-minute exceptions.

I took a deep breath. "Did you ever love me, Tandy?"

"I love you now, Zeke."

That's when I picked up the .38 Special and pulled the trigger.

*　*　*

Zeke's jury decided when he came into the house and saw his wife in compromising circumstances with another man, he first shot the man, then shot his wife. And at least one juror argued that Zeke took the time to beat Tandy between shooting the man from Trenton and shooting her. This, after Paul Wilkins testified under oath that Zeke had no bruises on either hand. The man from Trenton, by contrast, had bloody knuckles and two fractures.

Heroin was found in both the bodies. Zeke was subjected to a blood test, but no trace of drugs was found in him. He was convicted of two counts of second-degree murder and sentenced to thirty years in prison. The jury could not accept the possibility that a man might kill his cheating wife in a final act of mercy.

As Maggie assembled the pieces of the puzzle and worked on Zeke's story, she wondered often about the man in the ravine behind her cabin.

I died on a Monday—same Monday I broke out of prison. My name was Ezekiel Thompson. Everybody called me Zeke. I killed three people, but only one from hatred.

The more Maggie worked on Zeke's story, the more convinced she became that Zeke felt responsible for his mother's death, too—that his choices had "brought on the cancer" like Mr. Thompson feared. So the second person he killed was his mother, and the third was Rodriquez.

Zeke had told Maggie he was coming to the cabin because it shone with light. When he got close, had he seen Rodriquez lurking in the woods? Watching Maggie as she bathed?

The more she thought about it, the more convinced Maggie was that the *whack* she heard before Zeke knocked on her door was Zeke protecting her from danger. What did he stand to lose in killing that man if he'd already died thirty years ago? But what he stood to gain was a chance at some measure of redemption...through the telling of his story...through Maggie.

29

"Telling people you are writing a book, then letting people read it, is like standing naked on the high dive." English professor to a budding author

Saturday morning the skies were clear and, if the majesty of the sunrise was any indication, it promised to be a glorious day.

Maggie wore the teal dress.

Canon had texted the evening before. "Pick you up at ten. I'll be designated driver in case you want to try the cherry wine."

"There you go again," she texted back, "making me out to be a lush."

At 9:45 Maggie checked the mirror one more time: cute teal dress with pockets, comfortable flats, and a white shrug sweater. Easter had passed, white was allowed, even Dot Jenkins couldn't argue with that. At 9:50 Maggie shot one quick spray of perfume with notes of vanilla and citrus in the air and let it waft down on her shoulders. At 9:55 when she heard him coming up the road, she grabbed her purse and sunglasses.

Maggie had repacked the purse three times.

One more look in the mirror. Makeup kept minimal, but she did put extra time into her hair, twisting the silk of it into a loose knot on her head and fastening it with bobby pins. If a wind blew up she'd be in trouble, but her phone and the skylights promised a calm day.

Maggie locked the door and tried not to run out to Canon's car looking too excited. He got out and held the passenger door open for her. *How romantic...his squad car.* At least Canon wasn't in uniform, and Maggie was glad. Jeans and a polo shirt again, with the sheriff's office logo.

"I hope you didn't eat breakfast," he said. "You're going to need a lot of room for all things cherry." Canon really did have nice forearms.

When he closed her door, walked around the car and got in, she could smell his aftershave. Maggie felt sixteen again. "I didn't eat." How could she with all the butterflies swarming?

Before starting the car, Canon held his keys a minute. "Can I get one thing out of the way before we leave?"

Maggie's heart dropped. *He's going to tell me it's not really a date.* That was sure to put a damper on things. Instead, he leaned over and kissed her lightly on the lips. Then he put the keys in the ignition and started the car.

Maggie smiled. "Thank God that's out of the way."

Canon laughed. *What a magical sound!* The kiss and his laughter broke through the tight web of Maggie's nerves, releasing the butterflies.

Canon parked at the sheriff's office. Music floated over from Main. It was 10:30 when they arrived. Everybody in the county must have turned out for the festival. They all seemed to know Canon and wanted to talk to him. Maggie met so many new people she couldn't keep track of their names.

She recognized Dot Jenkins, of course, in cropped white pants and a polka-dot blouse—cherry—to match the theme of the day. Paul Wilkins was there, and Rynell, though the two didn't share a distant-relation hug. Becky Renco worked the ring toss with an athletic man named Steve who turned out to be her husband.

Canon put a hand on Maggie's elbow, leaned close to her ear and murmured helpful information. "Steve's the local high school football coach. They've had a rough year."

He kept moving her through the crowd. It sent a shiver down Maggie's spine to have him walking beside her, men tipping their baseball hats to him, women eyeing Maggie like she'd won the door prize. Each time Maggie thought of his kiss in the car, she bit her bottom lip to keep from breaking into a silly grin.

They stopped and talked to June Hargrove and her husband, who wore overalls and a John Deere hat.

"Ed's a farmer," said Canon, as they moved along.

Canon pointed her toward Mabel Stevens' booth first thing for that fried cherry pie, because he knew she was going to be overloaded with options. As promised, it was a slice of heaven. But Maggie liked her lunch salad even better—spinach with dried cherries, apples, pecans and feta. The balsamic dressing was perfect. Or was her favorite the cherry beignets after lunch? Who had ever even *heard* of cherry beignets?

Maggie bought jars of cherry preserves, cherry salsa, and cherry chutney to try later in her cooking, and a bag of sour cherries for Yvette because she knew her soon-to-be daughter-in-law loved them. And she did try that cherry wine and bought bottles for the kids and a couple for herself. By 2:30 Maggie's feet and stomach begged for relief and Canon's forearms bulged carrying her shopping bags.

"You about ready to go sit by the pond and fish?" he said low under his breath as he dodged running children on the sidewalk. The music and revelers were dying down. Canon had planted his yearly tree at noon, adding to a row lining the east of the courthouse.

"So ready," said Maggie.

They made their way back to the car. Canon checked on things in the office while she settled her bags in the back, then he drove them out of town, turning off on a side road she'd never been down before.

Maggie was so tired she wanted to close her eyes, but she didn't want to miss the countryside. This was the route to Canon's farm. She wanted to experience it. Corn fields...hay fields...newly planted rows of soybeans passed outside her windows.

Canon pointed. "That's Ed and June's farm there." Acres of Ed's young corn lined the road.

After a while they turned off again, onto a dirt road this time, winding past houses of all stripes—trailers, red bricks, white cottages, a log house here and there. In the distance she saw a yellow farm house approaching and put a hand on his arm, "Oh, look at that one, Canon! That's the loveliest one yet."

"I'm glad you think so." He pulled into the long drive.

"This is your place." She said it as a statement, the way he typically did.

He smiled, looking satisfied...looking happy. "This is the farm."

There was instantly something different about him. Watching his eyes as he looked out over his farm, Maggie sensed this was where Canon felt his greatest peace. The Canon she had come to know ran constant surveillance and kept up his guard. Even in town at the festival, Canon's eyes had roved over the revelers non-stop, his head quick to turn at any loud sound. But here, coming up the driveway to his place, his shoulders relaxed.

The farm was every Tennessean man's dream...every Tennessean woman's, too. Yellow house with white wraparound porch. Matching garage, detached. Red barn set well back and off to the side. Pond in the distance. Cows on the hillside. Two horses she could see. And a profusion of flowers around the house with more dotted along the sweeping white fence lines.

How did he keep all those fences painted? There were the rows of buttercup stalks, a few lingering blooms on the forsythia, and groupings of peonies and oak leaf hydrangeas in side sections near the house, exactly where Maggie would have planted them. She recognized the stems for lilies popping along the fencerow, with sections of iris.

Canon stopped the car so she could take it in. "This is not the original house, but it was built to look like it. The original house only had porches on the front and back, not all sides. That one burned in a fire that started in the chimney."

And killed your grandfather, Thomas Buchanan Dale, the second, who went by "Tom." But your grandmother, Martha, survived, because she was visiting a sick friend. Tom was the only one home at the time.

Maggie had read about the fire in the special section of Brad Bybee's paper but she didn't mention this to Canon.

"My father rebuilt it as an anniversary gift to my mother..."

Whose name was Sadie.

"...but when her folks died, Mom and Dad moved into their house in town and I moved out here. After Dad died she came back out here and lived with me for a while, but when her health started failing, we moved her to Shirley's."

Canon looked at Maggie. "You do know Shirley's my sister."

"Took me a while, but yes." They'd seen Shirley and her husband, Bob, at the festival, too, and their youngest son, Keith, a stocky boy who played on Steve Renco's football team.

Canon grinned. "It's a family business. Shirley and Bob's oldest son, Kyle, is a senior at UT Knoxville. Studying criminal justice. Anyway, Mom died a couple of years ago. Stroke."

"My mother has dementia."

Canon frowned. "I'm sorry to hear that. What about your father?"

"He died eight years ago. Heart attack."

Maggie and Canon still hadn't talked about Canon's wife's death. He knew she knew, they'd been to the festival, after all. He had looked at Maggie and smiled before he dug the hole during the tree dedication.

Maggie stood by Shirley, who didn't say much other than, "Turned out to be a nice day." To which Maggie replied, "Yes, it did."

Canon drove onto a concrete patio in front of the garage and parked. The door to his workshop at the side of the garage stood open. He waved her over to see it. Maggie could smell the sawdust long before she stuck her head inside. Pieces of wood...table saws...a few paint and varnish cans lining one wall.

Next, Canon walked her through the yard, pointing out a small fruit orchard, the pond, then showed her the flower gardens. The remains of last year's vegetable garden, not yet tilled for this year, sat past a white gazebo. "That's my next project," said Canon.

The side porches held cushioned wicker furniture, the front and back porches white rockers and swings. Canon took her in the back door, into the kitchen, after they'd made a circle of the house. The inside was as lovely and manicured as the grounds. Maggie wondered if it always looked this nice, or if he cut the grass and mopped the floors because he wanted to impress her. The kitchen floor was tile the color of clay pots, the rest of the flooring lightly finished wood.

Maggie followed him in, marveling that a man who lived alone so long could have such an inviting home. The house was square, not overly large. "May I?" she asked, longing to see the layout.

"Of course!" Canon waved her on.

Coming in the back door, the kitchen was on the right—white cabinets, some with glass doors—with a large wooden butcher block island in the middle. There was nowhere to sit down and eat in the kitchen, but as Maggie walked through it, she saw there was a door that went out to a side porch with a table. An open area behind the staircase led to the formal dining room, then back around to the living room on the front. The windows were lovely. The fireplace sat across from the end of the staircase and was viewable from the kitchen.

That seemed a smart design, heat could roll right up the staircase. The wooden stairs had polished rails on both sides. That was it: laundry, kitchen, dining and living rooms on the main floor, open, simple, clean, and homey. It was quite a contrast to the house Maggie walked out of last August, but exactly the feeling she had wanted.

She made a circle of the downstairs and came back to him as he leaned against the butcher block island, arm crossed, watching her with amusement.

He looked down at her dress. "That okay for fishing?"

"Are you kidding? I fish in this dress all the time!"

"Alright," he laughed, "but you might want to borrow better shoes." He reached into the laundry room.

Maggie was enthralled by the kitchen. When he came out of the laundry holding a navy pair of rubber boots Maggie said, "You never told me you lost a wife, Canon." She felt it strongest here, standing in the kitchen.

He set the boots on the floor beside her. "That was a long time ago."

"You do all the cooking in a kitchen like this?"

He nodded. "I kept it updated for my mom, she liked to cook. And Shirley's real bossy. We have Thanksgiving dinner here every year. It's good for that. She lets me know when she thinks I need improvements." He smirked. "To the house, or otherwise."

A convection oven of Maggie's dreams was built into a brick section in the corner, with a warmer oven below it. If this was Maggie's kitchen the only thing she'd change would be to add a sink to the island and install granite countertops. The ones here now were getting dated. And it could have used a larger refrigerator for those Thanksgiving dinners.

Maggie stopped herself. What was she doing picturing herself in this kitchen, making updates, cooking holiday meals? But she couldn't stop herself from running a hand along one of the countertops, admiring the glass doors of the cabinets above it. Lights were needed under the cabinets, too. A kitchen could never have too many lights.

Canon went to the refrigerator and pulled out carrots, squash, and peppers. "There's potatoes and onions in the pantry, and pecans and breadcrumbs to coat the trout. I'll heat up the grill when we get back from fishing."

"I don't think I'll ever be hungry again," Maggie confessed.

"It's a hike to the pond. You'll work up an appetite."

Maggie slipped off the cute flats she'd worn to the festival and looked down inside the rubber boots. "Do you have a pair of socks I could borrow?"

He went upstairs to get them—men's white sports socks.

"Sorry." He handed them to her, eyeing her lips again. "Best I can do."

Maggie couldn't help but think of Zeke as she pulled them on and stepped into the boots.

"Where's my pole?"

"We'll cut you a pole. There's a stand of bamboo out there. It makes the best poles."

He pulled a tackle box from the laundry room that rattled with line and lures, and threw a quilt over his arm.

They walked out the back door, off the porch, and out to the pond. Canon laid the quilt on the grass for her to sit on and readied her pole. An hour later, Maggie had two good-sized trout.

Clouds began to roll in.

On the way back to the house they agreed Maggie would prepare the food inside while Canon fired up the grill out by the gazebo. She made an olive oil dressing, let the vegetables marinate in it while she coated the fish, then they grilled them on wire racks.

Night was just before falling when the food was ready. They carried it inside, fixed their plates, then took them back out to the table under the gazebo. Canon lit candles. The first drops of rain held off until they finished.

Maybe it was the way the wind picked up, stirring Maggie's senses. Or maybe it was the glow of the candles during dinner...the last of the cherry wine Canon poured...or Maggie's bare feet running through the grass after she pulled her boots and socks off. Whatever it was, Maggie felt alive as the rain caught her on her run back to the porch and the wet droplets drummed her body.

Then she was inside the house and Canon burst through the door behind her, his laughter welling up from deep down inside his chest, then he was behind her, his left hand brushing the waist of the teal dress, circling it, his right hand pushing wets strands of fallen hair off her shoulder and neck to make room for his mouth.

Maggie stood paralyzed at the butcher block counter, Canon's lips pressing against her damp skin, his tongue licking raindrops off the backs of her ears. She couldn't move, couldn't breathe with both his hands sliding around her waistline now, turning her until her lips met his.

Maggie's hands ran over his rain-slick arms, her body so grateful for his interest, responding despite the more sensible voices in her head. She hardly knew this man! No...she'd wanted this for weeks...months now...since staring at his forearms sitting in his office, the room so stark and bare compared to the warmth of his home...his body...his lips.

The wildness of the wind! The way the rain caressed her skin as she ran for the house—the way the moistness of it still trilled on the surface of her limbs. Now Canon was lifting her, setting her up on the island, shoving the vegetable shavings to the side, his hands pulling her knees forward, closing the distance between them.

As she ran her fingers through his dampened hair, she felt his thumbs grazing over her hip bones. Her body grew hopeful, her lips on fire kissing his, then his were traveling the open neckline of her blouse, and God help her, she wanted them to.

A radio buzzed.

Canon stilled, his breath hot on her collarbone.

He took a slow step backward and reached for the radio. Maggie hadn't realized there was a scanner in the room. It sat on a narrow built-in desk under the staircase where mail collected.

She straightened the hem of her dress and wondered if she should hop off the island, her heart still pounding against the teal fabric. What had become of Maggie's sweater?

Canon put his back to her. "What have you got?"

"Domestic. Drexlers' place. You're the closest. Shots fired. Call came in from a neighbor instead of Tina this time."

"I'll get over there."

Canon set the speaker down and turned to Maggie.

"I'm sorry about this." His sheepish look was more pronounced than normal. "Hope I didn't take liberties."

"Don't apologize, Canon. It means the world to me to think that you..." Maggie was going to say "want me."

Canon was back to the butcher block island in two strides, kissing her again, confirming without words that he did, in fact, want her.

It felt so good to be wanted.

"Will you wait for me?" he whispered.

"I don't have a car."

He smiled. "Smart thinking on my part. Make yourself at home."

Then he was pulling a bullet-proof vest from a hook in the laundry, strapping it on, looping a holster through his belt for a gun.

And he was gone.

30

We spend a lot of time with our oars in the water. Every now and then—exquisite and brief—we find our rhythm. And for that moment we are perfectly in tune with all that's shining in the universe.

Maggie's heart was as stirred by the image of Canon strapping on his gun as she had been moments prior with his lips traveling the edge of her neckline. Fear bled into her heightened emotions as quickly as pleasure departed.

She didn't know how long she sat on the butcher block island—long enough to become aware of her own breathing—long past the wail his siren made as his squad car sped down the gravel drive out onto the road, trailing into the wet night.

Finally, she eased herself off and put her feet on the cold tile floor. Maggie was still barefoot.

Canon might have left the house, but she could still feel his presence, the spirit of his late wife, and the spirits of generations of his family that had seeped into the walls of the farmhouse. They had bled into the very land. Maggie felt it the moment she'd gotten out of Canon's car when they first arrived.

Slowly, Maggie circled the downstairs again inspecting furniture, pictures, wondering who picked out this wallpaper, that paint color. Maggie could tell which knife Canon used most by how worn the slit was in the block on the counter. Did the old-fashioned dishes in the corner cabinet belong to Canon's mother? Grandmother? Had any items survived the fire? Or had Rita picked these dishes in her registry? Who first decided to place the green pillows on the sofa? Did Rita crochet the cream-colored throw on the back of the blue-checked couch? Who had worn the navy boots Canon kept in the laundry?

The laundry was covered in white bead board and well placed for coming in from the yard. It had a shower, toilet, nice counter that matched the ones in the kitchen, with a deep sink at one end.

Maggie padded upstairs, but didn't closely inspect his bedroom or bath that opened off it. That seemed too personal. But she could tell which one of the three rooms was his and did step inside to look at the red-haired woman dressed in eighties clothing hanging on one of the walls—same woman who smiled with a younger Canon on a side table in the hallway alongside several pictures of Shirley and her family over the years. Maggie looked closer. Shirley had given birth to twins, a boy and a girl. But by the time Keith had come along, only Kyle as a toddler was in the photos. Kyle graduating from high school. A younger Keith sporting a youth league football jersey, standing with a younger Bob and Shirley.

A man and woman Maggie recognized as Canon's parents from the news story hung on the wall in the upstairs hallway. Another frame featured only his father wearing a deep brown jacket pinned with stars and medals.

As she turned to leave with a final glance inside the bedroom, she noticed a picture without a frame lying loose on his nightstand. She stepped over to look. It was her, standing in the ravine behind the cabin bundled in her hat and jacket.

A warm wash traveled down Maggie's neck toward her naked feet on the hardwood floor. This must be the picture Becky Renco was talking about that day in the sheriff's office. Canon brought it home with him. Left it lying on his nightstand.

Maggie's warm wash turned suddenly cold.

Seeing Canon pull on a bullet-proof vest had been sobering. Maggie didn't like that sight at all, or knowing he was headed where shots were fired. Visions of the fight he'd broken up in the parking lot on New Year's Eve came back to her.

Maggie told herself Canon had a thirty-two-year tenure dealing with bad behavior. He knew what he was doing. But she couldn't seem to stop the cold finger of fear twining itself through her chest cavity, thickening, especially when she went back out into the hall and her eye landed on the picture of his father in his uniform again.

She kept moving, kept inspecting the house, reading the story of Canon Dale from the material items that surrounded him. Nearly an hour passed before Maggie went back outside. The rain had stopped. She gathered the dishes, brought them in, and washed them. She found her white sweater, damp and cold, and hung it in the laundry room.

Another hour went by. Still no Canon. How long did it take to resolve a domestic dispute?

Maggie didn't know what to do, didn't know who to call. The police radio in the kitchen was silent. Canon must have turned it off. She reached for the knob to turn it back on, then stopped. If something had happened to him, she didn't want to learn about it from eavesdropping on the radio.

So she waited.

Maggie curled herself on the checked couch in the living room, pulling the cream throw over her, feeling lonely, cold, scared. Then the ringing of the house phone was waking her—an old rotary dial on the kitchen wall.

She lifted the receiver with one hand, covering her mouth with the other, to stifle the moans she knew would come if the news was bad.

"Mrs. Raines?" Shirley drawled into the phone, "Canon's at the hospital."

What was Shirley saying?

"Just a graze, but it's protocol. Paul gave him somethin' and he's not supposed to drive. He said tell you there's a set of truck keys hanging on a hook in the far left kitchen cabinet. You're welcome to use 'em to get yourself back to your own car. He'll come pick the truck up later."

Silence on the line. Shirley was waiting for her to say something.

"Is Canon okay?"

"He will be. Lord knows, he's been nicked plenty of times before."

"What happened?"

"Tim claims it was an accident, that the gun just went off."

The clock on the microwave said it was 3:05.

Maggie couldn't drive back to the cabin without checking on Canon, even though that's what it sounded like Shirley was suggesting. "He's at the hospital in town? He'll be there the rest of the night?"

Shirley didn't sound like she appreciated having to call Maggie. Maybe she didn't like Maggie being at the farmhouse. "You must have been asleep," she said flatly.

Maggie nodded. "On the couch," she felt the need to explain.

"Well...Canon asked me to call you, so I called you." The phone went silent. Shirley was done talking to her.

Maggie stared into the dimly lit kitchen for several minutes, wondering what to do.

Suddenly she flipped on every light switch she could find—in the kitchen, in the laundry, in the dining and living rooms. She couldn't bear the darkness with so many ghosts lurking in the house. Then Maggie prowled until she found what was needed to make Canon a quiche.

Then, as dawn broke over the horizon, she used the truck keys to drive back into town.

Shirley was sitting on a plastic chair outside Canon's room when Maggie walked in. "You made him a pie? After all that sweet stuff at the festival?"

Maggie let the criticism pass. Shirley had a rough night, too. "It's a quiche."

Shirley scrunched her nose. "I doubt he's ever had quiche in his life."

As Shirley reached for the pie plate and looked suspiciously under the foil, Maggie peeped through the narrow window at Canon. He was asleep, a thick bandage wrapped around his head.

"Bullet grazed the back, behind his left ear. Lord help...same side as Daddy."

Shirley called her father 'Daddy'?

"Paul said gettin' shot in the head is like havin' it slammed against a wall. Concussion risk, even if it was only a graze. That's why he wouldn't let him drive home, much as Canon hollered to."

"How long has he been asleep?" Maggie whispered.

Shirley set the quiche on the chair beside her. "Not long. He makes about the worst patient you ever saw, plus they didn't want him to sleep right away because of the concussion risk."

This was the most Shirley had ever said to her. Maggie looked past Shirley back down the hallway, toward the door she'd come in. Early morning light shafts streamed in on the tile floor. Maggie felt a sudden urge to run. Get in that old truck, hightail it back to the cabin and pack her bags. Burn the manuscript she'd been working on in the metal barrel out back. Get out of here. Never come back.

The same gathering wave that hurtled toward Maggie when Tom sat her down on the sofa in August rushed toward her again. She had tried to work out the details while cooking. Cooking—the act of creation—always helped her think.

Drop off the quiche as a last goodwill gesture. Leave the keys with Mr. Thompson. Tell the old man she was sorry, but she couldn't tell his son's story after all. It was too hard. She lacked the constitution to stomach *this* much truth and fiction. The world had enough pain without her drawing attention to more. Best to bury the past in the ground and leave it. Stay safe in a high-rise condo. Alone. Because she wasn't buying into the old adage that it was better to have loved and lost than never to have loved at all. Better to wall off one's emotions and never get hurt again. That's what Maggie was thinking as she eyed the light shaft coming in on the institutional flooring down the hallway.

Shirley must have seen the struggle on her face, because she suddenly spat, "Why did you bring him food if you're just going to walk out of his life!"

Her words came out so uncharacteristically fast, they stopped Maggie as if the woman had slapped her.

Shirley eyed Maggie up and down. "Canon don't need some quiche-bakin' writer, a *city woman*, complicatin' his life. But I could tell from before I even met you—from the way he talked about you—you meant something to him. I don't know what you did, what kind of spell you wove so fast, but there it is. He *likes* you. If you go and break his heart..."

Shirley's voice broke. She scrunched her nose again.

To keep from crying?

Maggie didn't know what to say. Shirley was right, Maggie had been planning her escape. Because Maggie only had one heart herself, and was trying to protect it.

Shirley thrust a finger at Canon's hospital room. "That man has been through hell and back. You know why I think he never let himself love anybody in all these years since Rita? Because of this right here—this thing that's making you think of bolting. Because it's *hard* what he does. He's watched people act bad and hurt one another for thirty-two years. And he's had nothing to counter that 'cept the farm."

Shirley's nostrils breathed fire. She and Maggie stood awkwardly beside the two plastic chairs in the hallway, avoiding one another's eyes, not speaking.

Finally, Shirley said. "I'm the one they call. Lord, I'm used to it. I'm a Dale. Doing hard things is in our bloodline. But I don't know that you've got the stomach for this sort of thing."

Maggie didn't like Shirley smelling her fear.

Okay. *Yes.* She was rattled to see Canon lying in a hospital bed look-ing vulnerable. She might have enjoyed the feel of his thumbs over her hip bones, but Maggie was sensible enough to know passion was one thing, love was another. Anyone could muster passion in a heated mo-ment, especially two touch-starved people. But not just anyone would sit outside your hospital room or clean your vomit from the seats of their Camaro.

Love and passion were not the same things at all. But for Shirley to suggest Maggie couldn't go the distance? *The nerve!*

Maggie took a deep breath, willing her panic and anger to simmer down. *Shirley had a rough night, too.*

She glared at Shirley, picked up the quiche, and went to the door of Canon's hospital room. When Maggie looked inside she saw a man who made her heart clench. Tom. Zeke. Canon. All three knocking her off balance.

If Tom hadn't made his choices...if Zeke hadn't told me to leave the light switch down...I might never have met Canon Dale.

Maggie looked over her shoulder at Shirley. "I can do hard things, too. You don't own the market on that."

Shirley nodded with deliberation—or was it satisfaction—then reached for her purse. "Delores Hinton is on duty at the nurse's station. She knows to call me if there's any change."

Maggie watched her go down the hall and out the door. Then she leaned her forehead against the glass and studied Canon again.

What would Maggie have found herself doing today if Tom hadn't offered Bethany a job? Trim those hydrangeas by the pool? Rake out the winter leaves so the perennials could breathe?

Bethany had given birth to a healthy baby girl. Robbie called to tell her shortly after leaving the cabin on Monday. And there lay Canon in a hospital bed, never having had the chance to be a father before finding his wife dead in the yard.

Maggie didn't know how long she stood watching him before a nurse came down the hallway.

"Are you here to see Canon?"

Maggie nodded.

The nurse sniffed the air. "Did you bring him breakfast? That was nice."

When the nurse pushed the door open, Maggie followed her in. Canon stirred and immediately reached for her hand. "Maggie."

Delores checked the fluid bag and instrument readings on the machines next to Canon's bed. "Look at that heartbeat reading," she muttered as if to herself. "Went up a notch." She raised her brows. "Must be that good-smelling breakfast this pretty lady's done brought you."

"It's quiche," said Maggie.

Canon's eyes never left Maggie's as he reached for it.

"Do you want to know what's in it?" she asked.

Canon shook his head. "Not if you made it. You mind getting me a fork, Delores?"

"I'll bring two." The nurse smiled and left.

"You found the truck key?"

Maggie nodded.

"I'm sorry about this."

Canon looked as meek as Maggie had ever seen him, in a patterned hospital gown, with those strong, hair-covered forearms showing. She could tell Canon was going to be fine physically...only his heart was still at risk.

"Don't be," she whispered.

"Some date I am, to leave the girl home by herself."

Maggie bit her lip. "On the butcher block island, no less."

She was a goner when his look turned sheepish then serious. "It was the best part of my evening."

"Mine, too."

He stared at her a minute. "How long will you be in Marston this time?"

"I need to go back today."

"Oh." She watched his face fall. "Least you got to see the cherry trees in bloom."

"Yes." Maggie smoothed the top of Canon's hair. *Take that, Shirley Weems.* Twenty-four hours ago Maggie wouldn't have had the boldness to touch Canon like this, but now she knew she loved him—she'd made the decision in the hallway. How could she not, knowing he loved her?

Love changed everything.

"I got to see the cherry trees in town and the dozen or so out at your place. And the pond, and the peonies, and the gazebo. The sun comes up over your fruit orchard."

Light was coming back into his eyes. "Did you watch it from the porch?"

Maggie shook her head. "Saw it when I went out to get the truck."

Canon held the quiche in one hand, but still held hers with the other. "Maybe you can sit out there with me sometime to watch it. That's the best view." He pulled her hand to his lips.

Delores walked back in. "I declare, Canon Dale! How you goin' to recover if you keep gettin' that heart rate up?" She set the forks on his side table, shot Maggie a wink, then left again.

"Are you sure you feel like eating, Canon?"

He let go of her hand and peeled the foil off the quiche. "Of course I feel like eating."

They ate directly from the pie plate. Delores brought them each a cup of coffee and offered Maggie a handful of liquid creamers. "Wasn't sure how you liked it. This is the best we've got. I know he's picky about his coffee. He's been here enough times." She threw Canon a look.

Paul Wilkins came breezing in, obviously having had his morning coffee. "How you feelin', Canon?"

"Fine!" Canon barked. "Get me out of here."

"You can go by ten if your vitals stay strong, but will you take it easy for a couple of days?" Paul smiled at Maggie and checked under Canon's bandage. "On second thought, I don't like this swelling. Let me keep you here one more day."

"Good Lord, Paul! You know I'm not fragile." Canon scowled.

"You're bound to have a splitting headache."

Canon didn't deny it. Paul looked at Maggie. "Best thing for him is rest."

"You're right. I should go." Maggie had settled herself on the edge of his bed to share breakfast, but now stood.

"No." Canon reached for Maggie's hand again.

"Yes," insisted Paul. "Or I'll keep you *two* more days."

Maggie wrapped the leftovers back up.

"Can I keep that?" asked Canon. "It's so much better than the food around here."

Delores had come back in. "I take offense at that. But I'll put it in the mini-fridge at the nurse's station. Only because you're the sheriff."

"Don't do me any favors," said Canon.

"Well...I did appreciate you not giving Julie that speedin' ticket." Delores swept out of the room with Canon's quiche.

Maggie squeezed his hand. "I need to be home for a few days, but I'll be back."

"How soon?"

"I don't know exactly."

"Alright." Canon braced his jaw like a man who'd seen his share of disappointment, like a man trying not to get his hopes up.

That's why Maggie, ignoring Paul, who was still in the room, kissed Canon solidly on the mouth before walking out.

31

Frederick Buechner said "...humanity is like an enormous spider web, so that if you touch it anywhere, you set the whole thing trembling...

As we move around this world... we too are setting the great spider web a-tremble. The life that I touch for good or ill will touch another life, and that in turn another, until who knows where the trembling stops or in what far place and time my touch will be felt." Frederick Buechner, The Hungering Dark

Before Maggie left for Nashville, she stopped at Mr. Thompson's. She stood on his porch breathing in the fresh fragrance of April following the night's rain.

"I may take a little longer before coming back, Ollie. I need some time to think—time to work on all the pieces of information in my head. But before I go, would you mind if I asked you a couple more questions about Zeke?"

"Of course! Come in." He held the door open.

Notebook and pen in hand, Maggie took her spot in Irene's old recliner.

"I'd like to write this story from Zeke's perspective, from his point of view. Do you mind if I take that angle?"

Mr. Thompson thought a minute. "I don't mind. I imagine that's not easy, never having known him."

Maggie had decided not to tell Mr. Thompson about the two days she spent with his son. It was a decision born of compassion. If she told him, he might or might not believe her. Then he'd wonder why Zeke hadn't come to see him. The most compassionate way she could offer Zeke back to Mr. Thompson was to resurrect him on the page. She didn't think she would ever tell anyone except Canon about actually having met Zeke.

"After all this research, I almost feel like I did know him." She glanced over at Zeke's picture on the console. "But nobody knew your son as well as you did, Ollie. I'd love to hear why you think he stayed with Tandy."

The old man nodded. "I think Zeke knew pretty quick he'd made a mistake with Tandy. He was star struck with her at first, but...he knew. Me and Irene—Irene especially—hoped Tandy might change after they married. But it's a hard thing for a person to change...to outgrow their raisin'.

"On the one hand I was proud of Zeke for sticking it out. His mother stuck it out with me. Lord knows I tried to give up the bottle. If Irene had ever given up on me, I don't know what I would've done. She saved my life. Her faith in me is the only reason I'm here.

"You know, young people today, they don't seem willin' to put up with much before they leave. You could argue some of them have a right to—I reckon Zeke had a right to. But there's a part of me that's proud of him, all the same."

Maggie felt a pang of guilt. Should she have stayed with Tom? Forgiven his actions and tried to work it out? It wasn't the first time she'd asked herself those questions. But Tom didn't ask her to stay. Not once. Would she, if he had? She didn't know the answer. A person could always speculate, but until you found yourself actually living through a moment like that, you didn't know what you'd do, which path you'd choose.

"I'll never forget the call we got that night," Mr. Thompson went on. "Canon was a deputy then, real young, but it was him that called. 'Ollie,' he said, 'I got some bad news. Zeke's been arrested for murder.' I dropped the phone. Irene, she...she'd had a bad feelin' for weeks. Said she knew death was in the air.

"She grabbed the phone up and said, 'What is it? What's happened to our boy?' And when Canon told her she cried—cried—not for Tandy bein' dead, but for Zeke bein' caught up in it. Sometimes I wonder if that's what give her the cancer."

Maggie knew then she was on the right track with her opening lines. The story was knitting itself together, she just had to keep pace with it. Irene was diagnosed with breast cancer two months after Zeke was arrested, and died six months before his escape. Maggie had an Excel spreadsheet with all the dates.

"Zeke said that man from Trenton beat Tandy before he got there," continued Ollie. "And he was tellin' the truth. I *know* he was tellin' the truth. He never lied to us, not one time. He told the truth even when it broke our hearts.

"Tandy shot the man, right before Zeke got there, then she begged him to finish it. She was paralyzed, you see. From the beatin' that man had given her.

"Zeke never would have beat her like that, then shot her. She'd cheated on him lots of times and he never laid a hand on her for it. But the courts didn't believe a man would put up with that. So they convicted him. Gave him a thirty-year sentence, which was as light as it could have been. State of Tennessee calls for at least fifteen years on a second-degree murder charge. I didn't know if you knew that. I didn't know that before this happened.

"Zeke was at Riverbend in Nashville the first two years, then got transferred to Turney Center because he wasn't no trouble. Read everything he could get his hands on. Was taking college classes by mail, even a Bible correspondence course."

Mr. Thompson got a far off look in his eye. Maggie gave him a minute, before asking, "Will you be upset with me if I take some artistic license that differs from your memory of how things really were, Ollie?"

Maggie knew from talking to Canon, and from her own experience, that everyone's version of the truth was a little different. It wasn't her intent to manipulate any of the facts she'd learned about Zeke's life. But there were holes, and the only way to fill them was with her own imagination.

"What kind of artistic license? Are you going to say he didn't kill her?" Mr. Thompson's face clouded. "I don't think Zeke would have liked that, if you made him out to be more innocent than he was."

"No, I don't intend to change any of the information that the evidence points to. But I've worked on this enough to know there will be moments when I'm putting it all together that I'll need to fill in the gaps. I may not fill them in with my words the way you've filled them in with your own thoughts."

He nodded. "I see what you're sayin.'" Mr. Thompson leaned toward her rocker and patted her hand. "I trust you, Maggie."

Ollie Thompson had no reason to place such faith in her. His trust made Maggie all the more determined to do her best with the story. "I've had a promising conversation with an agent. The reason I need to go home today is to meet with her. Then I plan to sequester myself until the first draft is ready. When I get the manuscript in decent shape, can I bring you a copy? I'd like to have you read it before I submit it to a publisher."

"See?" Ollie raised a crooked shaking finger at her. "That tells me right there you're the person for this job, Maggie. That's mighty good of you. Not required, but mighty good."

"One of the biggest holes I have is why Zeke escaped. I understand how he got out, but several people have mentioned that he didn't seem like the type to try to escape from prison. Can you shed any light on that?"

"I wish I knew, Maggie, because if he had stayed put, he would have been out by now. He could have buried me, 'stead of me buryin' him. Sometimes at the prisons—a lot of folks don't know this—but the guards just don't come in. It had come a big snow and ice storm that day. Lot of the guards couldn't get to work. Zeke worked in the laundry, they all have jobs in prison. Don't get paid anything much for 'em, but it helps 'em buy toiletries and food from the commissary. They have commissary, like in the army.

"His mother had already died, and I guess he was worried about me. He evidently came here first, but I was passed out cold. Canon told me later." Mr. Thompson's lips quivered and he squeezed his eyes hard against the memory. "Canon found marks on my front door that proved Zeke came here first. He tried to get in. But I had the place locked up tight. There was a key in the shed—the shed never had no door on it—to that cabin down the road. That key was gone when we looked for it later."

Maggie and Ollie had been over this part of the story, but Ollie must have needed to tell it again. Maggie let him. She wondered how many times he'd combed over the details in his memory, as curved and shaking now as his fingers.

"I found Zeke curled up on the porch two days later, froze to death. The temperature dropped down into the single digits then exactly like it did that first week you stayed there. Christmas was on a Thursday that year, and Zeke escaped the next Monday night. I found him late in the day, last day of the year.

"I brought him home. Didn't tell nobody, but Canon stopped by. You know, Canon found his wife dead. That's an awful thing, to see someone slumped over and to realize it's the person you love most in the world.

"When the ground thawed back out, Canon helped me bury him in that old family cemetery behind the shed. Those other people out there aren't even our family. It goes way back, to the people who first built that cabin.

"I didn't put a marker on Zeke's grave for years, but I got worried something would happen to me and nobody but Canon would know where he was. So a few years ago I got Nate Carlson to make a head-stone. That's a guy in town who works for the funeral home.

"Canon comes by here to check on me ever' time it snows. It's good of him. He's a good sheriff." Mr. Thompson looked at Maggie slyly, "I think he's got an eye for you."

"I've got an eye for him."

Mr. Thompson smiled and put a gnarled hand on her arm. "I guess that knocks me out then."

Maggie and Canon were going to have to adopt him, seeing as how they were short on parents. "This may seem like a strange question, Ol-lie, but something else I haven't found information on is whether Zeke had any special markings or tattoos. Do you know if he did?"

Mr. Thompson's face screwed up. "Not that I know of. He never had any tattoos I ever heard about."

Maggie hadn't been able to confirm Zeke had the 'everlasting' tattoo running under his collarbone, but she knew it was there. She saw it. Yet nowhere in any of the information she'd combed through had it been mentioned. Seemed like a father would have known if his son had a blue word stamped across his chest, that he would have seen it peeking from a shirt when they sat in the recliners and talked.

She stared at Zeke's picture, then studied Mr. Thompson. How would it feel to watch your son be sent to prison? Maggie thought of Yvette, Cal's fiancé. She was a sweet girl. Maggie liked her. And she liked Mark. She wondered what the future held for her children. She also wondered how much it would have hurt her father to see her and Tom divorce, and to know that Tom had an affair with a girl his own daughter's age.

"Do you know what 'Ezekiel' means, Maggie?" Mr. Thompson asked suddenly.

Maggie shook her head. "Doesn't the 'el' mean God?"

"*God strengthens.* That's what Ezekiel means. Ezekiel was Irene's favorite book in the Old Testament. She liked that story about the bones. Our boy never did have a middle name. Irene said that one was enough.

"I don't know if folks will want to read about Zeke or not. I don't know if it will make any difference to anybody. But he was a good boy. And I like to think his life wasn't lived in vain."

Mr. Thompson studied his hands. "Took all the fight out of Irene for battling the cancer when Zeke was sent to prison. He was our only child, only child the Lord ever blessed us with."

The old man's voice caught then. It was an awful sound—the sound of an elderly man's heart breaking—the evidence in the pull of the vocal cords. Maggie wondered how many breaks there had been over the years, and marveled that the human heart had the capacity to keep on breaking.

"I hated I couldn't bury him in the cemetery where Irene's buried. I guess I was trying to protect him...or keep him close...something. I didn't want folks to know. I didn't want folks to have any more reason to feel sorry for me...or him.

"Canon didn't charge me with any crime for burying Zeke here. I'm glad of that. He let 'em know at the county records office, I guess."

"Canon's in the hospital," said Maggie.

Mr. Thompson looked up. "What happened?"

"He went to check on a domestic dispute last night and the man said his gun went off by accident. A bullet grazed the back of Canon's head."

"Well, I'll be." Ollie studied her. "You're not going to hold it against Canon for being a lawman, are you?"

Maggie shook her head. "No."

She had stayed longer than she meant to. Maggie closed her notebook and stood. Ollie was the first to reach out and hug her this time.

At the door she remembered the keys. "I almost forgot." Maggie held them out for him. "This is the cabin key, and the key to Canon's truck. It's parked there. He'll be by to get it in a few days."

32

"Those who cling to worthless idols forfeit the grace that could be theirs." Jonah 2:8, some NIV translations

Maggie didn't see Canon again for six weeks. His head wound healed, but from his text messages she knew his heart still stood on a precipice.

The day after she left he texted.

Thanks again for the quiche.
Did Paul let you go home?
Not yet.
How do you feel?
Fine.
Good time to catch up on reading? Movies? Sleep?

Too much time to wish I didn't have a scanner at my house.

A week later he texted again.

The cabin on Patterson Road misses you.

Then, before Maggie could think of a clever reply...

Ollie misses you.

And once more...

I miss you.
I miss you, too, Canon. I'm sorry I had to leave town while you were in the hospital, but I had an appointment scheduled with an agent.
How did it go?
I'm hopeful. She has my proposal. She's thinking about it.
When will you know something?
Couple of weeks.

After two weeks passed...

Been trying to think of something I could come arrest you for.
I paid my taxes.
Damn.
My car tags are coming due. I could hold off on those.
That's only a misdemeanor. Any word from the agent?
Not yet.

Another two weeks passed. Maggie was lying in bed one morning after staying up late working on her manuscript when she heard her phone ping. It was a picture from Canon, of the sunrise over his apple orchard. She stared at it a long time.

Nice.
Better in person.

If Maggie could have blinked herself to his porch, she would have. In fact, she considered running to her car and seeing how fast she could get there. She'd text him to say, *Hold on! I'm coming.* The condo was close to I-40. Her phone said it would take her seventy-two minutes. It was Saturday morning. Light traffic.

When she hesitated...

How's the book coming?

Maggie looked over at her desk in the corner. Should she snap a picture of those piles of books from the library? Or of her wastebasket, with all those papers ripped and wadded?

Slow, but sure. No word from agent yet. She may have decided to pass.
You'd rather she take her time and be sure about it.

Maggie wondered if he was telling himself the same thing about her. She knew it was only a matter of time until she and the Marston Country sheriff saw where things might take them. Maggie made a decision that morning at the hospital. She told Shirley she could do the hard things. It was a hard thing to take a chance on love again.

But Maggie had also made a commitment to the story. And if Canon couldn't live with her pursuit of a writing dream then he wasn't the next man she should fully give her heart to. Plus...it was still so soon...not even a year had passed since the day Tom told her about Bethany. Still, it felt like a lifetime, perhaps because Maggie spent so much time in her own head.

True. If she decides I'm the one, I want it to stick. I want it to be for life.
I'd want that, too.

*   *   *

For six weeks, Maggie wrote. She was neck-deep into the manuscript, typing the words as she heard them, then proceeded to edit, edit, edit until she worried she would edit the soul out of what she was trying to craft.

Marriage and love are curious things. I had a lot of time to think about each when I was in prison.

I remember standing at the courthouse with Tandy, both of us just kids, in that too-big jacket of my father's, looking into my future wife's green eyes, thinking I had the world by its tail. Tandy's hair was all fussed up in a perm, and she was wearing a cream-colored dress she'd made. I bought her a wrist corsage at the flower shop like we were going to the prom, a big white orchid.

If you had asked me that day if I loved Tandy, I would have sworn the answer was yes. And I was convinced she loved me, too. But what did either of us know then of love?

Love, I realized later, was more complicated than the way my knees got weak when Tandy Wilkins first smiled at me in English class, slamming my heart like a sledgehammer. And love went deeper than the tangle of our bodies on the vinyl seats of a car.

Here was my first test of love: when I found a white orchid in the trash the morning after going to the courthouse.

When I asked Tandy how come—did she not want to freeze it, or press it, or something—she laughed and said what for?

How did a writer ever get to the final stages and know the story was finished? Every time Maggie read back through her Scrivener files there was one more word that needed changing, one more line to be added, another to be taken away.

And the *research*! The research never seemed sufficient to the task. Intuition, gut feelings, and a lot of time on the treadmill in the fifth floor's exercise room were needed to fill in the gaps.

I died on a Monday—same Monday I broke out of prison. My name was Ezekiel Thompson. Everybody called me Zeke. I killed three people, but only one from hatred. Or maybe I killed four. Do you count yourself if your own bad decisions lead to an early departure?

Maggie long ago lost count of how many times she'd gone back through the opening lines, scrolled down through the chapters, checking the pacing, checking the grammar, checking the emotional pulse of the story. She was convinced those opening lines, which simply came to her, much as Zeke had—unbidden and unexpected—was what helped her get the final offer from the agent who called to sign her at the end of May.

This time Maggie called Canon instead of texting. She wanted to hear the deep timbre of his voice.

"Hey." He sounded surprised.

"Guess what," she breathed.

"She signed you."

"She *did!*" Maggie silently pumped her fist into the air. She had needed a win.

"I knew she would," said Canon.

"How could you be so sure?"

"Sometimes you just know. And because you're fabulous. And it's a story that needs telling."

Maggie held her breath. "You think I'm fabulous?"

He chuckled. The sound of it sent thrills running up her back. "Don't act like you haven't figured that out by now. You know what this means," Canon said. "We have to celebrate. My place or yours?"

"You would come to Nashville?"

"Woman, I'd drive farther than to Nashville to see you."

Maggie's heart was already in the clouds. Now it felt like it might burst.

"I'll cook," she said. They agreed on Friday night, 6:30.

Tandy and I got married on a Friday. Nobody came to our wedding. The judge called a cleaning lady in to serve as witness, but as we came down the outside steps when it was over I saw my mother at the end of the walkway crying. I figured Dad was off drunk somewhere. Mom knew as well as anybody the kind of life I had just signed on for.

At my trial, lawyers from both sides wondered why I would stay married to Tandy for so long. If my mother hadn't been sick by then, she could have told them. Seemed like I owed it to her to stick it out with Tandy. Seemed like the least I could do for breaking her heart.

Later, when Tandy had that first abortion, I found the cream-colored dress in the trash next morning. That time I didn't even ask her about it.

*   *   *

Canon was prompt. He wore a navy dress jacket over a white collared shirt, jeans, and his ostrich boots, holding up a 10-gallon bucket filled with gladiolus—yellow, red, orange—when Maggie opened the door.

"You should see the hummingbirds swarming around these things."

When Maggie kissed his cheek his shoulders relaxed. He didn't blend well with the contemporary design of the building or urban landscapes in the windows. This man belonged on a farm.

As he followed her to the kitchen while Maggie looked for large vases and arranged the flowers, he said, "I was afraid you'd given up on me."

"I needed time to finish the story."

"So it's finished?"

"I'm sure an editor will think it still needs work, but Julie believes in it, and that feels good."

"Always feels good when somebody believes in you."

Canon's eyes followed Maggie as she walked a vase of flowers to the living room table and another to the dining table. She left one on the kitchen counter, setting his 10-gallon bucket by the door. When she turned to look at him he was doing surveillance again, checking out her condo. The kitchen was open to the living and dining areas. The single bedroom and bath sat to the left of the entry. The layout always reminded Maggie of a nice hotel suite at the beach. It didn't feel like his place...it didn't feel like a home.

"How's your head?" Maggie asked. She stepped closer to him and craned her neck so she could see the spot they shaved. His hair was growing back over it.

Canon wouldn't be still for her to get a good look. "Fine. Hard as ever."

They exchanged awkward it's-been-a-while smiles, then she turned back to finish dinner. "My kitchen's not as nice as yours."

"I'd share."

Maggie stopped and looked at him. Biting her bottom lip, she pushed a cutting board with washed vegetables toward him. "You want to chop these for our salad?"

Canon took off his jacket and laid it on a nearby chair, rolled up his sleeves in that customary way he had, picked up the knife and got to work.

"I'm not good at being subtle," he said. "I'm not good at playing games or being debonair. I didn't mean to launch right into things, but I had an hour's drive...six weeks, seven days...to think about that kiss in my kitchen and I've got some things to say."

He made quick work of the chopping and pushed the cutting board back toward Maggie.

She slipped the Brown Sugar Salmon into the oven and reached for the asparagus.

"I'm listening."

"First, I've gotten clearance to take you out to Turney Center. I think it would be good for you to go out there and see where Zeke was. I got the current warden to go back and look up the original reports from his escape. Thought that might help you."

Maggie salted and peppered the asparagus, had the olive oil heating in the pan, and was ready with the balsamic glaze she liked to drizzle over it. She was going through another round of edits now. Seeing the prison that Zeke had escaped from would only deepen the story. "How soon can we go?"

He looked pleased that she was pleased, and nodded. "Soon as you're ready. Although I thought about this, and it would be good if we went on a Wednesday night. There's a group of volunteers that comes in to teach classes every Wednesday night that would be the most similar conditions to the night Zeke walked out."

"Would next Wednesday night work for you?"

He thought a minute. "I can make that work."

"I can, too." Maggie put the asparagus in the pan. "What's the second thing?"

Canon looked sheepish. "I'll wait on that one until after we eat."

"Okay. No hints?"

He only smiled at her, but it wasn't a happy smile, it was a tortured smile. So Maggie didn't press the point. She wasn't sure she wanted to hear what it was if it had him nervous. This was supposed to be a celebratory dinner for her signing with an agent. Had Canon forgotten that?

No... he'd gotten her clearance to visit the prison. He hadn't forgotten about her book. Canon wasn't the kind of man who forgot anything, and he wasn't the kind of man who acted afraid.

So what had him looking tortured?

Me and Tandy, we had some good moments. We fell into a rhythm, me and her. We'd do okay for a while, then I'd get a call from a bar...a hotel...the hospital.

I learned to hide the money. But Tandy was good at finding it. She could take us back to zero in one afternoon, all for one good high. I never did understand how she knew where to go to find what she was looking for. But I did understand that the thing she really wanted—the thing everybody wants—wasn't in those places she was looking.

Tandy never did figure out how to find the one thing that really mattered.

In the New Testament, Paul said love was what mattered most. More than faith, more than hope, love trumped it all. But you couldn't go buy it with the

last of your husband's paycheck. You couldn't smoke it, you couldn't drink it,
you couldn't shoot it into your bloodstream.

Love was right there for Tandy, all she had to do was accept it.

Maggie tossed the cut vegetables in with the salad greens, stirred the asparagus on the stovetop and turned off the oven. All was nearly ready. The table was set.

She pushed a bottle of her favorite Pinot toward Canon. "You mind opening that?"

"Glad to. I need a drink."

He filled two glasses and took them to the table while she brought the plates. Maggie's condo was on the eleventh floor. The views were spectacular. The dining table sat next to the windows with an unfettered view of downtown Nashville.

"Wow," Canon said. "I could tell it was a great view from the kitchen, but sitting here I have more appreciation for it."

Maggie picked up her glass. "It was the best view I could get with my severance package." The one thing she and Tom had argued most about in buying their house was the windows. So windows became Maggie's top priority when shopping for her next living space. Windows were helpful when trying to clear your vision in looking down the road toward your future.

"I won't be able to afford it forever...unless my book ends up on the New York Times bestsellers list."

Canon raised his glass. "Here's hoping it's a bestseller." Maggie raised hers. "But not so you can live *here* forever."

Surely Canon wasn't planning to profess his love, or ask Maggie to marry him. *Was he?* The thought caused Maggie conflicting emotions: joy, fear, warmth, panic. Canon was acting so uncharacteristically uncomfortable.

Or was there some chance his feelings for her had changed? Maggie might have made too many presumptions about that picture on his nightstand, and Shirley's words at the hospital. Had she read too much into his text messages? Or his "I'd share" comment about the kitchen?

They made stilted small talk during dinner. Canon praised the meal, grinning. "I've been wanting this meal ever since the morning I met you."

"I'm glad you like it."

His voice dropped. "That brings me back to that second thing."

Maggie would wait on the dessert and coffee.

"I need to be honest with you, Maggie."

She studied his eyes, trying to read the words on his face, waiting, hardly daring to breathe.

Canon opened his mouth to say more, but nothing came out. He tried again, his voice low. "I saw it."

She put her hand on his arm above the wrist, offering reassurance. "Saw what, Canon?"

"Everything. Zeke. Rodriquez. You. The cabin."

Maggie took her hand back, staring at him. He looked out at the Nashville skyline. Neither of them spoke while Canon threw back the last of his wine like it was a shot of hard liquor.

33

A woman goes to the woods to gain clarity and listen for a story. She's alone but for a ghost. Then a second man shows up with several ghosts of his own, looking for someone to mend his heart.

"Rita died thirty years ago, Maggie. I found her in the garden." Canon nodded toward the gladiolus on the corner of the table. "Near where those are planted. Paul wasn't the coroner then, Doc Anderson was. He said she had a brain aneurysm. We'd only been married a year.

I swore when I lost her I'd never love anyone like that again. And I kept my word."

Canon rubbed his forehead. "That night, the night I met you, I had a dream. Truth is, I'd had it three nights in a row. Wasn't the same every time, but parts were. Ollie drunk, passed out on his bed. His phone ringing. A woman undressing a man—a woman with brown hair." Canon's eyes bore into her now. "I saw it, Maggie. I saw you bandage his leg. I saw him take your cell phone—pin you to the bed."

Maggie's eyes widened. She had never told Canon that Zeke pinned her to the bed.

"Didn't you think it strange I knocked on your door at 4:30 in the morning? Or that I knew I ought to search the woods behind your cabin?"

Maggie's breathing was thin. "Are you telling me you saw that, too? You saw what happened?"

Canon nodded.

"Was it Zeke? Before he knocked on my door?"

Canon nodded again.

Maggie gasped. "Then why did you act like you didn't believe me, Canon? Why did you make me go down to the station? And talk into your phone?"

"Because it's so hard to explain, Maggie."

"You're telling me!" That came out harsher than Maggie meant for it to. But Canon's words were a shock.

"At least you're a fiction writer," he said. "A lawman depends on the facts, so I tried to gather the facts. I didn't have a ghost come see me, I had a *dream* and dreams are vague...wispy. Nothing was an absolute. I couldn't see Zeke's face. I couldn't see yours.

"All I know is I woke up at 3:38 in a cold sweat that morning worried about Ollie. I thought my subconscious made up some crazy dream to get me to go check on the old man. You know how a dream can be.

"Rodriquez had escaped from Turney Center. I'd gotten a couple of calls and been on the lookout for him for two days. I thought my mind was swirling with all that and I had this far-fetched dream, but I couldn't shake it. It rattled me. So I called Amos to cover the dispatch and I drove out to check on Ollie. He didn't come to the door, so I drove down to the cabin."

Canon's forehead pinched like he was in pain. "When you opened the door you took my breath away. I thought maybe I was still dreaming."

Maggie's eyes burned. Canon looked like he was going to cry. It made her cry.

"I checked that cabin," he said. "You know it, you were there—looking for someone, half-expecting to find him. And I was so relieved not to. I told myself it was just a crazy dream and a crazy coincidence. But I still had to check the woods behind the cabin at first light."

Canon waited for her to say something, but Maggie didn't know what to say. He rubbed the creases in his forehead again. Maggie wondered if his gunshot wound was really healed, or if he was rubbing the front of his head because the back was hurting.

"I almost told you when you started talking as we were coming out of the woods that day," said Canon, "and again standing at Zeke's grave. But then Ollie showed up. In late January when I stopped by the cabin, I was going to tell you then. But by that time..."

"What?" asked Maggie when he stopped. "By that time, *what*?"

"By that time I was afraid I would run you off. By that time, I was having other dreams, dreams of my own making."

There was that tortured look again.

"The day Robbie met you she claimed you were scared of me. Is that true, Canon?"

"Yes," he whispered.

"Why?" Maggie put her hand on his arm again, above the wrist. He covered it with his own, clinging to it like it might save his life.

"Because I swore I'd never love anyone again. And I can't explain you. I can't explain that dream."

"The same way I can't explain that Zeke Thompson was in my cabin."

"You're the only person I've told," said Canon. "You're the only person I can tell."

"Same here."

They stared at one another, emotional waters passing silently under the bridge.

"You know how a dream can change on you?" asked Canon. "First you'll be dreaming one thing, then it will change into something else?"

Maggie nodded.

"I dreamed a man was kissing you. Then I was kissing you. And I *felt* something." Canon's eyes filled then—tall, broad-shouldered Canon Dale. "I felt something so strong my heart wouldn't settle back down. And I felt it again when I kissed you in the car before the festival. I feel it every time I'm around you, Maggie, every time I think about you. When you opened the door that night, I *knew*."

"Knew what?"

"I knew you'd come for me."

Like a light in the distance. From a long way off.

Every hair on Maggie's arms was raised. Still, she said, "I can't believe you acted like you didn't believe me, Canon." She pointed to the bottle of Pinot. "You even suggested I might have had too much to drink."

He looked sheepish. If Maggie had any renewed misgivings about her own feelings for Canon, with that sudden sheepish look, they vanished.

"I hope you'll forgive me, Maggie. I did believe you, but the whole thing had me spooked. Plus, it's my job to prove things. I had nothing for the report but a ghost and a dream."

*   *   *

On Wednesday Canon drove Maggie to Turney Center. They went inside, through checkpoint. Hearing the clang of the heavy doors as they opened and locked again was sobering.

When I got to prison, I read everything I could find in the library on euthanasia. It's a real thing, one of those issues where morality, science, and the justice system clash. I know I'm not the only person who ever killed someone out of mercy. Still...I don't recommend my choices.

Another book I read when I got to prison was Hosea. God said his love was a love everlasting. Everlasting. That word seemed to be everywhere I looked in the Old Testament.

I liked that word so much I decided to tattoo it over my heart. You can do that in prison if you make friends with the right people. One guy gets the ink, the other gets the needles. I did it myself. Took a while, standing in front of the mirror, reading backwards. It hurt. But I got where I liked the prick of the blood on my skin. It became a nightly ritual until it was finished.

The New Testament says baptized Christians are stamped with the seal of the Holy Ghost, and that old bodies are discarded for new ones. Still, something in me wanted to mark myself to remind anyone—or any collecting death spirits who might come across my body one day—of the cross that had been mine to bear, and that I was promised God's love regardless of my sins. Or maybe I just needed to remind myself.

No man wants to think his life was lived in vain. Only time will tell the final outcome of my choices.

Canon showed Maggie the educational wing where Zeke had taken classes, keeping his hand on the small of her back, protective as they moved along hallways and sidewalks, Canon scowling at the inmates as they admired Maggie with their eyes.

I hope I'm not remembered as being a tragic figure. My story is not a tragedy to me. But I know I could have had a wider influence. That's the part I'd change.

The first day Tandy showed interest in me, the first moment, I would have said, "I'm going to medical school, Tandy Wilkins. If you want to wait for me, live life on my terms, great. And if not, I wish you well."

Maybe that's what heaven will be—a chance to do it over again, to get it right the second time around. I'm sure most folks would think, what do I know of heaven? What makes me think I'll ever find out? And they'd be right.

Of course...my chances are excellent if it all depends on mercy.

Driving back to Marston, Maggie said, "He walked all this way on foot? In the snow and ice?"

"As the crow flies, it was twenty miles. I've actually been over it in a helicopter. Dense woods most of the way. The fact that he kept moving and had some shelter from the wind in those woods helped him for a while. The snow didn't start until about the time he walked out. But when he came out of the woods near Ollie's and stopped to try to get in..."

"His body temperature started dropping," finished Maggie.

She'd only come up for the day, to ride out to the prison that afternoon with Canon. They met at the cabin, but she wasn't staying the night. She had an early morning meeting with her agent.

When they got back to the cabin, before the sun set, they walked up the hill to the ridge and peered down into the ravine where Canon discovered the body.

"In my dream, Rodriquez was staring into the windows of the cabin when Zeke materialized. He whacked him with a broken tree limb. Hit him in the head, then drug him up to this ravine and threw him in. As dreams are sketchy, I didn't see what he did with the tree limb. I came back out here after the snow and ice melted looking for it. Never could find it. No evidence to prove anyone else was ever here."

"Same as in the cabin," said Maggie.

Why did I leave prison that night? Because the door stood open. That's it.

True, in the days that preceded, I had longed to see my mother's grave. I longed to sit with my father and tell him he was not a failure. I longed to taste free air on my lips once more.

But in that moment, I didn't take a lot of time to think about all this. My departure wasn't planned, any more than I had planned to shoot Tandy that night I drove home from the fish place. Maybe that was the biggest part of my problem—I should have planned more, instead of rolling along where life took me.

Anyway, that's why I did it. That's why I walked out.

An unexpected opportunity fell into my lap. I found a badge on the sidewalk, for a man who looked a little like me—white, mid-thirties, brown hair. And I had a notebook because I was going to class. So I dropped that notebook on the ground like it was an accident, and scooped the badge up with it when I picked it back up, slipping the hard plastic inside the pages.

When I got down to C-School for class I told the officer on duty I'd forgotten a paper that was due. Because he knew me and trusted me, he said I could go back and get it. So I made it look like I was going back to my room, but I slipped inside the laundry, instead, where I knew there was a set of street clothes in a locked cabinet. They always had a few street clothes in that cabinet for guys being released. And I knew where the key was hid.

I grabbed the key, opened the cabinet, and stripped off. I put a set of street clothes under my prison garb, then redressed over them. Thankfully, my prison jacket was bigger than the jean jacket I put on underneath it.

Then I relocked the cabinet, hid the key again, slipped that badge down in my pocket, and went to class. Soon as class was over, I went to the bathroom—there's a couple of private bathrooms in C-School—one-person-only bathrooms.

I took off the outer clothes real fast and tucked them up under one of the ceiling tiles. I wet my hair and slicked it back, tried to look a little different, more like the man on the badge. Then, as I listened at the bathroom door to the sounds of the guys leaving out, and the visitors milling behind, in conversation, I heard the guard call down the hall, "time to go," and I opened the door a crack. He saw me as the last of the visitors turned the corner of the hallway to go back up to checkpoint.

"Come on then," he said. It was the new guy, and he didn't recognize me. I had the street clothes on and the badge. When I stepped out of the bathroom he pointed down the hall where the guests were moving out and said, "you don't want to get left behind."

I flashed him my best smile and said, "No, I don't."

I felt him watching me as I hustled to fall in behind the guests who were moving out of the building into the cloud-covered evening, up the outdoor sidewalk, toward checkpoint. They gathered at the doorway. I heard the lock click open. They filed inside a hallway, one-by-one, showing their hands under an infrared light.

A guy up in front of me realized his badge was missing. He felt in his pockets, then turned to look behind him. I heard him say, "My badge must have fallen off," then he stepped out of line to go back out the door to check for it on the sidewalk.

During the commotion, I moved up quickly and stuck my hand real fast under the light beside another man's, hoping the guard on the other side of the glass wouldn't notice. And he must not have, because then the main door clicked open. I listened to the heavy roll of it feeling like I was standing somewhere else, seeing my life play out in a dream.

A couple of the men stepped out of line to wait for their friend who'd gone out the door looking for his badge. I slipped up past them and through the door, watching the folks in front of me, doing like they did, handing their badges over to the guard behind the desk to get their driver's licenses back, signing their names in a book. I took the badge off and looked at the name, knowing I needed to get out the door before the guy outside got back in and they figured it out.

"Matthew Dyer." That's who I was for the next five minutes.

I handed the badge over, acting like I was one of the regulars, not saying a word to anybody. The guy in front of me, whose signature I couldn't make out on the paper handed me the pen and I signed Matthew Dyer's name and the date, then the guard handed me Matthew's license and I was past the glass of the door, moving into the parking lot, grateful for the darkness of an early night.

Folks in the group were talking to one another. "Where'd Matt go?" asked somebody.

"Dropped his badge. Went back to look for it."

"He's got my car key."

"He'll be here in a minute."

That's all I heard. I walked to the farthest car in the line, acting like it was mine, then I dropped and rolled on the ground to the bottom of the hill where there was a tree line. I never looked back—I was into the trees and running.

Snow started falling and piled quickly. Hypothermia must have started its process by the time I got to Dad's. He never came to the door. I knew he was in there—his pickup was there.

I went to the shed thinking I'd get in his old truck and at least be out of the wind when I saw the key hanging on the wall for the cabin down the road. If I could get in that cabin, I knew I could run a hot bath, start a fire, there might even be some food in the cabinets, left from a former tenant.

But somewhere between Dad's place and the cabin I lost that key.

The Bible refers to stolen water as sweet. I think it means a stolen kiss from someone who is not your wife. And those stolen clothes had looked so sweet, the bite was in the hole in the pocket of the jacket.

When I lay down on the porch of that cabin, realizing that the cold was reaching up to my throat with her icy clutches, I could see a light in the distance.

I thought of Ezekiel, my namesake in the Bible, and his vision on the banks of the Kebar River. Heaven. Splendor. An understanding of the vision God had in mind for His people. We're forever falling out of the rows and pulling our oxen through the muck.

Meanwhile, He never gives up hope on us, that we'll someday figure it out. I think Tandy saw right there at the end. I think she saw that my love for her, while flawed, was the best I had to offer. I wanted to believe she was grateful at last. That she wanted to end on a good note, and I wanted that for her.

As I lay on the porch looking at that light, I thought I could see Tandy whole in the distance, like Ezekiel looking at that vision. And my mother standing beside her, smiling. I envisioned myself with self-respect again, standing upright, somewhere out in front of me.

But it was a long way off, so I lay down there a minute to rest and thought back over my life and decided it was a good one, after all. About as good a life as any man could ever hope to have. I was offered imperfect love, and I gave it. That is something fine indeed.

*   *   *

It took Maggie nine months total, January to September, from the first words to the sending off of the manuscript to the editor—same as the gestation period for a baby.

"What happens now?" asked Maggie. She and her agent sat in the same hipster coffee house where Maggie so frequently met Cal or Robbie.

"They'll send you a schedule." Julie, a deep auburn redhead, smiled at her from across the table. "Maureen will send her suggestions back to you in a couple of months. You'll have a few weeks to review them and send her another revision. Then you'll do it again, but you won't need as long on the second go-round."

Maggie had known Julie was the right agent for her. An onslaught of emotion bubbled up, causing her eyes to fill. "And Maureen is a good editor? It's important to me that the final version is as strong as we can make it."

"She's great! And that's what editors are for."

It was hard to believe, after all this dreaming, listening, slicing and dicing, that it was time to let Zeke's story go.

"What are you going to work on next?" asked Julie.

"I'm thinking about a series of historicals called *Tales from Marston County*."

Julie cocked her head. "I like the sound of that. Tell me more."

34

And that's how story comes. Like a ghost. A wisp. An apparition. Like a snippet on a website. Love seeped into the walls of a cabin.

Romanticized. Imagined. A feeling you get when you walk into a lonely man's farmhouse. Gossip in a library. Memories etched into the wood of a door-frame. A memory...a smell...red hair...a promise. A dream that comes in the night and rekindles your hope.

Mark and Robbie's wedding was lovely the following April. Canon had informed the town planners he was done planting cherry trees around the square, but it was decided Marston would continue having an annual festival.

On the last Sunday in April...two weeks after tax season ended...Tom walked Robbie down the white steps of the Marston County Courthouse, and she and Mark were married on the lawn surrounded by friends, family, and thirty cherry trees shedding the last of their blooms.

Tom and Canon shared an awkward handshake after, while Maggie walked over to Bethany and asked if she could hold the baby, a girl they named Carmen, with soft tufts of blond hair.

Later, when Maggie, Yvette, Dot Jenkins, Becky and Shirley, who had long ago stopped giving Maggie a hard time, had cleaned up the last remnants of the couple's reception, and Robbie and Mark were headed to the cabin for their honeymoon, Maggie walked out of the library where Canon was waiting.

He offered her his arm. "I'm thinking about retiring early."

"But law enforcement is in your bloodline."

"I know. A day like this makes a man wonder about his future, though." Canon's voice dropped, "Can we be next?"

Maggie had held him off, not wanting to steal thunder from her children. Cal and Yvette had gotten married in a destination wedding to Jamaica in February. Maggie had gone alone since Canon couldn't get away that long. Now that Cal and Yvette's and Robbie and Mark's weddings had come and gone, it was time.

"Pick a date," Maggie said.

In your fifties, the urgency of love is different.

It's, how long do I have? And, let's get to it—to making a wooden sign together that says, 'Canon and Maggie'—sharing coffee on a white-railed porch watching the sun come up over your fruit orchard.

Epilogue

A month before her book was set to come out, as Maggie packed her things to leave the condo—her lease was up and she was getting married in a week in a little white country church, freshly painted, with new windows installed—she pulled her cookbooks from the shelf. The one with the Brown Sugar Salmon recipe fell open and a thin sheet of paper fell out. How had she not noticed it before? Maggie used recipes from this book all the time. But the paper was fine and must have clung to the back of the page.

She picked it up, not recognizing the sharp, slanted handwriting.

Don't judge me too harshly about the man they'll find in the ditch, Maggie. He was a bad egg, unlikely to convert.

You're going to be fine, you know, just fine in the end. There's a strong light in you, a light meant for sharing. I had that light once, or at least I like to think I did.

I didn't tell you this, I'm not sure why, but I tried my hand at writing, too. I tried to write my story. They let you have pen and paper in prison. I could never quite tell it like I thought it, though, and the pages got left behind. They're long gone to the incinerator by now. I wanted to explain I wasn't mean like some folks at the trial made me out to be, that I had my reasons for doing what I did.

Maybe you'll tell it for me, Maggie. But don't paint me with greater grace than I deserve. I don't justify my actions. They were wrong, and I paid dearly.

Here's the one piece of advice I'll offer—this is for writing, and for life in general. Don't try to write the truth exactly; the truth is slippery. A man—or a woman, I suspect—can go crazy trying to decide what the truth really is. Base what you write on what people need to hear, Maggie—on what you need to hear—or better yet, on what you need to say. I don't see how anyone can do better than that.

You're in there typing now. I won't be here when the snow melts, but you keep typing, Maggie. Whatever you do, don't fear your life. Don't fear your death, either. And don't fear whatever crosses you are handed between the two.

It's all meant to take you to the place you're supposed to be.

Zeke

Author's Note & Acknowledgements

I have fond memories of riding to Perry County from Nashville in the back seat of our family car—often tucked onto the back window shelf before seat belts were required by law—listening to my parents talk about the homesteads we passed as we traveled to visit extended family.

When I moved to Hickman County that neighbors Perry as a young bride, then moved to Gainesboro, then back to Hickman County, I came to understand how you do know people who live all up and down the winding highways. And like Norman Maclean alluded to in *A River Runs Through It*, words telling stories lie under the rocks of the rivers, and words are buried in the Tennessee soil.

I include this in an effort to help readers understand where I'm coming from as a writer. My goal is to weave a tapestry of stories connected to a common place—by homesteads and intersecting family lines—over time. Most of these will be in historical settings, but *Alone in a Cabin* takes place in 2016, the year my first book was published. The year Maggie turned 50 is the year I turned 50. A divorce wasn't my kick-start into writing (I am happy to report that Stan and I are solid), but there were other events that had me re-evaluating and finally leaning into the calling I'd always felt to write.

It is my privilege to teach Business Communication classes at Lipscomb University in Nashville. God knew I needed some business acumen, so He put me in the College of Business where I get to help students refine their career goals and give them practical advice on how to achieve them. What a blessing this is to me!

Thank you, LORD, for the many ways You have equipped and blessed me through the equipping and blessing of others.

Thank you Don (posthumously) and Joan for first planting the seeds of story in me.

Thank you DePriest Bend and the old Wood homestead (now an Amish farm) and the family lines that have extended from them for providing such a rich sense of place.

Thank you friends, family, and church communities of Hickman, Perry, and Jackson Counties for teaching me to love small towns and for fostering my early writing dreams.

Thank you to all the thought leaders and influencers, several of whom are quoted or mentioned in this work, for teaching and inspiring the rest of us.

Thank you Matt Hearn for giving me such a spot-on quote about the writing life, and Jennifer from LIFE who helped teach me that the bars of prison can be a source of freedom to some.

Thank you Dana Chamblee Carpenter for all the practical wisdom you've shared as my critique partner and propping my arms up when needed.

Thank you Julie Gwinn for believing in me and serving as my agent.

Thank you Andrea Lindsley, Jade Novak, and Patti Trapp for being my Friday morning walking crew/sounding boards.

Thank you Donita Brown, Denis Thomas, Holly Allen, and Tessa Sanders for being my fellow faculty writers group/sounding boards.

Thank you Shelby Mick, Kathryn Mick, Mary Beth Best, Joan Wood, Kathy Steakley and Andrea Lindsley for being early readers of this manuscript and offering such great feedback for improvement.

Thank you Randy Bostic for easing my mind on legal matters.

Thank you Ami McConnell Abston for being a great friend and a great connector for all those who love story and work in this industry, and Jenny Hale for the generosity of your time and wisdom, and Mary O'Donohue and Jenny Baumgartner for that great therapy session at

Ami's that served as a final nudge I needed to set this story on the waters.

Thank you Stan and Jo for offering me daily pep talks.

And thank you Shelby and Lincoln who kept me propped up on this one: pre- during- and post-pandemic. Watching the two of you continue to bravely create your art in the face of a challenging year did more to keep me moving forward than you know. My pride and love for each of you fills my heart and keeps me dancing.

Photo by Shelby M'lynn Mick

Alone in a Cabin is Leanne W. Smith's first contemporary romantic suspense novel. Her Amazon bestseller, *Leaving Independence*, and its follow-up, *A Contradiction to His Pride*, were post-Civil War historicals. Regardless of the time differences, all three inspirational stories have ties to the fictional Marston County in Middle Tennessee. In addition to writing, Leanne teaches in the College of Business at Lipscomb University in Nashville. She and her husband have two grown daughters and a son-in-law who each make the world more beautiful with their artistic talents. Visit Leanne's website at www.leannewsmith.com for more information about her books or for inspiration in pursuing personal and career-related dreams.

About the chapter headings

Most of the chapter headings in *Alone in a Cabin* are original to me. Others are a collection of thoughts and quotes that come from a variety of sources that have inspired me as a writer.

Readers will already be familiar with some, others may be new. Following is more context for each in case you find it interesting. If I were sitting with you in a coffee shop and you asked me to share what I've learned about the craft of writing, I would say, "Read *Alone in a Cabin*. It's my love story for writers. I put the best lessons I've learned in there."

1: A story begins with a disruption to the heroine's daily life—a major disturbance in the balance of things that throws her off her footing and sets her on her rump.

Stories typically focus on something extraordinary that happens in an otherwise ordinary life. The place to begin is in the middle of things (known as "in media res") where that extraordinary something happens. The other two goals of Act 1 (the first 15-20% of your novel) are to set the background and establish what the character wants.

2: "Rustic cabin. Built in the 1850s. Original fireplace. New windows. Only 70 miles from Nashville. Perfect writer's retreat." Airbnb description

I made this cozy little spot up—my own idea of the perfect writer's retreat—but real ones are out there.

3: After the inciting incident kicks the heroine to the ground, she has to decide whether to lie there or stand up and put one foot in front of the other. If she can rally the reader has cause to cheer.

Your main character can't be weak or the reader won't root for her. She doesn't have to be perfect—she shouldn't be perfect. But something about her should inspire.

4: Nothing can remain as it first appears. If it does, the reader won't turn the page. If the reader doesn't turn the page...well...what's the point?

Karl Iglesias wrote in *Writing for Emotional Impact* that movie audiences "pay to feel." And readers read to feel. So make them feel something.

5: An artist must prepare for the unexpected. Entering a new realm is frightening, a risky proposition with a real chance of failure, including the chance of harm and damage to your soul.

I don't know how to separate who I am from the story I'm seeking to tell. Things have a way of working themselves into the manuscript that I didn't even consciously know I was wrestling with. So for me, it takes courage to write, because I don't know all that it may reveal.

Even though *Alone is a Cabin* is my third novel, it's the story where I finally gave myself permission to be a writer—an affirmation that I've learned something about the craft. But also an admission that brilliant writing will likely always elude me. The critics will forever loom large, and I am my worst.

6: "Where can I go from your Spirit? Where can I flee from your presence?... Search me, God, and know my heart...lead me in the way everlasting." Excerpts from Psalm 139, NIV

Psalm 139 is my favorite passage in Scripture. The last phrase encapsulates what I want for my writing—that God would lead me to pen everlasting truths that glorify Him and help people feel less alone.

7: "It is not death that a man should fear, but he should fear never beginning to live." Marcus Aurelius

I do fear death. But like I think Marcus Aurelius was getting at, I don't want this to keep me from being courageous.

8: There is something sexy about a man in uniform. Prison garb does not count. Nor does clothing from the eighties.

Admittedly, Rick Springfield did look good in eighties clothing. That bit about Maggie seeing him in concert when she was sixteen? That was me and my friend Rhonda, fourth row, screaming with the best of them.

9: Stephen King said in *Secret Windows* that writing allows you to step into another world, to "be someplace else for a while."

In the movie adaptation of Isak Dinesen's *Out of Africa*, Karen von Blixen tells Denys Finch Hatton that she has been "a mental traveler." That's what books allow us all.

10: The Shirelles first asked the question in 1960 and women have been wondering ever since: "Will you still love me...tomorrow?"

This is the tune that popped into my head when I was here in the story. Sometimes you agonize over a name, a scene description, the right word to use. Other times the Rolodex of your life spins and shoots out a name, scene, or sentence fully formed, ready to go.

11: There can be no resurrection if there is no death. Conclusion drawn from the study of Ezekiel in the Bible

I always need a minute to let that sink in.

12: According to Sol Stein, the fiction writer's job is to entertain—to create pleasure for the reader.

This seems in conflict with what Stanley Williams says in *The Moral Premise*. (Great illustration of this is *Les Mis*. Every character's arc runs along the common moral thread of redemption.) I actually think Sol and Stanley are both right. Entertainment that has a point stands to resonate most with the reader.

13: Twice in Act 2 there should be a plot twist, a major turning point, something the reader is not expecting. Often it surprises the writer, too.

There are two camps of writers: the plotters and the pantsers. I secretly envy the plotters. They outline the whole story, the scenes, then fill in the details. Which sounds like a very smart way to go about it. But I write by the seat of my pants. The only picture I had of *Cabin* when I started was of a lonely woman in a remote place. And then a guy showed up.

14: "I will put my Spirit in you and you will live." Ezekiel 37:14, NIV

If God could bring a valley of dry bones to life in the book of Ezekiel, I thought He could resurrect one frozen mercy killer for a couple of days in Maggie's cabin...fictitiously speaking.

15: If a story comes to you and takes root, you are the keeper of the tale. You may never know how it truly sprang to life, but now your job is to feed it. See what kind of fruit it bears.

Elizabeth Gilbert talks about the origins of stories in her book, *Big Magic*. She suggests that ideas may not wait on you if you ignore them for too long. They'll go looking for another writer who has the time and inclination to pay attention to them. Thankfully, my stories have been longsuffering. They haven't given up on me, and I'm not giving up on them.

16: "Where, O death, is your victory? Where, O death, is your sting?" 1 Corinthians 15:55, NIV

One gift of story is that death is not the end of anyone's. All lives live on if someone tells their story.

17: "The job of the artist is always to deepen the mystery." Sir Francis Bacon

Mystery is part of the cord you pull. Tighten the narrative. Take out the dull parts. Give the reader a reason to turn the page.

18: "I died on a Monday—same Monday I broke out of prison. My name was Ezekiel Thompson. Everybody called me Zeke. I killed three people, but only one from hatred."

For years I had a book title in my head; *I Died on a Thursday*. I had no story for that title, but I kept it tucked away all the same, thinking it might come in handy one day. I couldn't make the date work out for Zeke to actually die on a Thursday, but Monday did work, so...now you know.

19: A writer pries open a lot of lids seeking truth for a story. Sometimes she closes them fast, knowing these are the contents that need to be brought to light, but sorry to be the one given the job.

I have a deep desire to capture truth when I write—to pen honest depictions—and still not offend anyone. But I'm not sure that's possible. We each have our own comfort level with imperfection. Mine isn't going to match every reader's, but I still grieve if I offend.

20: "Even though I walk through the darkest valley, I will fear no evil, for you are with me; your rod and your staff, they comfort me." Psalm 23:4, NIV

I didn't know Zeke murdered his wife when I started this story. I didn't know Tandy was going to be a wounded woman who hurt her husband. Tom got his receptionist pregnant. These are all dark things I have no first knowledge of, and I'm grateful for that. But I also know this: we all wound one another. At best, all any of us offers is imperfect love. And that is what we are offered in return by others. I'm not saying that is okay...it's not, which is why we need a Savior...but I am saying we all reside in the same boat of imperfection. "God with us," as He is in this psalm, paints the picture of our only hope.

21: Thoreau said the regularity of the news, in his case a daily stroll to the village to hear the gossip, was "as refreshing in its way as the rustling of leaves and peeping of frogs."

Isn't that rich? Artistry like that fills me up and makes me want to be a better writer.

22: In *The Artist's Way*, Julia Cameron recommends morning pages. Three, free-flowing, unedited pages. Get the toxins out of you and onto the paper—fear, worry—all that stands in the way of the story.

Thank you, Julia Cameron. My friend and fellow writer, Dana Chamblee Carpenter, was the first to introduce me to your books. And I have lost count of the artists I have now shared you with in my effort to pay it forward.

23: When your heart lies in shards around your feet you think you'll never breathe normally again. Then one day, you feel the vital organ pumping. Like the soar of a hawk's wings lifting in the air.

Time, God, and love. The best three healers I know.

24: If a story idea comes floating down the aisle and jumps inside your empty head (like J.K. Rowling says a boy wizard did for her), be the fertile mind most willing to water it.

Nancy Duarte says in in her book, *Resonance,* that an idea is the most powerful thing in the world. And ideas float down the aisles around us all the time. But you have to be willing to do the hard, steady work of cultivation for any ideas you hope will flourish.

25: One day you find yourself dancing in the kitchen and you know you're going to be alright. Every day won't be for dancing, but those few that are? Those few are all you need.

I have never been through a divorce, but I have grieved a few losses I felt deeply. When my body returns to dancing, I know the balance scales have tipped back into safe ranges again.

26: Anne Lamott said first drafts are excrement. (She used a different word.) The trick is editing—trying to shape the smelly pile into something more pleasing.

Anne Lamott's "Shitty First Drafts" chapter in *Bird by Bird* has given us all permission to write subpar on the first go-round.

Thank. The. Lord.

27: "Prison is where I finally became free." Former student in the LIFE Program at Tennessee Prison for Women

It's been my privilege since 2012 to teach periodically at the Tennessee Prison for Women in Lipscomb University's LIFE Program. Jennifer, a friend and fellow writer whom I first met when she was incarcerated, said this to me—that prison was where she finally became free. This is why I felt I could give this sentiment to Zeke.

If you have a heart to support the incarcerated (or formerly incarcerated) who now seek to change the trajectory of their futures, may I offer two organizations to consider?

Lipscomb University's LIFE Program provides an opportunity for high-performing students to take college courses for credit. Education is an effective, proven avenue to reform. If you agree, consider supporting LIFE or another educational reform initiative in your home state.

Tennessee Prison Outreach Ministry is a faith-based organization that provides transition housing following incarceration for both men and women, along with job search and life skills programs.

28: We fall, we get up. We lose, but we gain something in return. We love, in spite of the risk. So much of life is conquering fear to reach the gifts that lie on the other side.

This may be my favorite personal quote from *Cabin*.

29: "Telling people you are writing a book, then letting people read it, is like standing naked on the high dive." English professor to a budding author

My friend Matt Hearn was chair of the English department at Lipscomb University where I teach when he said this to me, and I've never forgotten it. Because it was so on point.

30: We spend a lot of time with our oars in the water. Every now and then—exquisite and brief—we find our rhythm. And for that moment we are perfectly in tune with all that's shining in the universe.

This is a subtle shout-out to Daniel James Brown who wrote *Boys in the Boat*, one of my favorite historical fiction novels of the past decade. It is so well written. I highly recommend it.

31: Frederick Buechner said "...humanity is like an enormous spider web, so that if you touch it anywhere, you set the whole thing trembling...

As we move around this world... we too are setting the great spider web a-tremble. The life that I touch for good or ill will touch another life, and that in turn another, until who knows where the trembling stops or in what far place and time my touch will be felt." Frederick Buechner, *The Hungering Dark*

Frederick Buechner, I am a fan. I've been quoting Buechner in the college courses I teach for years. Along with C.S. Lewis (with whom I share a birthdate—and Madeleine L'Engle and Louisa May Alcott), Buechner is one of the gentleman writers I most admire.

32: "Those who cling to worthless idols forfeit the grace that could be theirs." Jonah 2:8, some NIV translations

This is another of my favorite Scriptures. I once stenciled these words at the ceiling line of our living room, as a reminder to turn loose of idols and take hold of grace.

33: A woman goes to the woods to gain clarity and listen for a story. She's alone but for a ghost. Then a second man shows up with several ghosts of his own, looking for someone to mend his heart.

In the *denouement*, a writer ties up all the loose ends. It also felt like this was a good place to state the logline of *Cabin*, as Maggie was finalizing all the pieces for her own book.

34: And that's how story comes. Like a ghost. A wisp. An apparition. Like a snippet on a website. Love seeped into the walls of a cabin.

Romanticized. Imagined. A feeling you get when you walk into a lonely man's farmhouse. Gossip in a library. Memories etched into the wood of a doorframe. A memory...a smell...red hair...a promise. A dream that comes in the night and rekindles your hope.

Story is everywhere, and writers will never lack for inspiration.

CPSIA information can be obtained
at www.ICGtesting.com
Printed in the USA
LVHW020307160721
692872LV00007B/223

9 780578 922416